BLOODSHED IN THE FOREST

A VIKING WITCH MYSTERY

CATE MARTIN

Cover design by Shezaad Sudar.

Rune art by BettyStrange at Dreamstime.com.

Ratatoskr Press logo by Aidan Vincent Kise.

ISBN 978-1-951439-61-3

❀ Formatted with Vellum

CHAPTER ONE

ᚢ

FOR JANUARY IN NORTHERN MINNESOTA, we hadn't gotten much snow yet. Face-biting cold, on the other hand? We had had more than our share of that.

But if you dressed for the weather, it really wasn't that bad. The sun was shining brightly, and while it didn't lend the world below any heat, it did sparkle off of the snow in a way that warmed the soul. The sun glinting off of individual flakes in the drifts of snow created bright hints of silver and blue to what would otherwise be overwhelming whiteness or even grayness on an overcast day.

And the forest I was walking through was mainly firs and pines, their limbs as green as ever under their thin blankets of snow.

The glinting snow and the bright sun were probably why I didn't feel the slightest bit afraid, although I knew I should at least be a little nervous. Sure, I had been in these woods before, but never alone. And I had promised Thorbjorn never to walk to my little cottage in the forest clearing without him.

But I was breaking that promise now.

Not that my goal was getting to my cottage, although I was heading that way. No, the point of this little walk was to prove to myself that I could do it safely.

I had no weapons with me, but that didn't matter. The danger that I worried about in that moment came from within myself.

If I didn't learn how to contain the radiating attraction to supernatural beings that emanated from my own growing magical power, I wasn't going to be safe anywhere for long.

Nearly summoning fire giants into the village of Villmark had taught me that lesson all too clearly. Which was why I couldn't bring myself to tell Thorbjorn that I was breaking his promise now. I wasn't ready to tell him about my part in his encounter with those fire giants. I wanted to be sure, very sure, that I had solved the problem first. I wanted to be able to tell him with total confidence that it would never happen again.

It had only been a few weeks, and this was my first real test. But to my surprise, I was feeling more confident in myself than I had expected, given the circumstances.

My mentor Haraldr had no magic himself, which was a huge obstacle in his teaching me how to control my own magic. But he had read every single text in the village that pertained to magic as we volvas practiced it, as well as other tomes which I had no idea how he had acquired. Did he have an antique bookdealer somewhere in the modern world who found them for him?

Because they weren't from our Nordic ancestors; they came from cultures all over Europe and some from even further away. And they were clearly very old.

Most of them were written in languages I couldn't read, so I relied on him to tell me what they said. And for his part, he didn't understand the concepts he had read about in any visceral way. He had to rely on my personal experience, limited as it was.

It was like he was a blind person trying to describe color based just on what he'd read. He could connect a bunch of ideas, like knowing which paints to mix to get the color he wanted, but he didn't really know what the experience of implementing those ideas would look like. He couldn't see what he was painting.

But I could see it. So after a little trial and error, the two of us had worked out what I needed to focus on to keep my magic within a tight sphere around me. I still glowed to anyone who could see such power if they were close enough to me, but I no longer radiated like a pillar of light up to the sky and through even the densest of forests, visible for miles around.

It felt very strange, holding my magic in like that. As if in sympathy to that muffling, I walked with my head down, crunching through the icy snow. Powdery sparkles kept raining down on me from the trees as I passed under them. It was like I was in the world's largest snow globe.

The surrounding forest absorbed every sound so that my own footsteps seemed like they reached my ears from far away. There was no birdsong, no chattering of squirrels, nothing.

At least my own breath was quiet in my ears, because it literally *was* muffled. The air was hurt-your-face cold, so I had wrapped layer after layer of wool scarf around my head. My parka was zipped up to my nose, and my hat rested low on my eyebrows, but I had wrapped that scarf around both as well as nearly everything in between, leaving just a slit for my eyes. It was cozy under all that, even if it smelled like damp wool from the moisture of my own breath.

And I kept getting fibers from it stuck on my tongue. Wet wool is definitely not my favorite flavor.

At last I reached the clearing where my cottage stood. It looked so different since the last time I had seen it. All the wood carvings were gone, leaving nothing but an expanse of white snow. That undisturbed snow ringed by birch trees bereft of leaves made the clearing seem larger than before.

But there was one thing that was the same as the last time I had seen it.

Loke was there.

"Hey, you," I said. I'm not sure he heard a bit of that, so I pulled down my bottom layers of scarf and tucked them under my chin. "I haven't seen you in days."

"I'm sorry, Ingy. Esja told me you needed my help," he said. He was still dressed all in black, if a bit more warmly than usual in a long wool coat with a tall collar buttoned up over the bottom of his face. He even had a black knit cap on his head.

"I did. Days ago," I said. "But then I'm sure Esja has filled you in on everything."

"Indeed. You've been by every day, she tells me," he said. "Now you are heading out to the secret hamlet west of here, yes?"

"Trust you to already know all about a secret hamlet," I grumbled. "But, yes."

He made a gesture inviting himself to accompany me, and I nodded, then pulled the wool back up over my face. My cheeks were already aching from those few seconds of exposure to the frigid air.

"I don't suppose you'll tell me where you were?" I said.

"I had some things to attend to," he said vaguely. I barked out a laugh, and he looked over at me, both eyebrows raised high.

"Sorry," I said. "It's just when you say that, I remember how Gandalf kept disappearing when Bilbo needed him. It seemed random at the time, and it annoyed me more than it did Bilbo when I read that book as a kid. But when I got older and read the other books, I realized it was because Gandalf was fighting a greater danger than Bilbo ever knew. So tell me, have you been fighting ancient evil?"

"Nothing so exciting as all that," he said with a laugh, but then fell silent without telling me more.

"Are you coming on the hunting trip?" I asked.

"The big to-do with the Thors and their cousins the Freyas? Not really my sort of thing," he said.

"The Freyas?" I asked.

"You don't know your hosts?" he asked, raising an eyebrow.

"I know that Thorbjorn's mother and her sister inherited the lodge from their parents, and that they bring all their kids there every winter just after Jule to hunt. But that's it."

"Thorbjorn has five cousins, all girls," Loke said.

"All named some derivative of Freya," I guessed.

"Freyja, Freydis, Freylaug, Freygunnar and Frigg," he said. "Apparently four deep is as far as Jóra would dig down the Freya well."

"I've not met any of them yet," I said. "You don't like them?"

"I never said that," he said. "It's just not my scene." He looked over at me. "You'll probably fit in with them just fine. But a couple of them are married to the sort of men who hang at Aldis' mead hall."

"If that's the case, I'm *not* going to fit in," I said, suddenly miserable. I had been looking forward to this trip away from Haraldr and his daily lessons, but now I wasn't so sure this was going to be the break I wanted.

"You know, you might be looking at this thing all wrong," Loke said.

"What do you mean?"

"I know it's hard because they are prejudiced against you, and that's a big obstacle. But if you can win those guys over, no one else in Villmark will ever speak against you," he said. "You already have the council in your corner, after all. With these guys behind you too, you'll have the support of all of Villmark."

"But that's just it. I don't think I can win these guys over," I said glumly. "They still look at me like my Villmarker Norse is an assault on their ears."

"You just need the right opportunity," he said with a shrug. "A chance to show them what you can really do."

"It sounds to me like you're wishing trouble on me," I said. "Right after you told me you won't even be there if I need you."

"I never said that," he said, pretending to be offended. "I'll be there if you need me, and if I am able to answer your call. But for the hunting and feasting and the telling of tales around the fire? Sorry, I'd rather give it a miss."

"This isn't the way we went before," I said, suddenly realizing the surrounding forest was not what I remembered. The trees were all tall pines, the lowest of the branches high overhead. And we weren't walking up and down rocky slopes. The forest floor here was pretty flat.

"No, when you were following Solvi to the troll pass, you went nearly straight north," he said. "As much as such things mean anything in this part of the world. But that's a dangerous path, and not the way we're going. Look, see the sun up there?"

I nodded.

"We're going west," he told me. "The Villmarker families with hunting lodges all have them directly west of the village, scattered throughout the hills in that direction. Since we turned west after reaching your cottage first, we're north of all that, but not so far north as to be straying into troll territory. And that's where the outcasts hide."

When he said the last, he pointed straight ahead of us. It took me a moment to make out the outlines of a cluster of log cabins built in a rough circle, almost completely cloaked by tall pine trees with wide, dense branches that wove together as if to protect those homes from view from above.

"And there's Haraldr," I said, raising a mittened hand to wave hello to the old man waiting at the end of the path through the snow we were now following. He returned the gesture very briefly, then huddled back inside his voluminous cloak.

"You're here to see Signi. That's her cabin there," Loke said, pointing to the cabin just behind Haraldr.

"How many people live here?" I asked.

"Only about a dozen," he said. "A few couples share a cabin, but no one here has any children. They aren't happy people, Ingy."

"Why do they live here and not in Villmark?" I asked.

"I imagine if you asked them that, they'd all have a different answer," he said. "Some even have family back in town who think they're either long dead or gone for good, lost to the modern world. And yet here they are, all so close to home but never setting foot there."

As we trudged over the snow to Haraldr, a man appeared out of the forest to our left. He had a couple of dead rabbits slung over his shoulder, but no sign of a weapon. I supposed he must've trapped them. He stopped to speak with Haraldr at the side of the path.

"Hello," I said to Haraldr as we drew near enough for words. "Are we interrupting?"

"No, please," the man said, gesturing for me to take his place before Haraldr. Then he touched the edge of his hood like a man tipping his hat, and said, "thanks again," to Haraldr. He walked towards the center of the circle of cabins, then took a moment to get his bearings. All the cabins looked alike, with the doors and the windows the same size and in the same locations. It was like every cabin had come from the same kit, all matching with no hint of color or individuality at all. But at last he nodded to himself and walked up to one of the buildings, opening the door to disappear inside.

"That's Geiri," Haraldr told us. "He's our most recent returnee from your world. He's only been back here from the Twin Cities for a few weeks."

"How long was he out in the world?" Loke asked.

"Let me see," Haraldr said, tapping his mittened fingers against his lips. "Nearly two decades."

"How's he readjusting?" Loke asked.

"Well enough," Haraldr said absentmindedly, as if his brain had already gone on to something else. "Were you planning on joining us today, Loke?"

"Oh, no," Loke said with a dismissive wave of his hand. "I was just catching up with Ingrid. Don't mind me."

But as I followed Haraldr around the side of the cabin to the front door that faced the center of the circle of cabins, Loke stayed in step close beside me.

"Are you up to something?" I asked him suspiciously.

He looked like he was pondering his answer, and I stopped walking to turn and face him. Haraldr was tromping up the steps to the cabin door behind me, but I kept my own focus trained on Loke.

Then I heard a door slamming open. Not the one behind me, but the one from the cabin next door. Loke and I both jumped at the sound, turning our heads to watch a giant of a man dressed in layers of furs kick the door closed behind him before heading across the circular clearing to disappear into the woods on the far side of the little village.

"Didn't even say hello," Loke said with mock hurt.

"Who?" I asked.

"Oh, never mind," he said with another little wave. "I'm sure you two will cross paths soon enough, although I did hope to be here when it happened. Well, I still might. But in the meantime, Haraldr is waiting for you."

"Loke, what are you hiding from me?" I demanded.

But he just grinned. "Me? Hiding something? As if I would."

Then he turned and walked away. He disappeared from view long before someone wearing all black in a winter landscape should be able to.

But I wasn't frightened. Knowing Loke, his little secret was just some bit of mischief. Nothing of real danger.

I turned to follow Haraldr into Signi's cabin.

CHAPTER TWO

THE OUTSIDE of the cabin had looked quite rustic, the logs worn from the passing of many seasons, the stones at the foundation covered in moss as well as snow. I expected the interior to match it, or at least to be darker than the homes in Villmark. Although the shutters had all been thrown open, the few windows the cabin had were all small, the glass thick to the point of being opaque.

But it soon became apparent that someone had run electricity out to this little hamlet. The minute I stepped inside, I found there was no need for my eyes to adjust. The brightness of the lights in the interior matched the sun on the snow outside. Mainly this was because of the variety of lamps that were all warmly glowing despite it being midday.

But this was also because, while the exterior had all been roughly cut logs, the interior walls were all bookshelves painted a flawless white. The throw rugs were white, the furniture was pale wood with white upholstery. Even the knickknacks were all white and shining silver.

The door behind us closed, and I noticed the woman for the first time. She looked to be in her sixties with steely gray hair pulled back into a neat bun and dark blue eyes that radiated warmth. She hadn't said a word, and already I was sure she was a very good therapist.

"Hello. You're Signi, right?" I said, pulling off my mitten before thrusting out my hand.

"That's right. And you're Ingrid, lately of St. Paul," she said with a smile. "I went to school there, decades ago now."

"Which school?" I asked. St. Paul had a lot of prestigious colleges.

"Concordia," she said.

"Oh, sure," I said with a nod.

"Would you like some tea?" she asked.

"That sounds lovely," I said, and belatedly realized that Haraldr had already taken off his coat and boots and settled himself by the fireplace. Which was also white, covered in tile that barely showed signs of soot. How did she keep it so clean?

She gave me another smile, then crossed the living room to the little kitchen area on the far side. I hung up my coat and stepped out of my boots before joining Haraldr by the fire.

While we waited for Signi to finish the tea, I looked around at the bookshelves. She unsurprisingly had a lot of books about psychology. But there were also books about history and geography, philosophy and theology. And I guessed I was sitting in her preferred reading chair, because the shelf closest to me was over-stuffed with Stephen King paperbacks.

"Here you go," Signi said as she set a large tray on the table between me and Haraldr. Then she went to the back corner of the room where she had a little office area and rolled over a desk chair so she could sit between us.

"You have a computer," I noted.

"I do," she agreed as she poured out the tea. "I no longer see clients in the modern world, but I still submit articles to publications from time to time. And assist old friends with tricky research."

"You get the internet out here?" I asked, tempted to sneak a look at my phone. I could get cell service in Villmark, even better than I could down in the valley in Runde, but I always lost bars the minute I stepped into the woods.

"No, I have to go into town for that," she said. "There's a lovely new coffee shop close by that has Wi-Fi. I go there a few times a week to check in with my colleagues in the modern world."

"I know the place. My friend Jessica runs it," I said. "She even has some of my art up on her walls."

"The pen and ink sketches?" she asked. I nodded. "You have a fine eye for detail. I always see a little something new every time I study one of your pieces."

"Thanks," I said, feeling my cheeks flush. I was sure they were still bright red from being out in the cold, so I didn't think anyone noticed. But it had been a long time since I had talked to anyone about the art part of my life rather than the magic part.

"We're here to talk about Bera," Haraldr said, as if he had not only read my mind but disapproved of the path my thoughts were taking.

"Yes, Bera," I said. "Is she going to be okay?"

Signi paused just before taking a sip of her tea and gave a thoughtful frown. "I'm not sure that's the best question, actually," she said.

"No, I get it," I said. "There are no simple fixes in things like this. But there's better or worse, surely?"

"She is better," Signi conceded, then finally took that sip of tea before setting the cup down on the tray. She rubbed the palms of her hands over the knees of her dark gray wool pants, at first aggressively and then more slowly, smoothing out the wrinkles. "Bera has a long road ahead of her. But she has been a very willing patient. I do have a strong hope that she will be, by some definitions anyway, okay."

"Not a threat to others?" I guessed.

"Exactly. I hope to be able to return her to her family, but that's several months away yet."

"And her brother?" I asked.

"Her brother is responding very well to the medication I've prescribed for him," Signi said. "He's so fortunate that his parents are willing to even entertain such a course of action. Many in Villmark would rather leave him in total disfunction alone in his room for all of his days rather than rely on modern pharmacology.

"Certainly there is reason to approach such things with caution, but with me as his doctor, there is no danger of him being over-prescribed. He is still in the early days of being diagnosed, and I have to adjust his medication from time to time, but his outbursts are now safely a thing of the past. Hopefully soon it will even be possible for his mother to leave him alone for an hour or two at a time without worry."

"That *is* good news," I said. "Do you go there, or do they come here?"

"I go there," she said, reaching for her tea again. "Under cover of darkness. You knowing where this place is, that's a unique situation."

"I'll keep it secret," I said, glancing over at Haraldr. Was Loke even supposed to know about this place? And yet Haraldr hadn't seemed remotely surprised to see him walking beside me when I'd arrived.

Unless Haraldr thought I had brought Loke here?

"Don't worry about that. Some secrets keep themselves safe," Haraldr said with a little wave of his hand. "You had another question."

"Did I?" I asked. I gave him a puzzled look, then turned to Signi, who just raised her own eyebrows back at me. "We were here to talk about Bera. Is there more that I should know?"

"We're in a tricky area," Signi said. "I know there are no HIPAA regulations here, but I would still like to keep the details of my patients' cases private as much as possible."

"I don't think I need to know more than that they are doing well, myself," I said. I looked to Haraldr again, but he was studying the fire as if he found the patterns of the flames absolutely fascinating. No help there.

"You also work with Halldis?" I asked, lowering my voice as if that sorceress could somehow hear me say her name, even down where she was in her sealed cave deep under the village of Villmark.

"To a very limited extent," Signi said. "I'm not allowed to meet with her face to face, and she has no interest in anything I might do to help her. But I have spoken with her through her door on a few occasions."

"And?" I prompted.

Signi sighed. "Halldis is a very dangerous woman. You did us all a great service when you unmasked her and had her put away."

"No one suspected her until I got here?" I asked. It just felt so unlikely.

"She never seemed suspicious to any of us," Signi said. "She was untouched by time, but so is your grandmother. Most of us just thought it was a magic thing. Not that we knew she had so much magic. We knew she had some, because she would do little things to help people. Healing, scrying, harmless little charms. She always treated the rest of us with kindness and worked hard at what little craft she had. I confess, a lot of us were puzzled why your grandmother refused to take her on as an apprentice. But she must have sensed things we didn't."

"Sensed things like what?" I asked.

"Well, maybe that Halldis *is* dangerous, and in more ways than just magical ones," Signi said. "Halldis is very good at reading people and presenting herself how others expect to see her. She can very nearly make anyone believe anything she wants them to believe. Maybe even your grandmother, to some extent. Even now, warded against the use of magic as Halldis is, it is too dangerous to speak with her for long. She is devious and manipulative. Even I, with all my training, feel myself falling under her sway."

"And you're sure it's not magic?" I pressed.

Signi glanced at Haraldr, but he was still watching the fire, behaving as if he didn't even hear the two of us speaking.

"No," she said with great reluctance. "No, I'm not sure she's not somehow still using magic. But I am sure that even if she is, she's not using *just* magic. I know Haraldr has recommended that you not face her until you are far stronger and more disciplined in your own magic. I would second that advice. But more, I would suggest you study as much about abnormal psychology as you can before that day comes. She's going to try to manipulate you. That's a guarantee. You should be prepared."

"That day is far in the future, I'm sure," I said.

Haraldr turned from the fire to give Signi a brief glance.

"I have books I can lend you," she said, as if at Haraldr's silent behest. Then her demeanor brightened. "But I understand you're heading deeper into the woods today."

"Yes, I'm going hunting at a lodge with the Valkissons and some others," I said.

"Stop by again when you're back, and I'll have a few books ready for you to start with," she said. Then she got up from her chair and wheeled it back to her desk.

"Signi, may Ingrid and I have the use of your lovely home for a few minutes more?" Haraldr asked.

"Certainly," she said. "I usually go for a walk at about this time, anyway."

"Oh, but it's so cold out there today," I said, hating the idea of driving her out of her warm, cozy little cabin.

"Nothing I can't handle," she said as she put on a parka that looked even warmer than mine. The voluminous hood hid her entire face from view, and the hem of the jacket fell to below her knees. She flipped down a bench seat that was built into the wall and sat down. "You remember about my house guest, Haraldr?" she asked as she pulled on a pair of knee-high, fur-lined boots.

"Yes, I do," he said. "Is that likely to be a problem?"

"No," Signi said, but she didn't sound completely sure. She glanced at the clock on the mantle. "He doesn't generally get out of bed for another hour yet, so I'm sure he won't disturb you."

"And we shan't disturb him," Haraldr assured her. "Is it going well? His... transition?"

Signi frowned as she stood up and smoothed out her parka. "I'd prefer to talk to you about it later, if that's all right?"

"Certainly. I'll wait for you here, then?"

"Yes, that's fine. A half hour, I think. Is that enough time?"

"Ample," Haraldr said. "Thank you."

"Happy to be of service to the council, as always," Signi said as she wrapped a snowy white scarf around her neck then pulled on a thick pair of very modern snowmobile gloves. "And to the new volva as well. It was good meeting you, Ingrid. I look forward to seeing you again when you return for those books."

"Me, too," I said. Although abnormal psychology wasn't the sort of thing I normally wanted to put high on my personal to-be-read list, I could see the sense of being as prepared as possible before I faced Halldis.

Signi's parka swished against her thighs as she walked to the door, and the sudden rush of cold air when she opened it made the fire sputter and dance. But then the door closed again, and Haraldr and I were alone in that cozy little space.

"Should I be worried about the man upstairs?" I asked. Haraldr gave me a questioning look. "It's just, the way you said he was transitioning. It sounded different than when you were talking about that man outside."

"All cases are unique," he said. "Different reasons bring people back to Villmark. The adjustment is different. This one is a particularly tough case, but I have full confidence in Signi's abilities. But now," he said, slapping his hands together in a gesture I was coming to know all too well. "Ready for the next rune?"

"What, right this minute?" I asked, surprised. "I'm about to go on sort of a vacation, you know. For days and days. I thought we'd get to it after I got back."

"No time like the present," he said, reaching into the pocket of his tunic to present me a square of sturdy paper adorned with a single shape drawn in charcoal.

"No time like the present," I agreed with considerably less enthusiasm, then leaned forward to take the card.

CHAPTER THREE

THE SIGIL on the card was like the bottom half of a handwritten capital R, with a straight stroke vertical on the left but a sloping one on the right.

"It makes an 'u' sound," I said. I knew it wasn't much, and I wouldn't be surprised if he was rolling his eyes at me. But I didn't look up at him. I traced my fingertip over the shape on the card. The charcoal came off on my finger a little bit, but I had never minded getting my hands a little messy.

"And if I told you its name was Ur?" he asked.

"Well, that means the oldest thing, or the first thing, right?"

"Actually, not in this case. The Germanic prefix you're thinking of derives from something else," he said.

"It feels old," I said, still stroking the charcoal. "Maybe all runes do, though."

"The one Ur didn't lead to the other, but the meanings do have some similarities," he said. "But what impressions do you have based on looking at that shape and what you know about runes in general?"

"Well, we're still in Frey's group of eight, right? And this is still a rune of creation, related to the last one?" I said, looking up at him again. I waited for him to toss out that old staple of teachers, "are you asking me or telling me?"

But he didn't. Instead he asked me, "do you see how the shape resembles a yoke?"

I looked back down at the card, at the gentle curve to the top of the rune. "Yes," I said. I could see that, even if it was a little crooked for that function, being taller on one side. But if I drew another, reflected version beside it, it would make an even pair, just a bit taller in the middle.

I didn't know much about farm work, but that made sense. The harness or whatever would run up the middle of the pair.

"The first rune represented cattle as wealth, among other things," Haraldr said. "This one is an aurochs or ox, if you will, doing work. It represents colossal strength, a strength rooted in the earth itself." He curled his hands into fists and drew them back to his sides to demonstrate pulling strength.

"So less spontaneous creation, more like... farm labor," I guessed. I had just been thinking those words, hadn't I?

"Exactly," he said. "Both runes reflect aspects of the first cow, Audhumla. But Ur also relates to personal growth. If the first rune represents the moment you were born and the strength you were born with, in this rune you learn and grow, evolve and take up your personal mantle, find your own strength. Claim your place in the world."

"I'm not sure I'm ready for this," I said, looking at the shape on the card. It felt like an actual, physical yoke of heavy wood and metal that was about to be placed on my shoulders.

Mastering this new rune was going to be so much work.

"I know you were planning a few days away for a hunting expedition," Haraldr said. "That is good. I approve of your taking the time to engage in Villmarker activities, especially some of the older traditions. But I expect when you return to the village with enough meat to see us through the lean winter months ahead, you will also have something to report to me about your time spent meditating on this rune."

"I'll do my best," I said. He raised an eyebrow at me. "Nilda and

Kara said we'd all be bedding down together in the same hall. No separate bedrooms or even a shared one that I might get a minute to myself in. No privacy."

"Bedrooms are a rather modern invention," he said, as if he could personally remember a time without them being commonplace. I doubted very much he could. He was old, but there was no way he was *that* old. "You'll find a way to manage, just as your ancestors did."

"I'm sure I'll work something out," I said, tucking the card away. I started to get up from the chair when another thought kept me from moving. "Haraldr, are there creatures like fire giants that I might accidentally summon when I'm working on this rune?"

"There are always things that will be drawn to you. Which is why you are practicing keeping your glow contained," he said.

"I know. But still, anything specific I should watch for?"

He frowned, but I could see he wasn't frowning at me. He was frowning over his own thoughts as he mulled over my question. "Nothing dangerous," he said at last. "You might draw some allies."

"Allies are good," I said hopefully.

Now he *was* frowning at me. "Not every ally is friendly or easy to talk to. Or above taking offense at a diplomatic misstep."

"Right," I said. "I'll be careful."

"I should hope you wouldn't have to promise *me* that," he said.

"Of course, I'm always careful," I said.

I wished I could be sure that was true. But too often since coming to Villmark, I hadn't even realized there was something I needed to be careful about until it was too late.

"I should get going," I said. "I'm meeting the others at the Valkissons' house, and that's a long walk back."

"It's good practice," Haraldr said. "Have fun with your friends. Meditate as often as you can, which I'm sure will be more often than you *think* you can. I'll see you when you return to Villmark."

"Right," I said, then went to the front hall to get back into my boots and parka. Haraldr resumed studying the flames, and I slipped out of the door without disturbing him again.

There was no sign of Signi returning from her walk, but if she had gone to Jessica's café it was far too soon for her to be back already. I looked back at her cabin and saw a tiny detail that set it out from the others: her wooden shutters had little hearts carved into them. They were so small I doubt I would've noticed them if I hadn't still been standing on her porch.

It was a warm touch, but overall this whole little community felt remote and isolated, not just from Villmark but from each other. The glass of the windows of the cabins around me was all frosted, but by design, not by the cold. These people cherished their privacy. I could see light from lamps and other electric fixtures through some of them, but no other sign of life, not even a passing shadow.

It felt strange, being surrounded by those buildings and yet feeling like I was completely alone in the world. And a cold wind was blowing strongly, as if the buildings weren't there at all. Like I was just hallucinating them.

I adjusted the layers of my wool scarf over my face then took a moment to be sure I was once more dampening down my magical glow. But before I had even walked down the steps from Signi's door to start walking home, I got distracted by the sound of voices. Male voices. They weren't loud enough for me to catch any words, but I could tell that an argument was going on.

I skipped down the steps then headed to the center of the circle of cabins. Now I could see the two of them, standing on another forest path just south of the hamlet. The taller of the two was the man who lived in the cabin next to Signi's, the one Loke had wanted me to meet. The smaller one was turned sideways to me to look up at the taller one, and with his hood up I could see nothing of his face, but I recognized his coat. He was the new man in the hamlet, Geiri.

I stayed where I was, too far away to hear their words, because I wasn't sure if this was any of my business. I had a place to be, and was already late.

The taller man stopped talking, which seemed like a good sign. Then I saw Geiri's mittened hands closing into tight fists. His entire body was tense, so tense I could see it through the many layers of clothing that were protecting him from the cold.

But the tall man either didn't notice or didn't care about the smaller man's growing anger. He turned his back to him, heading for his cabin. His eyes glanced up and saw me standing there in the common area. He gave me a cursory glance, then a harder look, as if he was trying to figure out if he knew me. He opened his mouth to say something to me, but I saw Geiri behind him raise a hand as if he were about to stab the taller man in the back.

"Look out!" I cried. The tall man spun and caught Geiri's wrist.

But there was nothing in his hand.

"Let me go!" Geiri hissed. The tall man released him with a little shove. "You had no call to do that."

"Didn't I?" the man asked him with a sneer. Now that I was closer to him I could see he was not as young as I had thought. He certainly moved like a young man, and one with martial arts training at that. But his weathered face was deeply wrinkled, especially around his green eyes.

There was something awfully familiar about those eyes. It made me think of Thorbjorn for some reason, but they weren't the same shade at all. Was this a brother of Valki, perhaps?

"Who are you?" I asked him.

He looked at me in surprise. But he just shook his head. "No. This isn't the time. Please excuse me."

Then he just left, walking back to his cabin and going inside with a resounding slam of his door.

It was a good thing I had that scarf covering my entire face, because I would look pretty silly standing there with my mouth gaping open otherwise.

"His name is Frór," Geiri told me, making me jump. I had forgotten he was there.

"I don't know that name," I admitted.

"He thinks he's in charge here," Geiri said with a great deal of bitterness in his tone. "But no one is in charge here."

"No, I gathered this was a pretty loose community," I said, but my eyes were on his hands. "You had something before. Where did it go?"

He opened both of his mittened hands to show me he was hiding nothing. "You can pat me down if you like. I have nothing."

"Then why did you...?" I broke off, miming the stabbing motion he had made before.

But he just shrugged. "It was a stupid thing to do. In my defense, I didn't know you were there watching me. I just needed to vent a little."

"That's very aggressive venting," I said.

"I didn't have anything in my hand," he insisted. "Look, I'm sure you know I'm the new one here. I'm only here now because my entire life on the outside world fell apart pretty dramatically. I came here to have a little peace and quiet to process. Not to be micromanaged by the man who could've been king."

"That guy was a king?" I asked, looking back over my shoulder towards his cabin.

"No, he was never even close to being made king. We don't have those here," Geiri said. "He just thinks he should've been king."

"I get that you think he's bossy," I said. "What was he trying to tell you to do?"

"Nothing," he said, too quickly. Well, I suppose it really was none of my business.

And yet, something didn't feel right.

"Do you mind if I take you up on that pat down?" I asked him.

He looked at me like he thought I was crazy. Maybe I was. "I'd rather you didn't touch me," he said at last.

"I won't have to," I said. "Just stand there."

I fished through my pockets. I came up with a stub of pencil and the card that contained my rune. I turned the card over and drew a hasty sketch of Geiri on the back of it.

I was peripherally aware of his mood morphing from annoyance that I was delaying him to curiosity at what I was doing. When I finished my sketch and put the pencil away, he came around to stand at my shoulder and see what I had drawn.

"Nice likeness," he said appreciatively.

"Thanks," I said, only half listening to him. I let my eyes drift out of focus and waited for anything hidden in the pencil sketch to jump out at me.

At first I saw nothing. Then I noticed an image in his shadow on the snow behind him: a literal fish out of water. I chuckled.

"What?" he asked.

"Nothing," I said, putting the card back in my pocket. "You're all right."

"Thanks?" he said uncertainly.

"My name is Ingrid," I said, thrusting a hand out at him. "My grandmother Nora is the volva, and I'm sort of the volva in training."

"Oh, of course," he said and mimed slapping his own forehead. "I saw you just an hour ago coming up the path with Loke. I guess I didn't recognize you without him."

"I'm about to leave town for a week or so on a hunting trip," I told him. "But I'll be back here in this hamlet to pick up some books from Signi first thing when I get back. If Frór is still hassling you, let me know then and I'll see what I can do."

"I'm sure that won't be necessary," he said. "I'm just having a bad day. Lots of bad days. I'm sure I just took what he was saying wrong."

"Well, just in case. I'll be here," I said. "But right now I'm running late."

"Please, don't let me delay you," he said.

"It was good meeting you," I said, although to myself I thought "interesting" was probably the more appropriate adjective.

I gave him a smile he could in no way see through my scarf, although perhaps my eyes hinted at it. Then I set off back towards my own cottage in the forest. I felt him watching me leave, or thought I did, but when I turned back at the edge of the hamlet to wave to him, I realized he had gone.

I was alone.

CHAPTER FOUR

ᚾ

THE LONELY FEELING faded as I left those silent cabins behind. I was once more in a forest filled with life. I could sense it all around me, even though it was far too cold for birds to be singing or squirrels to be out of their drays.

But it wasn't just the smaller forms of life I was feeling. Those little creatures *were* all around me, but there was also something else, something more focused.

As I walked alone through the woods, I sensed a presence following along behind me. And I had that tickling feeling on the back of my neck, like I was being watched.

I couldn't just look back over my shoulder, not with my parka hood up and my hat down low over my eyes and all those layers of wool wrapping over everything. No, I had to stop walking all together and turn completely around to peer out of the slit for my eyes I had left in the layers of my scarf.

I had thought perhaps someone was looking out one of those cabin windows, watching me trek away from their hamlet. But I had already left the cabins far behind. There was nothing to be seen behind me but trees, snow, and my own footprints. No one could possibly be watching me.

But the minute I turned back and started walking again, that feeling of being followed returned, even stronger than before.

I kept walking, step after step through the snow, but inside my mind was racing. I double-checked my own magic, and I wasn't glowing or drawing anything to me. I was absolutely sure of that.

But whatever I was sensing behind me? That was clearly magic of its own.

No one in that collection of cabins should be able to use magic. They hadn't been able to when they left Villmark; I was certain of that. Only my grandmother and I and Halldis had any ability with magic.

But what if someone who had left had learned magic out in the modern world?

That was a chilling thought. I knew for a fact there were other kinds of magic. My friend Tlalli from México had an Aztec magical lineage. And I knew there was an Irish woman in Duluth who also knew magic. There had to be more. But how many? How prevalent was it?

The people of Villmark might not be able to use magic themselves, but they knew with certainty that it existed. If they left for the modern world and encountered something mystical, they would know better than to just dismiss it out of hand.

I suddenly had a lot more questions for my grandmother. But she was in Runde. She might as well be a world away from me now, forbidden as I was to go back to Runde.

In the meantime, that feeling of being followed was creeping up the back of my neck something fierce. It wasn't just magical power I was feeling. No, this felt like real malevolence.

I knew what that felt like. Halldis had been filled with it. But for once, I didn't suspect her. This malevolence was quite different from what I had felt coming off of her.

It was more... masculine? Was that possible? Every practitioner of magic I knew was a woman, some kind of witch, but I knew so few I didn't want to assume that warlocks weren't a thing.

Trollmenn. That's what they were called. From the stories, I had always assumed they were more common than volvas like my grandmother and myself.

But that was in the old world. What would a trollmann be doing in the woods so close to Villmark? It had to be some new presence, or I would've sensed it before.

That thought sparked a sudden panic in my mind, and I immediately stopped walking.

What if it was following me back to town? What if I was once again leading trouble towards my people?

I had to do something. But what?

"Ingrid! Hey, Ingrid!"

The voice rang through the surrounding trees, directionless, but that wasn't as unnerving as it might sound, because I recognized that voice. It was my friend Nilda, and soon her sister Kara was calling my name too.

Then I saw them through the trees ahead of me, running up the path towards me. The clearing and my cottage were just behind them, and that clearing was filled with people and horses and sleighs piled high with sacks of supplies.

"We were looking for you!" Nilda said as the two of them reached me.

But I didn't answer, because I was looking back again. Whatever had been behind me, so close behind me it had been running its spectral tendrils up my spine and sending magical shivers all over my body, it was gone now.

I closed my eyes and expanded my senses, but there was no sign of anything out of the ordinary anywhere around me. It had disappeared without a trace.

Which wasn't comforting. Had it come from the hamlet, or had it just crossed paths with me near there? Until today, I had never been in that particular part of the woods.

"Ingrid?" Nilda asked. I could hear the beginnings of worry in her tone and forced a smile as I turned back.

"Sorry, I thought I heard something," I said, but waved it away as nothing. "Never mind. I thought I was meeting you all in Villmark, though?"

"You weren't there," Kara said. Her voice was flat, not giving me any hint to what she was thinking or feeling. Just as it had been for weeks now, since the night Thorbjorn had left to fight off the fire giants.

"Loke said you'd gone this way," Nilda said. "So we figured we'd meet you here and save some time."

"I packed, but my bag is still at home," I admitted.

"We've got it," Nilda said. "Mjolner too. He's sleeping in a nest of furs in one of the sleighs."

"I didn't even know he was planning on coming," I said. I wondered if he had sensed what was behind me in the woods, but quickly decided he couldn't have. If he had, he would've been at my side. He was still in super-protective mode after barely saving me from Bera and her wicked stone-throwing arm.

"We should get going," Nilda said, gesturing back towards the sleighs in the clearing. "We want to get to the lodge before sunset, and we have a long way to go."

"Sure," I said, and followed the two of them back to my cottage.

Thorbjorn was staring off to the north when we emerged into the clearing. For a moment he looked just like a Thor I had drawn in ink once, guarding the world of men from incursions by the giants, staring off into the distance as he waited for them to approach. He had the same faraway look in his eyes. He even had his hand resting on the handle of the axe hanging from this belt.

But then he turned at the sound of our approach, and a wave of relief washed over his face, so intense I felt a twinge of guilt.

Nilda whispered something to her sister, then pulled her towards one of the sleighs. Thorbjorn waved an arm in the air and the other sleighs started moving out of the clearing, to the west but more to the south than where I had just come from.

"You thought I went that way?" I said to Thorbjorn, pointing to where he had been staring off towards where he had taken me before, to the mountains that were visible to the north even though they existed in Old Norway.

"I wasn't sure where you went," he said. "Loke wasn't clear. He only assured me that you were perfectly safe."

"I was. Perfectly. I was with Haraldr," I said. Did he know about the hamlet? If anyone in the village outside of the council knew, it was the Thors. But just in case he didn't, I decided not to mention it now. Instead, I said, "he's been teaching me how to hide my magic from the senses of others."

"Oh," Thorbjorn said, taken aback. "How's it going?"

"Good, I think," I said. "I don't know how long I can keep it up, though. Or if I'm still tamping down my glow when I'm sleeping. So I'm not ready to spend any nights in my cottage yet. More's the pity."

I touched the doorframe of my cottage with its subtle carving evoking the great lake's waves in the wood. The previous owner had been an artist. Wood had come to life under his tools, whether it was a statue of a bear or a troll or just a suggestion of water like in that doorframe.

I longed to spend more time in this home that hadn't belonged to my ancestors, that was just mine. But I was supposed to stay in town, in that ancestral home my grandmother had moved out of decades before.

But this cottage would still be here when my control was better.

"We should get going?" Nilda called to us from where she and Kara were bundled together in the back of the sleigh.

"Right," Thorbjorn said. "Let's go. We can shout a few introductions once we catch up with the others."

I climbed up into the sleigh and settled in among the piles of furs, careful not to jostle Mjolner, who was curled up at my feet.

Thorbjorn got in on the other side and flicked the reins. The sturdy horses in front of us took off at a brisk trot and we were zipping through the forest, the blades of the sleigh singing over the frozen snow.

And despite the cold, I smiled and then laughing in delight. There was more than one kind of magic in the world. This moment, like a winter postcard come to life, was definitely one of the good kinds of magic.

CHAPTER FIVE

ᚢ

It wasn't long before we caught up with the other sleighs racing through the trees, the bells on all the harnesses ringing brightly through the cold air.

"I wish it were warmer," Kara grumbled from the back seat. She was slouched low under a thick fur blanket, only her blue eyes visible from under the fur brim of her hat.

"It'll warm up tomorrow," I said. "Although it's likely going to snow in the next few days."

"How do you know that? Magic?" she asked. Again her tone was so inflectionless I couldn't tell if she was teasing, or attacking, or just asking for information.

I opted to assume the latter. "I have an app on my phone," I said. "I checked the weather forecast before I left Villmark this morning. I assumed I wouldn't be able to get any bars out at the hunting lodge."

"You assumed correctly," Nilda said. "But I'm glad to know it'll get warmer. I like the cold, but the last few days have been a bit much even for me."

"Are you warm enough now?" Thorbjorn asked, glancing back over his shoulder at the two sisters buried under furs.

"We're perfect," Kara said, although the fact that only her eyes were visible made her a little less than convincing.

"Introductions," Nilda reminded Thorbjorn.

"Right," he said, looking around at the other sleighs. "That one," he said, pointing to a sleigh painted blue and silver, pulled by two white horses. "That's my parents and Thorge and Thormund. But you've met them all before."

"Not your mother," I said.

"Are you sure?" he asked.

"Positive," I said.

"Her name is Gunna. You're going to love her," Nilda told me.

"I hope so," I said. I had to admit I was a bit nervous about that. I got on well with Thorbjorn's brothers, but I wasn't sure their father cared for me at all. Valki was on the council, and most of my interactions with him had been in that capacity, so it was a little hard to tell. After all, I hadn't thought Haraldr liked me much before we had started working on the runes together. Maybe spending time together in this less formal setting would make him regard me a little more warmly.

"And over there," Thorbjorn said, pointing beyond his parents' sleigh to a larger sleigh pulled by six horses, "that's my mother's sister Jóra driving the team. Beside her is her oldest daughter Freyja and Freyja's husband Manni, as well as their son Martin."

"He's just a baby," Nilda said. "Not quite one."

"I guess that's why I can't see him from here," I said.

"Sitting behind them is my cousin Freydis and her husband Yngvi. They're newlyweds."

"Yngvi looks familiar," I said. Trees kept passing between our two sleighs, and we were dozens of meters apart, but I was sure I knew that strong, slightly hooked nose.

"You might have seen him at Aldis' mead hall when we were there with Loke," Nilda said, barely over a whisper. As if he might overhear us from so far away over the sounds of the horses and the bells.

"Oh, right," I said. "Loke mentioned something about that. That the men here are the kind that don't mix with Runde."

"No one is going to be rude to you here," Thorbjorn said darkly.

"I know you'll look out for me," I assured him.

"Forget about that," he said with a laugh. "If they are anything less than cordial to anyone while under my mother's roof... Well, let's just say her temper is legendary."

"Oh," I said, not sure how to react to that.

"It's her place," he said, as if a question of ownership had been what had tripped me up. "Her and her sister's. They inherited it from their parents. It's been in the family for generations."

"Who's in the very back of that sleigh?" I asked. I could see three women huddled together, much like Nilda and Kara were behind me.

"The youngest of my cousins, Freylaug, Freygunnar and Frigg," he said.

"Jóra and all her daughters run a bakery together on the east side of town," Nilda said. "We don't get to see them much these days, since they're so busy with their bakery. But when we were kids, Kara and I hung out with them all the time. They're great."

"And that sleigh?" I asked, pointing at the red and gold one pulled by a pair of brown horses that was off to our right. Then I recognized the man holding the reins. "Wait, that's Roarr."

"Correct," Thorbjorn said. "And that's Sigvin beside him."

"It took a lot of convincing for her to come with us," Nilda said. "In the end, I think it was her parents that did it. But this will be good for her. She misses her sister so much." She looked over at her own sister with great fondness, and a little of the steel rigidity of Kara's posture softened, if only a little.

"And behind them?" I said conversationally, but then I recognized those men too. "That's Báfurr and Raggi, isn't it?"

"It is," Nilda said. "They're close with Manni and Yngvi."

"And will also behave themselves if they know what's good for them," Thorbjorn said, his voice almost a growl. I suspected objections had been raised to their presence.

I wondered who had overruled him?

"Are you hungry?" Nilda asked, digging down under the furs in the middle of the sleigh. "We won't be stopping for lunch, but I packed some food to eat on the go. Meat and bread and cheese. And," she paused until she found what she was looking for. She held a large thermos up into the air like an Arthur who had just freed his Excalibur from the stone. The chrome of the thermos even glinted in the sun like a silvery starburst. "Mulled wine!"

"See why I picked the three of you for my sleigh?" Thorbjorn said. "You can always count on the Mikkelsen sisters to keep an entire company of men fed."

"And yet, that's not the job I'm angling for," Nilda said with a laugh. "Hit me with the compliments when I've taken down the biggest elk of the party. Which I will."

"Not a bear?" he asked, glancing back at her.

"Ugh. I hate bear meat," she said, wrinkling her nose.

"Hunting a bear is just about telling the tale afterward," he said. Then he winked at me. "I always bag a bear."

"Here," Nilda said, nudging my shoulder. She put an enormous sandwich into my hands, then gestured for me to hand it to Thorbjorn.

"Ah, perfection," Thorbjorn said and bit into it with gusto. Then he glanced over at me. "You should probably eat something if you want any of that mulled wine."

"You're going to want some of my mulled wine," Nilda said, handing me a large, steaming mug of it. The heat felt wonderful in my hands, and the melange of spices in the air were warming just to smell.

"Careful," Thorbjorn said. "It's got more of a kick than you'd think."

I took a careful sip. It was sweet and spicy at first, but Thorbjorn was right. The alcohol content was quite pronounced.

"Sandwich?" Nilda asked me, and I knew that even though I hadn't sputtered or coughed, she knew I was feeling the effects of her special brew.

"Just cheese on mine," I said.

I didn't take another sip until half of that sandwich was gone. But when I did, I was instantly warm all the way down to my toes.

The wine warmed Kara up as well, and soon she was sitting up and leading us all in a singalong as we raced over the snow. Some of the songs I knew from my nights at the mead hall at the south end of Villmark, but many were new to me.

But not to the others. As the day darkened towards sunset, the sleighs drew closer together, and soon the people in the other sleighs started joining in with our songs. The bells on the harnesses set the rhythm, making every song a joyous one.

Then suddenly it all stopped. The drivers of the sleighs pulled the horses to a halt, and we all tumbled out of the warm furs into the air that had only gotten colder when the daylight had faded.

"Just in time," Thorbjorn said, looking off to the west. The forest here was too thick to see the sun directly, but it definitely had gone behind one of the rolling hills, leaving the valley where we had stopped in murky grayness that was creeping towards night.

"There's the lodge," Nilda said, pointing off to the left. I could just make out the shape of it through the trees, a tall A-frame structure made of sturdy logs. If it were decorated with carvings like my cottage or my grandmother's mead hall, it was too dark to tell. I would have to make a point to walk around outside in the morning.

"Can you three take all the bags in while I see to the team and the sleigh?" Thorbjorn asked.

"Of course," Kara said, and she and her sister walked around to the back of the sleigh and started untying the cargo.

I dug through the furs in the front seat until I found Mjolner, still sleeping in his warm little nest. But when I lifted the last fur to reach for him, the cold air disturbed him. He woke with an irritated meow, then glared at me before hopping out of the sleigh and heading towards the lodge, as if he knew exactly where he was going.

Well, he probably did.

I slung my duffel bag full of clothes over my shoulder, then my heavier bag of art supplies, before reaching for one of the bags that Nilda and Kara were stacking on the snow. It was even heavier than my art supplies and rattled and clanged as I moved it. Cast iron cookware, I was sure.

"Bring that to Gunna," Nilda said to me, and gave me a nudge toward the lodge. I certainly couldn't carry any more, even if I could somehow free up a hand. I tried not to grunt as I carried that bag into the open door of the lodge.

The inside was just as cold as the outside, but that wouldn't be true for long. Already Thorbjorn's father Valki was lighting a fire in the center of the hall, and Thorge and Thormund brushed past me with armfuls of seasoned logs ready to add to it once it really got going.

They had both taken off their hats already. Thormund's long hair looked like it kept his head warm enough, the three braids of his hair and two braids of his long beard thick and only a little frosted from his breath.

Thorge kept the sides of his head shaved and never allowed the longer red hair on top to fall over the knot work tattoos that curved over his ears. I still really longed to draw them. Perhaps I would have the opportunity some evening while we were all gathered together by the fire.

"Gunna?" I said as I approached the corner of the hall that served as the food preparation space. She was unpacking a crate filled with canisters of flour and sugar and salt, but looked up when she heard her name.

"Ah, Ingrid," she said, and rubbed her palms down the front of her apron before extending a hand to me. I shifted my duffel and art bag a little higher up my shoulder before taking her hand. She had a very strong handshake, but she stopped just short of crushing me in her grip. "What do you have there?"

"Pots and pans, I believe," I said.

"And Thorbjorn made you carry it?" she asked, clearly amused. I heard Thorge chuckle, but when I looked his way he was dutifully focused on the fire.

"Never mind, dear," Gunna said, taking pity on my inability to come up with an answer to that. "I'll take it. You can put your own things against one of the walls for now. We'll sort all that out later. We need to get everything inside before it's dark first."

"Okay," I said, and walked past a long, crooked line of benches to set my bags against one of the log pillars. The wood was gorgeously stained, brightening the color and bringing out the patterns in the wood's grain, but was otherwise unadorned. No Nordic patterns or fanciful carvings of animals here.

Talking and laughter drew my attention back to the open doors. Jóra's youngest three daughters were coming in, each with a great round sack in her arms. The aroma of fresh bread was so strong I could smell it even halfway down the hall. Raggi, Báfurr and Roarr came in behind them, each carrying a crate with an assortment of root vegetables inside.

The laughter was from the sisters, who were ostensibly talking with each other, but kept casting looks back at the three men behind them. Raggi and Báfurr clearly noticed but were playing it cool.

But Roarr, as usual, seemed completely oblivious to anything the women around him were doing. He just brought his crate over to Gunna in the kitchen. She pointed him towards a spot against the front wall, and he set his crate down then set to work arranging all the others around it that had been set there all pellmell.

I went back outside to find Nilda and Kara standing by the mountain of sacks watching Thorbjorn and the other drivers guiding the horses into the stable that was at the back part of the hall. The sleighs had been lined up under the overhanging roof. If it snowed like my weather app had predicted, at least the sleighs wouldn't get filled with cold drifts.

"Can I help?" I asked Nilda.

"Sure," she said, and tossed me a sack. I flinched, fearing another sack full of iron cookware was about to collide with my face, but the bag was flying through the air way too gently for it to be that.

"Bedding," Nilda said with a grin. "Bulky, but not heavy."

"I thought this was a family outing," I said to her as we picked up as many of the sacks as we could manage.

"It is," Nilda said, giving me a puzzled frown. "Are you asking why we're here or why *you* are?"

"It's not that," I quickly assured her.

"Then what is it?"

Another burst of loud giggles announced that the three youngest sisters were coming back outside to help with the rest of the baggage. They stopped and looked back, waiting until Raggi, Báfurr and Roarr finally appeared behind them. Then something set them off giggling again.

"It feels like a singles meetup," I whispered to her. "Seriously."

"That's just the Freyas," Kara said. She had a bag under each arm and another in each hand, and when she headed towards the lodge she waddled like a very round penguin.

"So they're always like this?" I asked Nilda.

"No, you're not wrong," she said. "The oldest two are married, and the five of them were always super competitive. It's probably a race among the last three not to be the last one to find a husband."

"So long as it's just them, then," I said. "I didn't come out here to pair off with anyone, or to watch everyone else pair off."

"I know. You're here for the culture," Nilda said with a teasing wink. "Come on, let's get everything inside so they can close the doors. I'm dying to feel warm again."

"You could just have some more of that mulled wine of yours," I said.

Nilda led the way inside to the far end of the room. I could just hear the sound of horses on the other side of the wall, but thankfully I couldn't smell them. I hoped they had a fire or a space heater or something besides their own body heat to keep them warm inside that stable, or they were going to be miserable indeed.

At least it was already getting warmer inside the lodge.

"We can just leave these here for now," Nilda said, dropping her sacks to the floor. "The bedding eventually goes in those cupboards while we're here, but that can wait until morning. No sense unpacking them until we need them."

I set my sacks down next to hers, and we headed back outside. But the others had carried in the last of the supplies, and the drivers were coming back around the corner of the lodge from the stable.

"I'm going to find my sister," Nilda said, then slipped back inside.

"Waiting for me?" Thorbjorn asked.

"I guess so. Are we all done out here?" I asked.

"Looks that way," he said. "Let's get in and shut these doors."

"Maybe I should stay out for bit," I said, looking back over my shoulder at the hall now filled with people. No quiet corners, no privacy of any kind.

Thorbjorn gave me a puzzled frown. Then a look of sudden understanding dawned on his face. "The outhouse is around the other side," he said, pointing.

"No, it's not that," I said, although that was useful information to have for later. "I'm going to need to be alone."

"Now? Why?" he asked.

"Not *now* necessarily, but at some point," I said. "I need to meditate or draw or whatever. You know, volva stuff."

"Oh, sure," he said, nodding. Then he gave me one of his intense looks. "But not now. It's night, Ingrid."

"I can see that, actually," I said.

"You don't understand," he said. "We're a lot farther away from home than you've been before."

"The trolls felt farther," I said, although I realized that couldn't be true. We had walked there in less time than it had taken to get here on horse-drawn sleighs.

"Distance doesn't work here like it does closer to Villmark," he said. "And the north is its own thing."

"Where are we exactly?" I asked. "If the north takes you back to Norway, where does the west go?"

"I don't know," he admitted. "It's just hills and trees, then more hills and trees."

"You patrol here?" I asked.

"Sometimes, but not often," he said. "Trouble comes from the north."

I nearly asked him about the hamlet, and if that was different too. But I still didn't know if he knew the hamlet even existed. I really should've asked Haraldr about that. If I knew I could talk to Thorbjorn, I could ask him all my questions about the different things that lurked among the trees. Maybe he could even tell me what I had sensed that morning.

But that would have to wait. "So it's safe here," I said instead.

"It's safe during the day, aside from the usual dangers from bears and wolves and the like. At night, it's still safe in there," he said, pointing over his shoulder into the lodge. "But not out here. You can come out in the morning if you like and do whatever you need to do on your own, but not at night."

"But what's out here at night?" I persisted. "Trolls? Giants? Something worse?"

"I don't know what's out here at night," he admitted. Then he grinned at me. "Because I'm always indoors at night. Does this really need to be the next mystery you investigate?"

"Of course not," I said. "I'm on vacation."

"It's a relief to hear you say that," he said.

"Thorbjorn!" his mother called from the doorway. "Get in the house. You know the rules!"

I started to laugh, but at the sight of her standing in that doorway, her weighty arms crossed over her chest, that legendary temper just barely in check, I decided I would be better off making all haste to get inside.

CHAPTER SIX

ᚾ

WHILE I HAD BEEN OUTSIDE with Thorbjorn, someone had put a massive cast-iron pot over the now-roaring fire in the center of the hall. One by one, Jóra and each of her daughters walked up to that pot and dumped in a bowl full of a different type of food. Jóra had sliced potatoes, Freyja sliced carrots, Freydis wedges of onions, Freylaug sliced fennel bulbs, Freygunnar chopped fresh herbs, and finally Frigg put in a bowl full of chopped dried meat.

"The last of last year's hunt," Thorbjorn told me as we stood with the others watching this little ceremony. "Our traditional meal before this year's hunt begins."

"It's going to take forever for that water to come to a boil," I said. "How late were we planning on eating?"

"We did get here late," Kara said. She left unsaid but clearly meant for me to know that we were late on my account.

"Can I try speeding things up?" I asked. "My little fireball is my only real spell, but it's reliable."

"Please do," Gunna said. I hadn't realized she was standing right behind me and Thorbjorn. When I hesitated, she gestured towards the pot.

Swallowing hard, I walked closer to the fire. I knew this spell well, but I usually used it for light. I had used it to warm my hands while drawing outside on a cold winter's day, but this was going to require a lot more than that. It was a lot of water. I was going to have to generate a lot of heat.

At the same time, it was probably best if I didn't burn this ancestral hunting lodge down to the ground.

I summoned the small version of the ball of light on my palms, then infused it with as much power as I dared. On impulse, I used some of the same techniques that Haraldr and I had been working on to contain my glow, only this time I was containing the power within the confines of a small, easily controlled ball.

When it got too hot to hold, I tossed it into the fire directly under the bottom curve of that pot. To my surprise, the flames of that natural fire leaped up into the air in a variety of colors, snapping like flags in a stiff wind and shooting sparks through the air. But just when I was certain I had messed up and really was about to set the lodge ablaze, the effects passed away.

I was looking at a perfectly ordinary fire now, burning hot within the red hearts of those logs under the cooking pot.

And the water in the pot was at a brisk simmer.

"That's a handy little trick," Freyja said. Her son was perched on her hip with a fist in his mouth, but at her words he threw both of his hands in the air and gave an inarticulate shout of delight.

"Did you like the show, little one?" I asked him. He just looked back at me with huge blue eyes, but I could see he was impressed.

"His name is Martin," Freyja told me.

"How do you do, Martin?" I asked, putting out a hand. Martin looked at it suspiciously for a moment, then slapped it with his own chubby little hand. The one that had just been in his mouth. I discretely wiped it on the side of my pants.

"Who's kill is in the pot?" Báfurr asked.

"Was it Nilda and Kara's elk?" Jóra asked. "They brought that elk down the morning we left last year."

"No, this was Thorge's kill," Gunna said, puffing her chest out with obvious pride. "He took down a deer while riding on the sleigh on the way home. That was the last kill."

"You shot a deer from a moving sleigh?" Raggi asked, clearly impressed.

Thorge tried to wave away the question, but Thorbjorn was having none of it. "We didn't even have to stop to track it or anything. It was a clean shot, right through the eye. One and done. We picked it up out of the snow and carried on back to the village. But I should let Thorge tell the tale."

"No, that's all there was to it," Thorge said. He was rubbing at the back of his neck, and he looked a little embarrassed by his older brother's bragging on his behalf.

"Don't tease him," I whispered to Thorbjorn.

"I'm not," he whispered back to me. Then he spoke aloud to the room. "But it is time for the telling of tales. My brother is being modest. He doesn't want to brag about his superior skill with the bow. It makes me wonder if he's really a Valkisson at all."

Some of the others tittered at that, and Thorge flushed even redder than before.

"A fine tale could be made of it, sure enough. But it needs a better poet than I to do it justice," Thorbjorn went on. "In the meantime, I know a tale that needs no poetic skill to make exciting. Thorge and Thormund here know it as well as I, for they were there with me. I could tell it well enough, but my part in the events was small."

"If you're talking about what I think you're talking about, you're underselling yourself," Thormund said, his voice a low rumble that might have been meant just for his brother but filled the entire hall all the same. "You were in that fight as much as the rest of us."

"At first, at first," Thorbjorn conceded.

I looked around and saw everyone gathering on the benches nearest the fire. The flames lit up their faces, but so did the excitement of what they were about to hear.

"This is about the fire giants, isn't it?" Kara asked with genuine eagerness.

Thorge flushed even more deeply as he nodded, and I finally realized what Thorbjorn was up to.

He was playing matchmaker for his little brother.

"Indeed," Thorbjorn said, ignoring my attempts to catch his eye. "But as you all may know, I was conked on the head almost at once and slept through the whole thing."

"Not remotely," Thormund said.

"Yes, I remember it quite differently, brother," Thorge agreed.

"I have the scar," Thorbjorn said, touching the still-visible wound on his forehead.

"Oh, you took one to the head all right," Thormund said. "But clearly, you're not to be trusted with this tale."

"Well, someone tell us," Kara said, her eyes darting from Thorbjorn to Thorge and back again. Thorbjorn made a show of throwing up his hands, then settling back on the bench beside me. "Thorge?" she prompted.

"Did you want to...?" Thorge said, gesturing towards Thormund.

"No, you tell it," Thormund said, also settling back on his bench to listen.

"Well, it's a rare thing, to go out into the hills with all four of my brothers by my side," Thorge said. His words started out halting, but he quickly grew confident in the telling of his tale, and by the time he had described each of his brothers and the weapons they carried and started in on the moment they had first seen the fire giants, he had every listener in that hall in the palm of his hand.

Except for me, but then this was not a high tale of adventure to my ears. It was the story of how I had nearly gotten one of my closest friends and all of his brothers killed through sheer negligence. I wasn't going to enjoy this story, no matter how entertainingly it was told.

"I see what you did there," I whispered to Thorbjorn. He glanced over at me.

"What do you mean?" he asked with feigned innocence.

"You're not fooling me, Thorbjorn Valkisson. I can see clear as day that you're looking out for your little brother," I said.

"It's not a lie that I was knocked unconscious and missed most of the fight," he said. I must have flinched at his words, because his eyebrows drew together in concerned confusion.

"I don't like to be reminded of that," I said.

"I have a hard head," he said, rapping on it with his knuckles to demonstrate.

"Don't joke," I said. "Head injuries are not joking matters."

"They are if nothing bad came of them," he said.

"No, they're not," I said.

"Fine," he said, and turned his attention back to his brother's story. Judging by the way everyone around us was leaning in, he had reached an exciting part of the narrative.

I let the words wash over me. I didn't want my guilt at hearing them to show on my face, so I just tuned them out.

But I watched Kara as she listened to this story. She glanced at Thorbjorn a time or two, but otherwise her eyes were glued to Thorge. There was nothing in her gaze that spoke of love or even attraction. Nothing like the way she always looked at Thorbjorn, or the way she looked when she just talked about Thorbjorn. But she *was* looking at him, which was more than she had done just weeks before.

And when she glanced at Thorbjorn, that customary besotted look in her eyes wasn't there either.

I hated how pleased that made me feel. Thorbjorn wasn't mine in any sense of the word. I had no right to wish ill on any potential suitors of his, least of all one of my dearest friends.

"Thorge has been fond of her for some time," Thorbjorn whispered close to my ear. "Longer than even he knows. I have spent years waiting for him to realize it, and now that he has, I wait for her to realize it too."

"That she loves him?" I whispered back. I hated to break it to him, but I had seen no sign of that.

"No, I don't know what's in her heart," he said. "I meant I'm waiting for her to notice his feelings. I truly hope she feels the same, but I don't think she's even considered it before. Is she noticing him now?"

"I think she is," I said with a smile. "How long have you been trying to cook this up?"

"I've only been waiting and keeping out of it," he said. "It's called for so much patience. If only I could've shipwrecked them together on some island for a month or two, this would've gone much faster."

"You knew she liked you," I guessed.

"Of course I knew," he said, offended. "I don't like to talk about such things."

"But you're talking about it now," I said. My tone was teasing, but the look in his eyes was completely serious.

"Yes. I am."

I didn't know how to respond to that and was immensely relieved for the distraction as Gunna declared the stew ready for eating. It was a warm and filling meal. Despite my help with the cook time, it was still quite late by the time we'd finished, and it would be an early morning.

After cleaning up the dishes and stacking the benches aside, everyone pulled out the bedrolls from the back of the hall and started spreading them out on the floor around the firepit. I found myself between Nilda, with Kara on her far side, and Sigvin.

"There's a pot behind that divider there," Sigvin whispered to me as I pulled off my boots and set them at the foot of my bedroll.

"A pot?" I said.

"No going outside after dark," Nilda said sleepily. She was already in her bedroll, the blankets pulled up past her ear. "I know you know that rule. We all heard Gunna yell at you and Thorbjorn."

"Got it," I said, and was grateful I didn't have to go.

But at some point during this hunting trip, I was likely to. The idea of doing anything with nothing between me and a hall full of people trying to sleep but a flimsy little divider was mortifying. I'd rather go out and do it on the snow, cold be damned.

But it wasn't just the cold. It was the unnamed danger that lurked in the night.

Why hadn't Haraldr mentioned it before I'd left that morning?

Perhaps the two of us could've come up with some sort of protective magic.

That thought led me to remember that I hadn't done any meditating that day. I had to be sure to do it in the morning. No slacking off.

But Haraldr had also told me to dream on the rune. The card was in my pack on the far side of the hall from where I was now. The idea of tiptoeing around everyone and digging through my bag now didn't appeal. It would be rude to wake everyone.

Plus, I was exhausted. My eyes were already closed, and I could feel even the racing of my thoughts slowing down.

I tried to at least call to mind the shape of the rune. I think I did it, but I can't say for sure, because before I knew what was happening, sleep blotted out my mind.

Only it wasn't a proper sleep. I was lying perfectly still, but my awareness never left my body. I could feel myself lying there, my arms and legs heavy, too heavy to move. My pillow was scrunched up under my head in a way that wasn't entirely comfortable, but I couldn't stir myself enough to fix it.

My last concrete thought was that Mjolner wasn't there. He had been sharing my pillow, but now he was gone.

Then suddenly my awareness expended out of my body, out of the lodge itself. I was spreading out through the night, higher than the treetops.

I was everywhere.

Then I felt it, that presence I had felt before, the one that had been following me to my cottage that morning. It was here, here in these woods. And it definitely didn't belong. Its energy wasn't connecting with anything around it.

It had followed me here, somehow, without me even knowing it.

I got control of my awareness, but I didn't wake up. Instead, I retracted myself to focus on just the lodge around me.

Yes, that thing was there, just outside the walls. It was closing in around us, searching for cracks, for any way into our protected space. It wasn't finding any.

Yet.

Then my magical awareness contracted, once more outside my control, and I was trapped in my body again, too heavy to move, but that thing was pressing in on the walls all around me.

Around us. Me and all my friends.

And I couldn't move.

I couldn't even breathe.

I summoned every bit of power I could find within myself. I focused all of it on just drawing in a breath.

I felt a blackness closing in around me. My consciousness was slipping away.

Then suddenly I was sucking in breath. I was sitting up in my bedroll, pulling in long breath after long breath. It was such a relief, that cold morning air.

And there was something warm and furry pressed close to my hip. Mjolner, sleeping away as if nothing had happened.

But I didn't want to open my eyes yet, not even to look at him. That cold air I was still struggling to breathe made me sure that when I did open my eyes, I would be staring into complete darkness. With the fire gutted out, the glow of the embers that had lit the room when we'd bedded down would be gone.

But when I finally gave in and opened my eyes, I saw the hall around me dimly illuminated by the gray light of dawn. And that light was streaming in through the open door. Then the light was gone.

Then it was back again, as someone else opened the door and slipped outside.

I looked around and saw that nearly everyone else was awake already. Most were gone, but a few were still getting dressed.

"Are you all right?" Nilda asked me. She was standing over my bedroll as she redid the braid in her hair. "You were breathing kind of funny. I wasn't sure if I should wake you."

"I'm all right," I said, although I felt like I was *still* breathing funny. "Just a weird dream. It's nothing," I insisted when I could see that the worry wasn't leaving her eyes.

"If you're sure," she said. She didn't look like she quite believed me, but she just tied off the end of her hair then pulled a fur cap down over the top of it. "We're all meeting outside to split up into hunting parties. You should get dressed."

"Oh, I thought I might stay here," I said.

"On the first day?" Nilda asked incredulously. "Just what *was* that dream you had?"

"Nothing," I said. "It's fine. I'll be out in a minute."

"Well, hurry up," she said. "It's almost dawn already, and I have a feeling Thorbjorn is going to make everyone wait for you before we head out."

"Got it," I said and reached for my boots. Mjolner opened a single eye and regarded me. "You staying in or coming with?" I asked him.

He shifted his position on my bedroll, turning just far enough to not make eye contact with me before going back to sleep.

"I thought so," I said as I pulled on my second boot then got to my feet. "See you tonight. Enjoy your nap."

Then I went outside to join the others.

CHAPTER SEVEN

THE SUN WAS NOT YET visible in the east when I stepped outside. I was sure it must have risen over the lake, but not yet over the tree-covered hills that stood between us and the shore. Its light was filling the clearing in front of the lodge, if diffusely, but the forest beyond was still in deep shadow.

But it was warmer, finally. I loosened the wraps of my wool scarf and left it draped around my neck in case I needed it later. It was a relief to breathe fresh air without that damp-smelling filter in the way. The air smelled subtly of clean snow and more sharply of pine trees.

"There you are," Thorbjorn said, leaving the other men who had gathered in a rough circle to talk together. He came towards me, but as he approached the warm smile on his face became a frown of worry. "What is it?"

"You and Nilda both? Do I really look so bad?" I asked, touching my mittened hands to my cheeks.

"You don't look like you even slept," he said. "Was it too crowded in the hall? Too noisy?"

"No, that was fine," I said. But I caught hold of his sleeve and drew him a little farther away from the others. "I had bad dreams."

"Normal dreams or something more?" he asked. I had been walking backwards, towards the door to the stables, but now he took the lead, pulling me to the very edge of the clearing, just inside the tree line and all the shadows lurking beyond.

"I'm not sure," I said. "I felt like there was something all around the lodge. Some menacing presence."

"Because of what I said last night?" he asked.

"It was you and your mother both," I reminded him. "But you were both so vague. What exactly is out here at night? Because I don't see any tracks in the snow besides what we've made ourselves."

"The stories vary," he said. "We aren't closer to Old Norway here, not like in the north. But there are other things that haunt these hills. Some of them are familiar from our old stories. Men who can take the shape of bears or wolves, that sort of thing. But other things aren't from our stories at all. They might be Ojibwe things. Our two cultures were closer once, before the later settlers came and we had to hide more. I don't really know."

"Stories and tales," I said, "like things told to children, do you mean?"

"They are based on real things," he said firmly.

"But you've never seen these real things," I said.

He sighed. "You should ask my mother about it. She knows more than I."

"I'll do that," I said, and started to head back towards the hall.

"But not now," he said, catching my arm to pull me back. "It's the first day of the hunt. It's very bad luck to miss out on that."

"Really?" I asked. "Bad luck for me or bad luck for everyone? I'm assuming this is just luck with hunting, and as I didn't really think I was going to actually hunt anything myself, I can take the bad luck."

"Come on, Ingrid," he pleaded. "You came all this way. You can ask my mother a million questions tonight, but for today I want you to go out hunting with us. Don't stay here." He was pressing his hands together pleadingly and practically hopping from foot to foot.

"All right," I relented. "But tomorrow I will have to stay back. I do have things I'm supposed to be working on, and the hall is too crowded and too loud in the evenings for me to do it."

"Tomorrow you'll stay behind, but the day after you'll come out again?" he asked.

"We'll see," I said. I tried to give him a reassuring smile, but I couldn't quite get my mouth to turn up more than a smidge.

"That dream really bothered you," he guessed, his face somber once more.

"It might just be any normal nightmare, fueled by the events of the day," I said.

"I didn't think you'd scare so easily, just being told to stay indoors after dark," he said.

"It's not just that," I said. It was time to tell him about what I had sensed the day before, if only a carefully edited version. "When I was walking alone through the woods yesterday, practicing containing my magical glow, I felt like something was following me. What I felt around the lodge last night was I swear the exact same thing."

"What kind of thing?" he asked.

"I'm not sure," I said.

"Should we set guards at night?" he asked.

"No, I don't want anyone to lose any sleep because I had a nightmare," I said after thinking it over for a moment. "It's probably something only I can sense. No point in posting a guard for that. But I'll put up some protection spells before I go to bed."

"Hey, you two!" Nilda called to us. "Get over here!"

"We're holding up the hunting, aren't we?" I guessed.

He shrugged as if suddenly hunting didn't matter to him. "You'll tell me if you need anything more from me, right? If you don't want to tell the others, I can keep watch myself."

"I'll tell you if I sense anything again tonight," I promised. "But if I do, we're telling everyone. I won't have you sitting up alone keeping watch."

"Of course not," he laughed. "I'd make my brothers take their turns."

"Thorbjorn!" Thormund called with real impatience, and Thorbjorn jogged across the clearing to where the others were waiting.

I followed more slowly, reaching out with my magical senses. But there was no sign of what I had felt the night before. There was nothing around the lodge but the usual forest creatures, and most of those weren't even stirring yet. I doubted I would find any trace of the malevolence during the day even if I stayed at the lodge in meditation. Whatever it had been, real or dream, it was gone now.

The only thing I could do if I stayed behind would be to meditate on the rune, which I wasn't particularly fired up to do. And the hunt itself was important. Haraldr had emphasized that more than once.

"You're with us," Nilda said when I had reached the fringe of the group.

"Who's us?" I asked.

"Kara and I, Roarr and Sigvin, and of course Thorbjorn," she said. "We're heading to a meadow south of here."

"You don't have a bow, do you?" Kara asked.

"No. I don't even know how to use one beyond the basics," I said. "I shot one once at summer camp. Just one time, a long time ago."

"I have a spare," Roarr told me as he and Sigvin drew nearer to the three of us.

"Can she even draw it?" Kara asked.

I was about to indignantly declare I could draw anything, and even had the supplies to do it. Then Roarr squeezed my upper arm through the thickness of my parka, and I remembered that word had another, more archery-relevant meaning.

To my chagrin, he didn't seem impressed by what he felt. "I guess we'll see."

"I really wasn't expecting to shoot anything," I said. I didn't want to tell a group of hunters that I wasn't even sure I could murder some poor woodland creature, but my lack of archery skill was not all that would be holding me back.

"All right," Thorbjorn said, slapping his mittened hands together as he joined us. "It's the southern meadow today, but we're rotating tomorrow so we'll be going to the western grasslands then."

"Does it matter?" I asked.

"The other hunting spots tend to get more game," Kara said, her voice as inflectionless as ever. But there was longing in her eyes as she watched Thorge and his hunting party take a northern path out of the clearing. He looked back, saw her watching, and raised a hand in farewell. But she just looked away without responding.

"This is the best place for Ingrid's first day," Thorbjorn said. "She can get some target practice in before going on a proper hunt." It was only slightly obvious that he was putting a good face on it. I knew he wanted to have a proper hunt today as well. And I was afraid the others had probably assigned locations while he was talking to me.

As if I didn't feel bad enough, Haraldr's words came back to me, about how I would have little time for rune work, if more than I would claim later. I had responsibilities beyond providing the village with meat.

"But tomorrow I'm staying here," I reminded Thorbjorn in a low whisper after the others had started towards the southern path.

"Of course," he said. "But the day after tomorrow, we're going north. And I'm sure you can take a break or two from your magical work to shoot a few targets here at the lodge tomorrow."

After nearly an hour's worth of walking, we reached the trunk of a massive tree with wide, level branches. Beyond the tree was an open meadow that dipped down below the small hill the tree stood on. Nilda, Kara, Roarr and Sigvin dropped their day packs against the trunk of that tree, then spread out to take positions under the cover of the trees and leafless undergrowth.

But Thorbjorn tugged my sleeve, and after dropping our packs, we continued on around the meadow to a smaller clearing. Then he handed me Roarr's bow and quickly went over the fundamentals.

The bow that looked so tiny in Thorbjorn's hands became suddenly massive when I was holding it. It took all my strength to pull back the string, and my arms trembled too much for me to take any time at all aiming it.

I hit the target more than I expected to, but it was extremely tiring.

By the time we joined the others back at the tree for a quick lunch, my shoulders were already aching.

And by the time we got back to the lodge that afternoon, my whole back was stiff and sore. I regretted every time I had laughed at the commercials for training equipment made to replicate pulling back on a bow. Sure, that equipment looked flimsy, but the real thing? I doubted even rowing on the Viking ship out on the lake would be more of a workout.

As tired as I was, the others were not in much better spirits. All we had to show for our first day out in the woods were three rabbits that Kara had snared. They'd be added to the stew pot back at the lodge rather than dried and stored for the rest of the year. Fresh meat was always nice to have, but taking down a rabbit was never going to be a tale for around the fire.

We reached the clearing just as the western group was also returning. Raggi and Báfurr each had a deer slung on their backs, and three of the Freyas rushed towards the open doors of the lodge to tell those inside all about it.

I was really going to have to make a point of telling the sisters apart. From a distance, they were just a blur of long blonde hair, bluish-green eyes and sturdy bodies, but I was sure they were no more alike in personality than Thorbjorn and his four brothers were to each other.

Nilda and Kara took the rabbits to the kitchen to butcher them for the pot, and Roarr and Sigvin went to help the other hunting party hang the deer in the shed on the far side of the clearing. I could see other deer already hanging from the rafters through the open doors, but even if the doors had been closed, I would know the other hunts had been successful.

The coppery smell of fresh blood was almost overwhelming.

"Ingrid?" Thorbjorn said to me. "Are you all right?"

"I'm fine," I said. My voice came out all nasal, on account of trying very hard not to breathe through my nose. "I'm not going in there," I added, nodding towards the shed.

"No, we have nothing to take in there yet," he agreed, although he sounded regretful of that fact. "But what do you want to do first?" he asked.

"What do you mean?" I felt like I could collapse on my bedroll and sleep for a million years, but I doubted that was an option.

"Talk to my mother about the stories? Or do that protective spell you mentioned? Do you have to be outside for that?"

I'd have to raise my arms for that, which didn't feel like something I could do. But that worried line was back between his eyebrows. He wanted to help me with something, if only I would give him a task.

"I'll do that before I go to sleep," I said as we walked into the lodge together. The fire was almost too hot now that the weather had turned warmer, and I was in no hurry to get closer to it. I looked around at the scattered groups of people throughout the hall, and my eyes fell on Gunna and Jóra hard at work in the kitchen. "And your mother looks like she's got her hands full with dinner. No time for stories, but I'll catch a moment with her tomorrow."

"So what then?" he asked.

I looked around the lodge and saw the three Freyas who had been with Raggi and Báfurr sitting together at one of the tables, already drinking ale from huge mugs. Their conversation had reached a lull, but I could see from their rosy cheeks and smiling faces that this was no awkward silence. They would be chatting again the minute any of them started a sentence, and would be laughing together a heartbeat after that.

"How about you properly introduce me to your cousins?" I asked.

"Certainly," he said with a grin and led the way towards their table.

I followed behind, stuffing my hat and mittens into my parka pockets before taking it off and putting that wool scarf down one sleeve. I tossed the whole thing towards my art bag against the wall as we walked past it.

Then I fluffed up my hat hair as best I could and put on my brightest smile of greeting as I quickened my steps to catch up with Thorbjorn.

It was time to make some friends.

CHAPTER EIGHT

ᚾ

"Cousins," Thorbjorn said when he had reached their table, and all three of the youngest Freyas looked up at the two of us with wide smiles. "May I present Villmark's newest volva, Ingrid? And Ingrid, this is Freylaug, Freygunnar and Frigg, the youngest of my cousins."

Like the Thors, they all had strawberry blonde hair and blue-green eyes. Unlike the Thors, they weren't working to differentiate themselves by any prominent choice of weapons. It was going to take a bit of work to remember who was who.

Luckily, as an artist, I had an eye for detail.

"Freylaug," I said to the first young woman. She had the widest smile of the three of them, and her hair was left loose, wildly tangled and yet somehow still attractively arranged.

"Freygunnar," I said to the second. She had her hair in a thick braid down her back, not a single strand out of place, and had a quieter energy than her sisters. She wasn't wearing glasses, but she felt like the sort of girl who would favor something horn-rimmed, or possibly even cats-eyed if she did.

"And Frigg," I finished. Frigg was the youngest of the sisters, with her hair in two braids that she then pulled back and fastened on the top of her head, leaving loops around her ears. She looked like she was just out of high school, with a little lingering teen-aged awkwardness.

"Good to meet you, Ingrid," Freylaug said. "Ale?"

"None for me, thanks," I said. I seriously doubted I could heft one of those mugs. Reaching a hand up to brush back my hair was almost more than I could manage.

"Mead?" Thorbjorn offered instead. "We have some around her someplace."

"Mother has a few bottles in her pack," Freylaug said, and started to get up from the table.

"No, really, it's fine," I said, catching her arm to keep her from leaving. "I need to stay clear-headed."

"Oh, right," Thorbjorn said, drawing out the words in a way that announced to everyone at the table that the two of us had some mysterious secret.

"It's just a small bit of magic," I told them as I sat down on one of the benches. "It's part of my training. Nothing to worry about."

"I thought mead helped with magic?" Freygunnar said.

"Some magic, it does. Mainly divination," I said.

Thorbjorn started to sit down beside me, but froze halfway as his brother Thorge called out his name from the doorway.

"Ingrid?" he said to me.

"I'm fine. Go ahead," I said.

The three Freyas watched him walk across the hall to join his brother. They spoke together very briefly, then disappeared outside.

"Oh, dear. I hope this isn't a sign of trouble on the way. It's nearly sunset," I said.

"No worries. Thormund is just over there, drinking with his father," Frigg said, pointing to a table behind me, closer to the fire. "If it was trouble, he'd be going too."

"You're right," I said, turning to look where she had pointed. Valki and Thormund were sitting shoulder to shoulder facing the fire, not speaking to each other as they contemplated the flames but occasionally taking long sips from their mugs.

"He sure looks out for you, doesn't he?" Freylaug asked in a teasing voice.

"Freylaug," Freygunnar chided her. "Of course he does. He's always considered himself the chief protector of the volva. Now that isn't just Nora, it's also Ingrid here."

"I miss Nora," Frigg said, frowning down at the ale in her mug.

"What do you mean?" I asked. It's not like my grandmother had gone anywhere.

"She used to be around town more," she said. "She would stop in at the school and visit with all of us students. Sometimes she'd teach us the old stories, the ones Haraldr doesn't bother with."

"Those were always the best stories," Freygunnar agreed.

"She stopped when I got here?" I asked.

"No, it wasn't you," Freylaug assured me, even reaching out to squeeze my wrist. "She's been tapering off over time. We've seen less and less of her each year for years now."

"When you've finished your training, perhaps you can take her place from time to time in that other place, and she can come back into Villmark for more than an hour or two," Frigg said hopefully.

"I certainly hope so," I said. "At least, that's the plan."

"Are you going to be like her, then?" Freylaug asked. Her tone was jaunty, but I sensed she was asking a more pointed question than that tone was conveying.

"What do you mean?" I asked.

"Are you going to be volva for us Villmarkers, but divide your time between us and the people down there?"

I didn't know quite how to answer that. I knew the council wanted me to choose to be in Villmark full time, but I wasn't sure I could do that. I loved my Runde friends. More than that, I had grown up in that outside world. I wasn't sure I could give it up forever.

"It's going to be years and years before Ingrid has to make that choice," Freygunnar said. She was speaking kindly, but when her sister Frigg sputtered out a laugh while taking a sip of ale, her cheeks flushed a deep crimson. "I didn't mean to say it would take you years to finish your training," she rushed to add. "Only that it will be years and years before you are the only volva. Nora will be with us for decades to come, I'm sure."

"I hope so. I'm in no rush to make any of these big decisions," I said. "I don't understand anywhere near enough about any of it to make those choices now. But I think I could do far worse than to carry on as my grandmother has done." Those last words came out more forcefully than I had intended, especially as I had directed them at Freygunnar. Of the three of them, Freygunnar felt like she was on my side.

Freylaug, on the other hand, kept not quite meeting my eyes. And she hadn't joined her sisters in praising my grandmother's stories.

I felt a shadow fall over me and realized someone was standing behind me, someone who didn't feel like Thorbjorn. But before I could turn around to see who it was, he moved around the table to slide onto the bench next to Freylaug. It was Raggi. "You could certainly do far better," he said as he threw an arm around Freylaug's shoulders, then helped himself to half of the ale still in her mug.

It took me a moment to put his words together with the last ones that had come out of my mouth. Then I felt the blood rush to my cheeks, my indignation clear to all even as I held my tongue.

He smirked at me. Freygunnar got up to fetch him a mug of his own, then refilled all the mugs from the massive pitcher at the center of the table before sitting back down on the bench beside me. She shot me the smallest of glances, but if she meant for me to understand something in her eyes, I missed catching it.

"I see your party had better luck than we did at the hunt," I said. There, that was nice neutral territory.

"Raggi and Báfurr both took down a deer before we even broke for lunch," Freylaug told me. Then she gave Raggi an adoring look. "But Raggi got his first."

"All that matters is who bags the most in the end," Báfurr said as he too joined us at the table, sliding in between Raggi and Frigg.

"Did Roarr not shoot anything?" Freygunnar asked me.

"No, we never saw a sign of anything except those rabbits Kara brought back," I said.

"It's that southern meadow," Báfurr said between sips of ale. "It's too close to the edge of Villmark's hunting grounds."

"What's beyond the edge?" I asked. I was imagining trolls or even giants hunting the game before the Villmarkers got here. But the dark scowl that appeared on first Báfurr's and then Raggi's faces told me a different tale. "Oh. The modern world," I guessed.

"Don't use that word," Frigg said.

"What word?" I asked.

"*Modern*," Freygunnar said to me. "Time has passed here the same as it has out there. We are no less modern than the world where you came from."

"I suppose that's true," I said. "But you've kept more of your old ways than most."

"By design," Raggi said. "By deliberate choice. And we shall continue to do so."

"Oh, let's not argue," Freylaug said. Then she stood up to refill his and Báfurr's ales. Which didn't seem to me to be the optimal way to bypass arguments, but I said nothing.

Raggi and Báfurr started debating the best place to start hunting the next day, and Frigg and Freylaug joined in with opinions of their own. None of the places or methods of tracking meant anything to me, although I could tell that the Freyas knew as much about it as the men did. And yet I had seen none of them carrying bows when they left this morning or when they had returned.

I was still puzzling out what that might mean when Freygunnar beside me sucked in a quick breath. It was a small sound, and when I glanced over at her, she was blushing again.

"Sorry, It's just, there's Roarr," she said, making the smallest of gestures with her chin towards where Roarr was coming in through the open doors. He was hunched over, hands deep in his pockets. I had no idea if that had always been his posture, but it was certainly what I had associated with him in the short time I'd known him. Like he carried an enormous weight everywhere he went.

But all the time I had known him had been after the murder of his fiancée.

"And Sigvin," Freygunnar added, considerably less excited to see her. I looked again towards the door. Roarr was clearly waiting for Sigvin to reach his side, then the two together crossed the hall to a table closer to the fire.

They looked for all the world like two people, both heading to the same destination that just happened to find themselves walking side by side, then sitting on the same bench. They didn't talk or even look at each other. Two people getting off a jet at the airport then heading to the same Starbucks to wait for their connecting flight to board showed more camaraderie.

And yet, from the look on Freygunnar's face, she was completely heartbroken.

"They aren't a couple," I told her.

"Really?" she asked too eagerly. "They've been together since they got here, so I thought maybe I'd already missed my chance."

"No, they're definitely not together like that," I said. "But I have to tell you, I don't see Roarr being with anyone else for a long, long time. He's still not come to terms with losing his fiancée, Lisa. Did you know her?"

"No," she said. "We five don't mix with anyone from Runde. We don't even mix with the crowd that mixes with the people from Runde. I'm sorry; I hope I don't sound judgmental. I'm sure Nilda and Kara are good people. When we were all kids playing together, they were great friends of ours. But, you know, trying to mix our two societies is a recipe for trouble. Like what happened to Roarr."

"What happened to Roarr wasn't caused by anyone in Runde," I said.

"On the face of it, no. But if he hadn't fallen in love with a Runde girl, would he be grieving now?"

"Probably," I said. I knew my tone was harsh, unkind even. And defending Roarr was not something I'd ever thought I'd be doing. But the truth was the truth. "Halldis would've killed any rival for his affections. If it had been a Villmark girl, it would've likely just been easier."

"His Runde girl was going to take him away from here. That's why she died," Freygunnar said.

I opened my mouth to argue, then closed it without saying a word. I was here to make friends.

But they weren't making it easy, were they?

"It's clear you care about Roarr," Freygunnar said, sending my brain into another overload of fighting off the urge to argue that *that* was certainly not the case. But she just kept talking. "I know he'll be grieving for some time. But it doesn't matter. I'm in no hurry. I can wait."

Then she turned away from me, directing her attention back to the conversation happening on the other side of the table. I had less interest in that than ever and got up from the bench.

I hovered in the middle of the hall for a moment, not sure where I wanted to go. Thorbjorn was still outside with his brother, and the kitchen was crowded with Gunna, Jóra, and the two oldest Freyas hustling through the last of the meal preparation. The smell of roasting potatoes hit me, and my stomach cried out for food with a rumbling roar.

Then suddenly I was being steered across the room, Nilda holding one of my elbows and Kara the other. The next thing I knew I was sitting at the same table as Roarr and Sigvin, and Nilda and Kara were slamming down frothing mugs they had been carrying in their free hands.

"This one is for you," Nilda said, pushing the only foam-free mug towards me. It was warm when I wrapped my hands around it, and I could see a curl of steam coming out of the top of it. "Tea," she told me with a wink. "Thorbjorn asked me to fix it for you."

"Thanks," I said. I took a sip that tasted of blueberries, lavender, and lemongrass sweetened with honey. "Lovely. I hope it wasn't any trouble?"

"Not at all," Nilda said. "We have a lot of it on hand this trip, as Freyja is still nursing Martin." Then she leaned closer to me, waving for me to do the same so she could whisper close to my ear. "Between you and me, I saw Freydis drinking it as well instead of ale. And she's only been married for a few weeks. Either she's very optimistic or they got an early start."

"Surely not our business either way," I said, but couldn't help returning her conspiratorial grin.

Then the food was served, and as starved as I had fancied myself, I ate far too much of it. Especially the potatoes, roasted to crispy perfection.

The carb coma that followed was profound, and even without indulging in the flow of ale, I found myself drifting off to sleep without ever doing the slightest bit of magic.

It was just as Haraldr predicted.

I couldn't quite roust myself back awake to rectify that, but in that moment I wasn't really bothered. I was staying at the lodge the entire next day, after all. Time enough then for all I wasn't doing now.

I would soon regret that decision.

CHAPTER NINE

ᚾ

IF I WAS DREAMING before I woke up, I didn't remember a bit of it. There was no lingering image or feeling of unease like I had woken with the morning before.

But it wasn't morning. It was still completely dark, dark and colder than ever. My breath hung in the air before my face. I sat up and looked around. I could see the dark reddish glow of the last of the embers of the fire, but none of their heat was reaching me.

This cold didn't feel natural. The others were still sleeping around me, but I could hear them rustling, turning over and groping for more blankets or snuggling deeper into the ones they had, all without waking.

Had a sound woken me? I didn't think so. I didn't remember hearing anything. But now that I was thinking about it and listening as hard as I could, the silence outside too seemed unnatural.

Maybe I didn't remember dreaming before I woke just now because I wasn't awake at all. Maybe this was still a dream.

I found that thought hard to dismiss. I threw back my blankets and got up. Mjolner wasn't there on my pillow. He hadn't been at the lodge when we had returned the night before, but I expected he'd turn up at some point. He usually did. Was this another sign of trouble? Or just Mjolner being a free cat?

I pulled a blanket around my shoulders to keep out the chill, then tip-toed my way on stockinged feet through the sleeping bodies to get to the doors.

Before I had quite reached it, the wind suddenly picked up, howling and shaking the walls. A glittering dust of frost rained down on me from the roof overhead, shaken free from the quaking wooden beams.

A dog barked, far off in the distance.

Then another answered, from right outside our door.

That bark was ferocious and ended in a snarl as something snuffled outside the door. I could see the bar that held the doors closed had been dropped into place before the last of us had gone to sleep. It rattled in its brackets but held firm.

For now. But what would happen when the other dog came?

The wind was still howling all around the walls of the lodge, but I could hear another sound, more rhythmic, buried under that howl. It was percussive, like the hooves of galloping horses.

I closed my eyes and sent my magic senses out beyond the walls of the lodge.

The walls I had failed to magically protect, but I willfully thrust that thought aside. Time enough for guilt and self-recrimination later.

For now, I wanted to know what was out there. I already knew this wasn't like what I had felt the night before. This was something much, much bigger. Older. More powerful.

But whatever was out there, it didn't want me sensing it. The very second I started to expand my awareness, it seized my consciousness and flung it back into my body. It was a magical throw, but my body physically stumbled back from the violence of it.

I was left gasping for breath a few steps back from the door. But before I could even gather my thoughts about what I had just felt, I realized the dog was trying to bash its way in again. I lunged back towards the door.

"What are you doing?" someone called out. I turned to see the others starting to sit up, looking around with wide, frightened eyes. Then I saw it was Raggi who had spoken. He was glaring at me.

Then I realized my hand was on that bar across the double doors. I had only intended to make sure it was secure, but the narrowing of his eyes told me he suspected I was about to throw those doors open and let whatever was outside in.

"Ingrid," Thorbjorn said, putting his hand on the wrist of my outstretched arm, then drawing me away from the door.

"Something is wrong here," I said to him.

"It's the Wild Hunt," he said to me.

"Oh," I said. I knew lots of folklore about the Wild Hunt, but a lot of the specifics varied by region across the northern part of Europe. Some tales were darker than others. "What does that mean specifically?" I asked.

"Odin's riding through the forest with his hunters and his dogs," his mother Gunna said. She was standing between me and the door now, also with a blanket pulled around her shoulders.

"Is this why we have to be indoors before sundown?" I asked.

"It's a good enough reason," she said sternly. But then she gave her husband a nervous glance. "We've never had one here in my lifetime, though."

"Not for centuries," Valki said. "There were a few recorded instances in the early days of the settlement, but nothing since."

"Why now?" I wondered aloud.

"What I want to know is why you were about to let them in?" Raggi said. He had a drawn sword in his hand, barefoot and shirtless but ready for battle. I flinched back from the sight of that blade, and Thorbjorn scowled at Raggi.

"Put away your weapon. There will be no fighting here," he said.

"Not until she tells me what she was doing," Raggi said, stabbing a finger of his swordless hand at me.

"I was making sure the door was fast," I said. "There was a dog just outside. Didn't you hear it?"

"Sure, we all heard it," he said. "Friend of yours?"

"Enough with the baseless accusations," Thorbjorn snarled at him.

"Baseless? She was standing by the door before the rest of us were even awake," he said.

"That doesn't mean she summoned it," Thorbjorn said. "She's a volva. She's more sensitive to magic than any of us can imagine. Of course she would feel the hunt coming before the rest of us."

I said nothing in my own defense. I wasn't sure I had actually sensed anything, except maybe the smothering silence before the wind had picked up.

And I wasn't sure that I *hadn't* summoned it, at least subconsciously. I closed my eyes and looked at my own magic, but I was containing the glow still, just like Haraldr had taught me. It was automatic, just like it was supposed to be.

"We'll all be perfectly safe so long as we stay indoors," Valki said. He was using his council voice, commanding and reassuring both at once. I had to use magic to get that effect when I spoke, but he just naturally summoned it. He started to speak again, but had to wait until another gust of howling wind had passed to be heard. "We'll pass a safe night here, if a sleepless one."

There was a murmur through the crowd of resigned agreement. Thormund and Thorge were building the fire back up to roaring life, and Gunna headed towards the kitchen, doubtless to find some drink or snack to help pass the time until the storm and the hunt passed.

I was just heading back to my own bedroll when I heard Jóra ask, "Where's Freylaug?"

The first time she asked it, she sounded merely curious and also still half-asleep. The second time held a note of rising panic.

The third time was nearly a shriek.

"She was just here, by me," Freygunnar said. I turned to see her on her knees, tearing apart her sister's bedroll as if she might find her hiding in the folds. Frigg crawled over to help in the futile search.

But then Jóra lunged to her feet, knocking me back as she barreled to the door. Thorbjorn caught her just in time before she could lift the bar to throw open the doors.

The dog outside rattled the doors harder than ever, nearly dislodging the bar on its own. Valki put his hands down on it and leaned into it. Raggi finally put his sword away, then rushed forward to help.

"Let me go! Let me go!" Jóra yelled as she struggled to free herself from Thorbjorn's bear hug.

"You can't go out, you know you can't," Gunna said. She caught her sister's flailing hands and held them still. Then she put a hand on her sister's cheek, and finally Jóra began to calm, slumping in Thorbjorn's grasp.

"She went out there. She must've done. But why?" Jóra asked.

"Perhaps she was lured out," Nilda said.

"By what? The hunt wasn't here yet," Jóra said.

"There's a bigger problem with your theory than that," Raggi said, and slapped his hand on the bar. "How did she close this door again behind her?"

"Ingrid, did you do it?" Thorbjorn asked. "Did you find the door open and secure it while the rest of us slept?"

"No," I said. "When I got up everything was dark and still, no one else was awake, and that door was mostly definitely locked."

The dog stopped its assault on the door, although we could still hear it breathing through the gaps in the boards. Thorbjorn handed Jóra off to his parents, then took my elbow to pull me to the most remote corner of the hall.

It wasn't really private. Everyone could see us, and half the lodge could probably hear us if they made an effort. But Thorbjorn gave the few looking our way a quelling glare before turning his attention to me.

"Is this what you felt last night?" he asked me in a whisper.

"No," I said. I was absolutely certain about that. "What I felt last night felt... human. Or human-controlled. This, going on out there now? It's not remotely human. It's something so other I can't even wrap my mind around it."

He gave me a wry grin. "Well, that would make sense, wouldn't it? If it's Odin and his band of taken souls, out for a hunt? That's definitely not remotely human. Or like anything you've encountered before."

"There are a few other possibilities," I said reluctantly.

"Tell me," he said.

"What I felt last night might be some sort of precursor to this," I said. "Like a warning I didn't know enough for us all to heed."

"I've never heard of such a thing, but that doesn't mean it isn't true," he said, stroking at his beard. "One of the taken souls that won back a measure of freedom, perhaps? It's not unimaginable."

"Or," I said, and then stopped again, swallowing hard even though my throat was quite dry.

"Tell me," he said again. He looked over his shoulder to be sure no one was trying to listen in, then moved closer to me, blocking out the sight of me from the rest of the room. No one but he would know what I said next.

I appreciated the gesture. The problem was, he was the one person I really didn't want to know.

"Maybe," I said, with such slowness that even I found it agonizing. "Maybe Raggi is right. Maybe they are here because of me."

"You didn't summon this thing," he said with absolute certainty.

"I know I didn't *try* to," I said. "I'm worried I didn't try hard enough *not* to."

"You're not making any sense," he said.

"I'm saying maybe I lured it here," I said.

"I know what you're saying, but it doesn't fit with what's happening here," he said. "If this thing was looking for you, it would be working a lot harder to get inside to get you."

That only made my cheeks burn hotter. "That's the other problem. I never did the protection spells I said I was going to do."

"Does it look like we need them?" he asked with a twinkle in his eye. "My mother's ancestors built a strong house. And the magic of our line, while not remotely the same as what lies with your family, still infuses these walls. My father is right. We are all quite safe here."

"Except for Freylaug," I said.

His face fell, and I realized he had forgotten about her, if just for a moment. "Perhaps she is well, too. I don't know how she could've gotten locked outside, especially without waking anyone. But if she did, she would know to get inside any of the other buildings. The stable on the back of this house, the shed we use to clean the animal carcasses. In a pinch, even the outhouse would protect her."

"Assuming she could get to any of them in time," I said.

"Until tomorrow morning when we can get outside and look around, assuming is all we can do," he said.

I nodded. I couldn't argue with that.

But I didn't have to like it.

CHAPTER TEN

WE PASSED a long night together in that lodge. The wind never ceased to howl. The drumbeat of horse hooves would fade but then return, stronger than ever. Sometimes there was even the sound of metal weapons striking the sides of the hunting lodge, as if the hunters were striking the logs of the walls around us, trying to scare us even more.

It worked. Oh, how it worked.

But the sounds started to fade away even as the first gray light of morning started peeping in from around the shutters, which were closed over the few windows.

I helped Gunna, Nilda and Kara make porridge enough for everyone and passed the bowls around. By the time it was safe to lift the bar and open the doors, we all at least had a belly full of warm food to ground us.

I for one felt like I was going to need it.

And that feeling intensified when I got my first glimpse of the newly fallen snow outside. It wasn't much deeper than it had been the day before, but the top layer was like no snowfall I had ever seen. It was blown in feathery strands, creating a glittering pattern that repeated over and over again as far as I could see. Under the eaves of the lodge, under the trees on the far side of the clearing, everywhere.

If you've ever seen a mark on the snow from where an owl or a hawk has snatched up some hapless little mammal, you have an idea of what we were all looking at. Like a multitude of birds had flown low enough to catch something in their talons, then brought those wings down with a mighty stroke to launch themselves back up into the sky.

At least there was no blood that I could see. No sign of death. But no sign of Freylaug either.

"Freylaug!" Jóra called. Her voice echoed through the forest around us, reverberating again and again until it faded into nothingness.

There was no reply.

"Let's look for her," Raggi said. He was dressed now, as we all were, prepared for a long day out in the weather doing whatever ended up being needful. But before he could step out onto that snow, Thorbjorn caught his arm and pulled him back.

"Ingrid?" he asked, looking to me.

"I should go first," I said. I tried to sound confident and not at all like I was fighting to keep my knees from shaking.

Raggi struggled against Thorbjorn's grip and looked ready to argue, but Jóra put a hand on his shoulder and he grew still.

"Let the volva look first," she said.

Raggi narrowed his eyes at me, but stepped back out of the way.

"You can all follow along behind me. I'll wave for you when I'm ready for you to come," I said.

Then I stepped out onto that haunting snow.

The surface was like ice, but only a thin sheet of it. My boot went right through it, ruining the pattern.

That was almost a relief. It was just snow. In the spring, it would melt. The strange patterns didn't change that.

I took another step, then another. I was ruining the snow where I stepped, but I was looking carefully before each time I moved to be sure I wasn't missing any possible clues.

"Ingrid, go north," Thorbjorn called out to me. I stopped and turned to look at him, and he pointed out the direction for me. I nodded, then continued on that way, towards the taller trees with the denser undergrowth. They were all dry now, nothing but bare scratchy branches that caught at my parka and, when it was tall enough, my hair.

I was just out of sight of the lodge when I saw the first footprint. It definitely wasn't from a bird. It looked large enough to be from a bear.

But I was really afraid it was from a dog.

I circled around the footprint but found my way blocked again, this time by the marks of horses' hooves in the snow. First from a single horse, then from a bunch of them all trampling over everything. Then another set of dog prints, even larger than the first.

I could also see a few deep holes thrust through the snow, as if from the staff end of a pole axe or something.

But that was all. No sign of any human footprints. Not from the hunt, and not from Freylaug.

Which didn't make any sense.

I turned around and looked again, back towards the lodge, just out of sight through the dense underbrush I had pushed my way through.

Yes, I could see something now, almost lost in the bird wing pattern, but easier to see from this direction, looking back towards the clearing that was slowly filling with the light of dawn. They were faint, and I suspected the bird pattern was meant to hide it, but they were definitely there.

Human footprints. From bare human feet that hadn't broken through the icy top layer of the snow. Perhaps during the deep cold the night before, that layer had been firmer.

Or perhaps it was just part of the magic that had lured her out to meet the hunt. She had danced over the snow like she was half a spirit already.

The footprints came through the hedge a little west of where I had pushed through, but they looked to have come from the lodge. Which made sense.

The other end of the trail ended in the most churned up stretch of snow. It looked like the horses here had been riding around in a circle, over and over. Then I saw, in the center of that circle, a single bit of unbroken snow. The bird wing pattern was missing here, but the human footprints stood out clearer than ever.

The toes were particularly deep. As if she had put all of her weight forward before leaping up into the air.

I didn't like the implication of that, like she had gone gladly. And yet, if she had fought, wouldn't it be her heels that stood out starker? If she had dug in and refused to go?

At last I went back to the hedge of undergrowth and waved for the others to follow me. Soon the space under the trees was crawling with people examining every trace of what had happened the night before. There was some murmuring, a few soft exclamations of shock, but no one truly spoke out loud.

"Jóra, are you satisfied?" Valki at last asked. Jóra was at the heart of the circle marked by the hooves of the horses, looking down at the final set of human footprints. She nodded without looking up. "Then let's gather around the fire and discuss this."

"What are we going to be discussing?" I asked Thorbjorn as we followed the others back to the lodge.

"Whether to finish the hunt or to return home with what little meat we have," he said.

"Finish the hunt?" I repeated. "Like nothing even happened?"

"No, not like that," he said. "But we still need the meat. And Frey-laug is not coming back."

"That sounds so heartless," I said.

"Welcome to winter in the north," he said humorlessly.

"But shouldn't we do something?" I persisted.

"Do what?" he asked. "Ingrid, this isn't a murder to be solved. We know what did this. And as far as we can ever understand such things, we know why. It's done."

"It's not like we won't mourn Freylaug," Kara said as she and Nilda fell into step beside us. "Even with no body to bury or anything, we'll still have a remembrance for her. Just not here and now."

When we crossed the threshold into the lodge, we saw the others were already gathered at the tables, but no one was speaking. We were the last to come inside, and Thorbjorn pulled the doors closed behind us, as if the clearing even by daylight was not to be trusted anymore.

"Jóra," Gunna said to her sister. "If you wish to return to Villmark, you have only to say so."

"No, it would be very bad luck to cancel the hunt," she said. Her eyes were red with unshed tears, her gaze glassy and unfocused. But her voice was firm and resolved.

"If you wanted to go back, the rest of us will stay to carry on the hunt," Gunna said. "There is no reason for you to stay if your heart would be easier at home."

"I would be honored to escort you back to Villmark," Thorge said, resting his hands on the hilts of his long knives.

"No, I will stay," Jóra said again. "It still doesn't feel real. It still feels like at any moment Freylaug will just walk back in through those doors."

"Jóra," her sister said admonishingly.

"I know she won't," Jóra said, raising her chin. "But I won't go back without her. At least, not today."

"We agree," Freyja said, and her sisters beside her were each nodding, although Frigg and Freygunnar had tears in their eyes. "We'll stay until the hunt is done. Then we will return to Villmark and plan the best way to remember our sister. Our sister, the first person to be taken by the Wild Hunt here in centuries."

"Are we all in agreement?" Valki asked, looking from one person to the next, never moving on until he had made eye contact with each of us in turn and gotten a nod. "Then we should divide up for the hunts. Or should we all stay together?"

"No, three groups, as before," Raggi said.

"Too many people together, we'll frighten off the game," Thorbjorn said.

"Very well. Gunna, will you need me here?"

"No, Freyja and I can handle things just fine," she said. "We'll check for damage to the walls and make sure everything is sound before nightfall. The rest of you just be sure to bring us back plenty of fresh meat."

"Assuming the Wild Hunt didn't frighten it all off," Roarr grumbled from where he was sitting behind me. But he spoke so low I doubted anyone heard him but me.

"I'll be here as well," I said, raising my hand as if volunteering to stay after school.

"We'll be quite all right," Gunna insisted, but I had seen the relief that had washed over her face the moment I had spoken. My presence was going to be appreciated.

"Actually, I need to do some things of my own," I said. "Volva things. And honestly, I'm not much for hunting. I know Thorbjorn would've bagged something if I hadn't been slowing him down."

He flushed red but said nothing, and I knew I had confirmed his own thoughts on that score.

"Bag more deer than Raggi for me," I whispered to him.

"You just stay safe," he said.

"I thought this *was* the safest place," I said.

"For anyone else it would be. Somehow, I have the feeling you're going to start digging up trouble."

"I need to study my newest rune. And I'm definitely adding some magical protection to this house, strong as it already is," I said. "Where's the trouble in that?"

He started to answer, but then looked around. I looked around too and saw we had quite an audience of people who were trying a bit too hard to look like they weren't eavesdropping on us.

I once more found myself propelled across the room by his hand on my elbow.

"I really wish you wouldn't do that," I said, wrenching my arm free. "Just tell me you want me to go with you."

But he ignored me, leaning in to whisper, "don't do anything about the Wild Hunt. Don't even *try* to do anything about the Wild Hunt."

"I wouldn't even know where to begin with that," I said, which was true.

Sort of. I had some thoughts.

"Listen to me, Ingrid," he said as if he could read my thoughts. "This wasn't a murder."

"She was taken before her time," I said. "It's not *not* murder."

"The Wild Hunt is part of the natural order of things," he said.

"More like the supernatural order of things," I said.

"Take my point, please," he said.

"I take your point," I said with a sigh. "It doesn't feel right, but it also doesn't feel like something I can set right. Good enough?"

"Not remotely," he grumbled, but I could see he was going to have to accept it. The others were already making their way outside, bows and quivers at the ready and cold lunches packed for midday.

"I'll see you at sundown," I said. I had walked with him as far as the door, but I had no reason to go farther. And I still had that strong disinclination to erase the bird marks from the snow.

"I'll see you," he said. Then he ran to join the rest of our party. They were heading west today, towards the better hunting grounds, and although they were trying to keep their exuberance tampered down, I could tell they were excited for whatever the day might hold.

Particularly Kara, who already had her bow in her hand. She fell into step beside Thorbjorn, matching his stride far more easily than I ever did. She looked up at him as she said something to him, and the happy glow on her face was like a kick to my stomach.

But I had to let that go. Again. Because I had work to do.

I had a rune to master. Spells of protection to weave.

And, whatever Thorbjorn said, a murder to solve.

CHAPTER ELEVEN

AFTER THE OTHERS had disappeared among the trees, I turned away from the doors and towards the lodge's shadowy interior.

And saw Mjolner sitting primly in the middle of the room, washing his ears and acting for all the world like he'd been there the entire time.

"I probably could've used your help last night," I said.

He ignored me.

"Not going to tell me what you were up to at that hour?" I asked.

He finished washing his ears and gave his six-toed paw a final vigorous shake. Then he curled up right there in the middle of the aisle between the long tables and promptly fell asleep.

Typical.

I grabbed my art bag from where it was resting against one of the sturdy pillars, then looked around me. Without more than a moment's thought, I made my decision and settled on a bench under a sunlit window. Gunna had thrown all the shutters wide open to let in the daylight. Soon I had my sketchpad on the table in front of me and my pencil in hand.

But I wasn't sure if I would be able to get into a flow state.

Not that the others in the lodge with me were being disruptive.

Gunna and Jóra had finished rolling up the bedding and storing it in the cabinets and were currently sitting together on a table near the kitchen area with mugs of coffee and a little plate of cookies between them. The breakfast cleanup was done, and it was early yet to start dinner, so the two of them were sharing a quiet moment. They were speaking too low for me to catch more than a murmur of their voices and the occasional sniffle from Jóra.

I didn't know how I'd feel losing a daughter, but I doubted it would be the calm acceptance that Jóra was showing.

Unless it *was* just for show. I had had practice myself, not showing my grief in front of others, months before when my mother had finally passed after being sick for most of my lifetime. But if Jóra really was holding it all inside, she was going to explode before this hunting trip was over.

The only other people still in the lodge were Freyja and her son Martin. She had spread a blanket on the floor in another sunny patch and the two of them were building with wooden blocks together. He was just old enough that he was starting to pull himself up to standing with the help of the many handy benches. He would then bounce in place. Sometimes with just one hand on the bench for support, but he wasn't quite walking yet. His words were still all just babble, but he had a surprisingly deep voice for such a little guy.

I found myself drawing the two of them playing together, and then Gunna and Jóra sitting in companionable silence. It was nice just to sketch for once, simple sketches I wouldn't be searching for clues later.

But I *did* have a job to do. I turned over to a blank page and traced out the shape of the Ur rune. It had a very solid shape to it, grounded and strong. It wasn't hard to feel the associations with cattle and yokes as I drew. It made me feel assertive just to draw it over and over again.

I turned to yet another blank page and let the pencil in my hand do what it will. It started drawing Freyja and Martin again, but more abstract than before. I switched from pencil to charcoal and drew them again, rubbing at the contours with my fingertips or the side of my hand.

Martin felt like a living example of Ur to me. But with his red hair and deep, happy voice, he reminded me of someone else. I drew in his uncle, Thorbjorn, standing over him. Not in a protective way, I realized as the drawing took shape. More like he was waiting for Martin to stand up, take those steps he was so close to taking, and join his uncles out on the hunt.

The sun had been climbing in the sky as I drew, and it reached a point high enough to shine over the tops of the trees, directly into my eyes as I sat near the window. I squinted against it long enough to finish my drawing of Martin with his chubby hand on a bench, reaching out with the other towards his mother, but then I stopped.

Was I bonding with this rune? Probably not on the first day with the first try. But it felt like it was going smoother than it had with Fe.

I turned to another blank page, but got up from the window and moved closer to the open doors. The sun was reflecting off of all the snow, but it wasn't directly in my eyes here. I settled my sketchbook on my lap, then looked out at the clearing.

The bird wing marks were still everywhere, although I suspected the full light of midday was going to be strong enough to melt most of them in a few hours. I swapped the charcoal for my pencil again and started sketching them. The feathery reach of the wings, the overlap of the pattern.

Every bit of it, every trace of a feathery touch on the gleaming snow, was glowing with magic. It wasn't diminishing in the bright light of day. It also didn't feel malevolent. I wasn't sure when amongst all the sounds of the night before that birds had made an appearance, but from the way the wing patterns covered everything, I had to guess they'd shown up just at the very end.

Was that deliberate? Were they some sort of clean-up crew, there to remove the traces of what had passed in the night?

And yet all the horses' hooves, dog prints, and holes from the pole axes were still there. If they had hidden something before we stepped out at dawn, what had it been? Even Freylaug's footprints were still visible.

I was barely aware of my physical body now, just a vague sense that I was turning to a blank page again, then putting my pencil tip down on the paper to start drawing the trees on the far side of the clearing.

Then my awareness was totally out of my body, and I was drawing the far side of those trees where the marks from the Wild Hunt marred the snow. I wasn't drawing from memory; I was drawing what my mind's eye saw as it hovered above everything at the level of the tops of the tallest pines.

Then I started another drawing, this one from ground level, looking to the spot where Freylaug had last stood. My mind's eye within that clearing swept over every branch, every print in the snow, every broken branch, while my hand back inside the lodge took it all down.

Someone behind me sucked in a breath, and I snapped back inside my own body so suddenly I nearly fell off the bench.

"Sorry," Jóra said, resting a hand on my shoulder to steady me.

"It's all right," I said, but I was disoriented. My vision was all starbursts, like I had been staring into the sun without blinking.

"Here," Gunna said, pressing a mug into my hands. I took a large gulp, remembering too late how strong her family liked their coffee. My heart started racing at once, but my mind cleared just as fast.

"I'm all right," I said again.

"I didn't mean to interrupt you," Jóra said.

"If she hadn't, I would've," Gunna said. "You looked like you weren't even breathing, and you didn't even notice when I stood right in front of you. I would've been blocking your line of sight if you'd actually been looking at anything."

"I was... somewhere else," I said vaguely.

"That's Freylaug you were drawing, isn't it?" Jóra asked. I looked down at the drawing and felt the world rock beneath me.

It was indeed Freylaug, standing on her bare toes amidst a circling ring of men on horses, two dogs running around them all.

And I had thought I was just drawing the trees and snow.

"I guess so," I said.

"That's what happened?" Jóra asked. "It really was the Wild Hunt?"

"Was that even in doubt?" Gunna asked her.

"It was for me," Jóra said, lifting her chin at her sister defiantly. But her face softened as she turned to me again. "Did you see this? Like a volva prophecy or memory or something? Is this what happened?"

"I think so," I said.

"Look at her face," Jóra said, and Gunna came around to stand behind my other shoulder and look down at the sketchbook on my lap. "She looks so... what's the word?"

"Swept up in rapture, I'd say," Gunna replied. "Did she go outside on purpose?"

"I don't know," I said. "I didn't see that far back."

"Maybe you will if you draw again," Jóra said, with such confidence that her tone contradicted her use of the word "maybe." In fact, it sounded almost like a command.

"Let her catch her breath, won't you?" Gunna said to her sister. "She still looks so pale."

"She always looks pale," Jóra said. But she gave me the smallest of smiles to soften her words. "We're all red-heads here. We know all about always looking pale."

Freyja at the other end of the room snort-laughed at that.

"Do you need more coffee?" Gunna asked me.

"No, this is fine," I said, doubting I'd even finish the mug I was still holding.

"We're going to start dinner. If you want to help, you can join us when you've recovered," she said. Then she thumped a plate full of butter cookies down on the table beside me. "But eat those first."

"All of them?" I squeaked.

"Enough to get your color back," she said. "Come, Jóra. We have a mountain of potatoes to peel. Then there're the carrots. And the turnips."

"I'll be along in just a minute," I promised, but Gunna just pointed at the plate of cookies again before she and her sister left me to head back into the kitchen.

Was she serious? There were a lot of cookies on that plate.

I took another sip of coffee, grimaced at its bitterness, then took a bite of one of the cookies.

Then I looked at what I had drawn. I wasn't surprised that Jóra and Gunna had been fixated on the image of Freylaug at the center of the drawing. Her face was the bright, white sun at the center of a whirl of darkness. It was a nice juxtaposition, and I was pleased with my own work, as unconsciously rendered as it had been.

But something else had caught my eye, something neither of them had remarked on. Perhaps they hadn't seen it. The lines that made up the trees that framed the image with their interwoven branches were so heavy and dark.

But here and there in the patterns of the bark were the faces of women. Or something like women. But every single one of them was within a tree, as if she were part of it.

I swallowed down the last of the coffee and grabbed a couple of cookies, then casually strolled out the door. I wasn't dressed for outside, but my wool leggings and knee-length sweater were warm enough for a short walk.

I once again pushed my way through the undergrowth to the clearing where the Wild Hunt had taken Freylaug. I stood at the spot where my mind's eye had been and looked at all the trees.

They just looked like ordinary trees now, as they had that morning.

I put my hand against the bark of one tree and closed my eyes, reaching out with my magical senses. The tree was alive, of course, but it was in a deep winter sleep, its warm heart low down in its trunk, almost completely dormant.

It didn't feel remotely like a woman was living within it.

I tried a few more trees, but they all felt the same. Finally, I just stood in the middle of the clearing near where Freylaug had been.

"Hello?" I called out, feeling a little foolish.

There was no answer. I didn't try again. I just put the last of the cookies in my mouth and headed back towards the lodge.

Maybe everyone else was right. Maybe this hadn't been a murder.

The face of the Freylaug I had drawn certainly hadn't looked like a victim.

But why was she outside in the middle of the night in the first place?

I hated the thought that I might never know. I went back to the hunting lodge to put up the protective spells I knew and then help with the peeling.

CHAPTER TWELVE

ᚾ

FOR THE SECOND night in a row, I found myself awake in the wee hours, heart pounding, not sure what had disturbed me. The silence was profound, pressing painfully against my eardrums, and the air was again frigid in a way it hadn't been when I had climbed into my bedroll hours before.

The others around me were tossing and turning in their sleep. At first I thought they were again mostly reacting to the sudden drop in temperature without quite waking. But a few of them whimpered or cried out like they were trapped in the throes of a nightmare.

And Mjolner was gone. He had been purring against the back of my neck when I had drifted off to sleep, but there was no sign of him now. Something was definitely going on with him. I only wished he could tell me what was so important he kept not being there when I faced things alone in the middle of the night.

And I was alone. No one else was showing any signs of waking, despite the disturbances to their sleep.

I got out of my bedroll and started walking down the center of the lodge, checking that each bedroll had an occupant.

And quickly realized that one didn't. I looked to either side of the empty bedroll. I saw the loops of Frigg's braids peeking out of the top of the next bedroll over and remembered that it had been Freygunnar who had laid down to sleep beside her, on the far side of Nilda from me.

Freygunnar was missing.

I spun around and looked to the door, which was still barred, just as it had been the night before.

Only this time I must be awake sooner, because everything was still deadly quiet. No wind, no dogs, no horses.

I half-closed my eyes and expanded my magical awareness to the spells I had cast that afternoon. They still held, although the older magic I had interwoven them with, the magic from Gunna and Jóra's ancestors, didn't seem to need the help from my puny spell craft.

I pulled on my boots then ran to the door, setting the bar aside then pushing my way outside into the moonless night. I closed the doors behind me. There was no way to bar them from this side, but with all the tossing and turning the others were doing, I was sure one of them would be awake before long.

Soon enough, they all would. I could feel that old power drawing nearer from somewhere just over the horizon.

I held the door handles closed behind me but took a moment to close my eyes and focus on my magic. I was still standing on the threshold. I wanted to be absolutely sure I had contained my glow before I left the last bit of shelter from the lodge behind.

But that effort had already become automatic for me, even though Haraldr and I had been practicing it only for a few days. There was no more of a supernatural gleam about me than there was to anything else out in this forest.

Which wasn't exactly nothing. Every living thing has at least a little bit of a glow. Lots of things were out here with me that I didn't have time to look at more closely now. But I didn't stand out, and I wasn't drawing anything to me.

That was the best I could hope for.

I opened my eyes and started walking away from safety. I knew I didn't have much time.

There wasn't a cloud in the sky above, and the stars were bright enough to light up the clearing in front of me.

I saw a single track of footprints in the snow. They weren't deep; like Freylaug's from the night before, they rested on the icy top layer without breaking through.

I had no such luck. Every step I took following those footprints found my boots crushing through the ice, then getting mired in the softer snow beneath. It was slow going, and just when I needed speed.

I followed the footprints through the tangle of dried underbrush, but they didn't stop in the clearing beyond. They kept going, past the point where the Wild Hunt had rode the night before. Deeper into the woods.

Did the Wild Hunt ever come twice in as many nights? I wasn't sure.

And I still didn't know exactly what else there was to fear in these woods after dark. I probably should've tried to wake someone to come out here with me. But I'd come too far to backtrack now.

I started to re-evaluate that assessment as the cold sank into my bones. I had pulled on my boots, but my coat, hat, mittens and scarf were all still back in the lodge. The sweater and wool leggings that had been enough for a short walk in the afternoon were woefully inadequate for a long midnight hike.

But then I saw something ahead of me, at the top of a small hill just barely visible through the trees. Someone's pale face had reflected the starlight, if just for a moment.

"Freygunnar!" I called out and tried to break into a run. The snow wouldn't cooperate, and I stumbled and fell into a tree whose branches promptly snagged the sleeves of my sweater. I pulled myself free and looked back up towards the hill.

There was no sign of her now, but I was sure I hadn't imagined her. "Freygunnar! Stop!" I called again. I sprinted as quickly as I dared up the hill.

I could see her clearly now, her long braid of red-gold hair catching the starlight as she continued to walk away from me.

Towards what, I had no clue. I ran down the far side of the hill until I had caught up with her, then grabbed her arm.

"Freygunnar, stop," I said, nearly out of breath. It hurt to pant like that. The air was so cold, and the stitch in my side was brutal.

She jerked her arm out of my grasp and continued walking without so much as a word to me. I pushed on after her again, this time running around to stand directly in front of her and block her path.

"Freygunnar. Stop," I commanded.

I was flat on my back, sprawled out on the snow before I even realized she was pushing me. But that wasn't the most startling thing.

No, that had been her eyes. Her blue-green eyes had been wide open but totally unseeing. Like she was sleepwalking, or worse.

Like she was hypnotized or under some sort of spell.

I could feel bruises forming all over me as I struggled back to my feet to go after her again. Whatever was happening to her, it seemed to have also given her a measure of super-strength somehow.

Maybe it wasn't the best plan to try to stop her. Maybe I should just stay with her and make sure she was safe until she woke.

Then, as cold as the air had been, it suddenly dropped another dozen degrees in a heartbeat. My eardrums hurt worse than ever, like the air pressure was changing as well.

My fingers were going numb, and so was my face. I was in real danger of frostbite.

And so was Freygunnar. I couldn't just walk with her. I had to get her back to the lodge somehow.

I started to run after her again. Then the wind picked up around me, strong enough to bend the trees and send their branches snapping in all directions.

A dog howled, far off in the distance. That remote sound chilled my already freezing blood.

Then the second answered from right behind me. I didn't dare turn to look. I just put my head down and ran for all I was worth.

The thunder of horse hooves was growing louder. And still Freygunnar kept walking. Where was she going? Where was she being summoned to?

"Freygunnar!" I yelled over the roaring wind. "Stop!"

I could only yell once. I didn't have enough breath to do it again. It hurt so much, to be short of wind in air so cold. It was burning my lungs.

But that burning was nowhere near as worrying as the lack of feeling in my hands.

Even if I wanted to abandon Freygunnar and run back to the warmth and safety of the hunting lodge, the sounds of the Wild Hunt racing up behind me were between me and it. I was trapped or was about to be.

I forced myself to keep running, but I knew I didn't have much stamina left in me. I was going to fall down into the snow soon, and when I did, I doubted I would get up again.

I needed to find shelter, but there was none. No caves in the sides of the hills, no fallen trees making tents of their branches under a blanket of snow. Nothing.

I nearly collided with Freygunnar as she stopped suddenly and turned to face whatever was behind us. I skidded to a halt, captivated by the rapturous look on her face. It was just like the one I had drawn on Freylaug, only the eyes were wrong.

I had drawn Freylaug with her eyes closed. Freygunnar still had hers open, but as much as she should be looking right at me, she didn't seem to be seeing anything. Not me, not anything behind me.

But I could hear the snapping of tree branches growing ever louder, and the dog's panting breath must be very close indeed to be heard over the thunder of the hooves.

"I'm so sorry," I said to Freygunnar. Then I ran past her, hoping to find some small protection in a thicket of leafless branches at the bottom of the hill.

But when I got there, I realized they were not as dense as they had appeared from the top of the hill. There was no protection here at all.

And when my boot skidded over an icy patch of snow, I realized that I was all done running. The stitch in my side had become a knife angling up from my diaphragm, through my lung, heading for my heart. I could barely catch my breath standing still. Running was out of the question.

It hurt so much to breathe.

I bent over, hands on my knees, trying to suck in enough air past that stabbing pain to make the starbursts in my vision stop.

I could hear the horses coming up behind me, and the inarticulate shouts of men as well as the baying of the dogs. But while the percussive beats of the hooves went on and on, they drew no closer.

I realized they were riding in circles, as they had the night before.

Then Freygunnar cried out, just once, a cry of pleasure and pain intermingled, neither quite dominant.

The beat of the hooves slowed, the horses blowing out their breaths and the dogs snuffling. I didn't dare look up, but I knew what was happening. I could see it so clearly in my mind. They were still circling, but not so fast as before.

They were looking for their next target.

And I still couldn't catch my breath. I couldn't even see properly, the edges of my vision starting to go gray. Not only couldn't I run, I was in real danger of fainting dead away. It was all I could do to make sure that I still wasn't exuding magic, but my defenses were still up. I wouldn't draw anything to me magically, but surely it wouldn't be long before they saw me physically. And there was nothing I could do to prevent that. There was simply no cover.

Suddenly a hand fell on my shoulder and jerked me forward, pulling me through the thicket. The short, spiny branches tore at my sweater, caught at my hair, scratched bloody furrows across my face.

Then everything went dark.

But it was a warm, nurturing dark. At first I just accepted it. Then I thrilled at the deep breaths of air I could take here where it wasn't so cold that it burned my lungs.

I could still hear the sounds of the hunt. It sounded like it was all around me now, like I was surrounded by it.

But it also seemed so very far away.

At last my heart slowed from a gallop to something closer to its normal rhythm. Although I couldn't tell in the darkness, it felt like the grayness was no longer threatening to consume my vision.

I put out my hands and felt dried wood splintering away under my fingertips. I was inside the hollow of a tree. A very large tree, I realized, as I moved my hands in a circle around me. I looked up and could just see a patch of the starry sky far above me. I took another deep breath and discerned the slightest whiff of ozone in the wood around me.

A lightning-struck tree, still standing in the forest after what given the dusty dryness of the wood must have been years and years.

I shuffled my feet, but there was nothing below me but earth and a crumbling layer of dry leaves.

I moved my hands over the inside of the tree again, making a more thorough search this time. But how I had gotten inside, I couldn't tell. There didn't seem to be any opening but the one yards and yards above me. I groped around with my feet, poking my toes into any concavity in the trunk around me, but felt no trace of a crawl space.

I didn't know how I had gotten inside, and I really didn't know how I was going to get out again. But with the sound of the hunt still all around me, as if they were circling my very tree in search of me, I was in no hurry to figure that part out.

Something had grabbed me and pulled me out of danger. I was grateful for that. But whoever they had been, they were gone now. I was alone, inside that dead tree.

And the hunt gave no sign of passing on any time soon. I found myself slumping a little, resting my back against the wood behind me, my knees pressed against the other side.

It was more comfortable than it sounds. And the smell of old tree, faint ozone, and the dry, clean smell of faded leaves were a comfort as well.

I soon found myself drifting off to sleep. And as my consciousness slipped away, I swear I heard the sound of a lullaby sung in some old, forgotten language. It syncopated with the persistent sounds of the

Wild Hunt, making those terrifying sounds just a harmless part of its soothing narrative.

When I woke, it was dawn, and I was outside the tree, sitting with my back against its trunk.

And all around me for as far as my eyes could see was the repeating pattern of bird wings pressed into the snow, not quite concealing the traces of the Wild Hunt that had failed to catch me.

CHAPTER THIRTEEN

I EXAMINED every inch of that tree, but there was no sign of how I had gotten myself inside of it the night before or how I had gotten back out again. I could tell by rapping on it that it was hollow in the middle, but that was all.

There was certainly no sign of what had put a hand on my shoulder and pulled me to safety. If it had left any trace on the snow the night before, it was lost under the overlapping pattern of bird wings.

I closed my eyes and looked at the magic around me. The tree had a definite glow to it. It felt protective to me, but it didn't have the weaving pattern I associated with spells. Had it been some sort of magical tree before it was struck by lightning, or had the lightning imbued it with power? Or maybe the power had drawn the lightning. There was no way for me to know.

I wanted to sit down in the snow and sketch it all out, but I didn't have so much as a stub of a pencil with me.

And the moment I thought of my art bag, waiting for me by my bedroll back at the lodge, I realized I had no idea where the lodge was. It was east of me, but beyond that, I just wasn't sure.

I climbed the hill and saw the spot where Freygunnar had last stood. Her bare feet had imprinted the snow much as her sister's had, deeper at the toes, as if she too had leapt up into the air and then never come back down.

I looked around at the other tracks in the snow, but there was no new information there. Horse hooves, impossible to tell how many. Two different sets of dog prints. And a scattering of places where pole axes had been thrust through the snow to the ground below.

But I had the nagging feeling that something was wrong with those tracks. I inched my way around that hilltop for quite some time before I realized what was bothering me.

The tracks never came down to my tree.

And yet I would swear I had heard them all around me the night before.

I looked around again and saw that the tight circle around Freygunnar's last footprints became more dispersed as horses broke away singly or in pairs. I followed one trail as it traced a lazy circle through the forest, the pair of horses sometimes together but often farther apart. It led back to the hill. I followed another trail that did the same thing, wandering through the trees as if searching for something it wasn't finding before circling back.

Many of them did this, and the tree I had been hiding in was always within the borders of their circles, but apparently only coincidentally. If they had been looking for me, they had no idea where I had been.

But they had made a straight line towards Freygunnar.

I suppose I should've been relieved. This was the best proof I was ever likely to find that I hadn't lured the Wild Hunt to the lodge. They had been pursuing Freygunnar, not me.

But I didn't feel relieved. Because if they had been pursuing me, I would understand that, and I would have some idea what I should do next.

But why was the Wild Hunt targeting the Freyas? And what could I do to protect them?

I heard a soft inquisitive meow behind me and turned to see Mjolner making his way towards me over the feathery snow.

"Mjolner!" I said, dropping to my knees to catch him up in my arms. He purred like mad, ramming his head again and again under my chin. "So you came back to bed and found me gone, did you?"

He gave a sheepish meow, not quite looking at me. I mean, most cats don't, but Mjolner isn't most cats.

"Well, trust you to be the one to find me," I said to him. "Do you know the way back? Of course you do. No, you don't need to get back on the snow unless you want to. I can see your trail and follow it myself if you want to ride home in my hood."

He purred happily, settling himself into the hood of my parka as if it were his own personal hammock. And sleeping against the back of my neck was his very favorite thing. He was soon curled up in a tight, warm ball, purring away in his sleep.

I followed the trail of his paw prints back towards the lodge, but before I was even in sight of the building, I heard voices crying out my name throughout the woods around me.

"I'm here!" I called, although I couldn't see where any of the voices were coming from. But no one seemed to hear me. I could still hear my name echoing through the trees, but always from so very far away.

Then a thicket beside me rustled. I stepped back and started to raise my fists as if I could somehow defend myself from whatever might be about to jump out at me with my bare hands. I remembered there were bears in these woods in addition to the many small creatures who had been glowing magically when I had looked around the night before.

But what burst out of the thicket was only Kara. Relief washed over her face, and she pulled me into a tight hug.

"I'm okay," I said, patting her arm. Mjolner meowed in objection at the way she was jostling him about, and she stepped back from me with a sniffle.

"We thought we'd lost you," she said.

"We did lose Freygunnar," I said.

"You saw it happen?" she asked.

"I didn't see it, but I was close by," I said. "And this morning I saw the marks on the snow, the same as yesterday after Freylaug was taken. I'm sure she's gone."

"Jóra is going to be heartbroken," Kara said. Then she looked up at me with a different sort of sadness in her eyes. "But Thorbjorn is going to be so relieved."

"Kara," I started to say, but she just shook her head.

"Never mind," she said. "We should get back." Then she turned and started to head east at a fast pace.

"We can walk and talk," I said after I had run a few steps to catch up with her.

"There's really nothing to say," she said, not looking over at me. "I never had any claim to him. Never even tried to make one. He never seemed ready. I always thought something would happen, in the fullness of time, but it didn't." Then she did sneak a quick glance my way, but only for an instant. "You didn't do anything wrong, and I have no right to feel sore at you."

"Kara," I said, grabbing her arm and pulling her to halt, which she reluctantly allowed me to do. If she hadn't, I would've been dragged behind her for sure. She was a lot stronger than me. But she looked me in the eye again, waiting for me to say my piece. "Kara, I'm sorry for how you were made to feel. I didn't intend to get in your way, or to make you feel like I was trying to take your place or anything."

"I know," she said with a sigh. "Thorbjorn talked to me this morning, during the long, torturous hours before we could go outside to look for you. He told me some things I wished he would've told me a long time ago."

"About how he knew about how you felt?" I guessed.

She nodded, but then she added, "to be fair, I'm not sure if he had been more direct that I would've heard him anyway. I think my heart would still be sure that at the end of the day, he'd come around. I suppose in the long run I'll be relieved that I didn't wait around any longer."

"But not yet," I guessed.

She shook her head. "No, not yet. It still hurts."

"I'm sorry for that," I said.

"I know," she said. "Let's go. The others are out of their minds with worry, and we shouldn't leave them like that longer than we have to. And we have to tell them about Freygunnar."

"No, you're right," I said, and fell into step beside her again as we continued through the woods.

"Ingrid, can I ask you something?" she said suddenly several minutes later.

"Of course," I said, although my stomach knotted in instant tension.

"Have you decided where you will remain when your training is done?" she asked. "Will you stay in Villmark like your ancestors did, or will you live in Runde like your grandmother does? Or even leave this part of the world entirely like your mother did?"

"Definitely not the last one," I assured her. "For the rest, I honestly don't know yet. Both worlds feel like my world to me. I don't know how I can choose."

"Or why you should have to, maybe," Kara said.

"I would like to be free to move between both," I admitted. "But I don't know if that will be possible."

"And until you do know, I suppose there are a lot of other things you can't decide about yet," she said. I knew she was thinking about Thorbjorn again. I hoped she wasn't looking for one last reason to keep carrying a torch for him, but I couldn't figure out any way to say so that wasn't way too blunt.

"You're right," I said simply. "I have lots of decisions in my future, but I can't make them yet."

Then we were in the clearing in front of the hunting lodge and there was a clamor of voices as the news of my arrival was shouted from the shed to the stable to the lodge itself.

Then I was caught up in a tight bearhug that ended only at Mjolner's very irritated yowl of protest.

"Sorry," Thorbjorn said as he set me back down on my feet. Mjolner dug his claws into my back as he launched his way out of my hood and zipped off into the lodge. Thorbjorn watched him run away, then turned back to look at me. The look in his eyes made my stomach knot tighter than ever. "I thought I had lost you."

"Something saved me," I said.

"What? Who?" he asked.

"I don't know," I said, but before I could say more, we were surrounded by the others. Nilda pulled me into a tight embrace, but even as I hugged her back I could see Jóra looking all around me and seeing no sign of her daughter.

"I'm sorry," I said. "Freygunnar's gone."

Jóra said not a word. She didn't cry out or shed a tear. She just collapsed onto the snow as if her legs could no longer carry her. Then she just sat there, staring dully straight ahead as if she could no longer hear me.

"What happened?" Roarr asked, elbowing past some of the others to stand closer to me. I saw Thorge had also come closer, and although he was standing beside Kara, that didn't seem to be why he had picked that place to stand. His body language was more combat-ready than besotted youth just wanting to be near his crush.

Then Thormund too came up close behind Thorbjorn, and I realized they were all putting their bodies between me and the others. I couldn't exactly look over any of their shoulders, but when I leaned over to peek around Thorbjorn, I saw the dark looks on Raggi's and Báfurr's face.

And the expressions on Manni's and Yngvi's faces were darker still. Clearly, they blamed me for the loss of two of their sisters-in-law. And I hadn't even told my story yet.

"I woke up in the middle of the night," I said. "The Hunt wasn't here, but it felt like it was coming. The rest of you were like you were trapped in nightmares, unable to wake. But I saw Freygunnar was gone. She wasn't in the lodge, and yet the bar was still over the doors."

"It wasn't," Raggi said.

"No, not when the rest of you woke," I said. "I opened it to get outside myself. Whatever brought her outside without disturbing the door, I didn't have access to the same means."

"What's that supposed to mean?" Raggi demanded.

"She's talking about magic," Roarr hissed at him.

"Oh, I suppose you know all about that," Raggi shot back.

"Enough!" I said, raising a single hand to quiet them. I knew I could compel them to do it if I put the magical power in my voice, but that felt like the wrong thing to do just then.

"You went outside without waking me?" Thorbjorn asked.

I didn't answer right away. I wasn't sure how to tell him that the thought had never entered my mind. I had just gone outside, alone, because that had felt right.

He was never going to understand that.

"You were all caught in sleep," I said instead. "I could see it wasn't natural, but I didn't have time to figure it out. I knew the Hunt was coming, and I wanted to get to Freygunnar first."

"Did you?" Manni asked. His voice was less aggressively distrustful than Raggi's, if not particularly friendly.

"I did," I said. "It was like she was under someone's spell. She wouldn't stop walking, not even if I tried to physically restrain her. She was superhumanly strong. But her eyes were like she was blind. She didn't respond to me. She just kept walking and walking until the Wild Hunt caught up with us."

"Then what happened?" Thorbjorn asked.

"I couldn't save her," I said. "I had to leave her, but I was still close by when they caught her. I heard her cry out, but I didn't see it."

"You *couldn't* see it," Thorbjorn said. "If you had, you would've been taken too."

His eyes darted towards Jóra, and I saw him bite back another expression of gratitude that I hadn't been a victim of the Wild Hunt. But I gave him a little nod to let him know I understood him.

"She was lured out by magic," Roarr said. "You're sure?" He had a haunted look in his eyes, but also a fiercely determined one. I understood both emotions. He and I had both been compelled to behave like puppets in Halldis' power. It had been a horrid experience, and not one to be wished on anybody.

"I think so, yes," I said. "I didn't have time to examine things at the moment, but that was certainly what it looked like."

"So you can fix this?" he asked.

"I don't think I can bring them back," I said. "I don't think that's how it works."

"No," Gunna agreed from where she was squatting beside her sister, who was still sitting numbly in the snow. "That's not how it works. They're gone."

"But you can stop it from happening again?" Roarr pressed.

I felt all those eyes on me, the ones that looked to me with suspicion, the ones that looked to me with unquestioning faith, all of them.

"I will," I promised. "I will figure out what's happening here, and I will stop it."

CHAPTER FOURTEEN

THE OTHERS WENT BACK inside the hall to confer with each other and take another vote. But it didn't really matter to me whether they decided to stay or to go. Either way, I wasn't going home until I knew what had happened to Freylaug and Freygunnar.

Well, it didn't matter to me if *everyone* stayed. There were a few I'd rather keep with me.

As if reading my mind, Thorbjorn lingered by my side. So did Nilda and Kara. Thorge was close beside Kara, speaking quietly to his brother Thormund.

Roarr and Sigvin made it halfway to the lodge doors, then turned back to look at me.

"Do you need our help at all?" Roarr asked.

I thought he was only speaking for himself and Sigvin, but the way everyone else was watching me, I realized they all wanted to ask me the same question.

"Don't you want to go in and place your vote?" I asked, looking mainly to the Thors.

"It doesn't matter," Thormund spoke for them. "Whatever the others decide, we'll be staying here as long as you need us."

"Thank you," I said. "But I don't know what I'll need. I don't even know what I'm going to do."

"Maybe we should start with what you learned yesterday," Thorbjorn said.

"It wasn't much," I said. "I have no idea why Freylaug was taken. And then her sister. It feels like a pattern, but I don't understand it. Does it bring anything to mind with any of you? They are your cousins."

They exchanged looks, but in the end just shook their heads.

"None of them have ever dabbled with anything that might bring them trouble," Thormund said.

"They were looking for husbands," Nilda said. "But who isn't?"

"In Villmark, sure," Kara said. "But here? Of those of us in the hunting party at this lodge? Not me."

"Or me," Sigvin said.

"Me neither. You're right," Nilda said. Then she looked to me.

"No, nor I," I said. "But wait, are you saying Frigg will be next?"

"She's a bit young to be looking to marry, isn't she?" Thorge asked.

Kara turned away from him before rolling her eyes at her sister. Nilda pressed the back of her hand against her mouth to just hold back her laughter.

"So she *is* next," Sigvin said.

"Maybe not," I said. "Two data points don't really make a pattern. Not yet. If anyone is staying, which I guess at least those of us still out here are, we'll have to set a watch to guard the rest of us while we sleep."

The Thors all exchanged glances again.

"What?" I asked.

"We tried that last night," Thorbjorn said.

"After our conversation where I said that wasn't necessary?" I asked.

He shrugged, unashamed.

"And you fell asleep?" I asked. It didn't seem possible. None of them would ever shirk their duties. "Who? No, the important question is how?"

"All three of us were planning to stay awake," he said.

"It would've just been one night of missed sleep. We've done that plenty of times," Thorge said.

"So what happened?" I asked.

"We just fell asleep," Thorbjorn said. "Every single one of us."

"That has to be magic," Kara said.

"I didn't sense anything," I said. "Not inside the lodge."

"But you were already asleep, so why would you?" Kara said, not unkindly.

"We'll set a watch again tonight," I said. "But I'll be staying awake as well. Then I won't have any excuse for not seeing what's happening."

"No one blames you, Ingrid," Sigvin said.

"No one out here," Roarr grumbled.

"Maybe it would be better if they all went home," Kara said darkly.

"No," Thorbjorn said. "No, we need the meat. We need to continue the hunt." Then he looked at me, even though I hadn't been planning to speak my thoughts about that out loud. "I'm well aware that we can get food from outside of Villmark, but I don't want to have to do that. Relying on ourselves is what makes us who we are."

"I wasn't arguing," I said, although I had indeed been imagining filling up a cart full of frozen meat at the nearest supermarket.

"So, what do we do now?" Nilda asked.

"Can you go inside and fetch my art bag for me? I'll need that," I said. She nodded and headed towards the open doors. "Kara, you're the best trapper I've seen since we've been out here. I think you should focus on making sure there's enough fresh meat for dinner, no matter how many choose to stay."

"I'll go with you," Thorge said before she'd even agreed. She blinked in surprise, trapping rabbits not being an occupation usually associated with a Thor, but just nodded.

"Roarr, Sigvin and Thormund, I'd like you to go inside and join the discussion in there. Make sure the others know what we're planning for tonight. Keeping watch, I mean. Anything you can do to keep everyone calm and not accusing each other would be great."

"Surely," Thormund said with a little bow of his head, and the other two followed him through the doors.

"That just leaves me," Thorbjorn said. "What service will I render?"

"Don't feel slighted, but I really need you to just stand behind me."

"Just stand behind you?" he repeated, puzzled.

"While I draw," I said. As if summoned by my words, Nilda appeared in the doorway and started to cross the snow-covered clearing, my art bag over her shoulder. "I want to see if I can summon any details by drawing, like I've done before. But I've always had the best success with that when I've done it beside the ancestral fire."

"That's very far away," he said.

"I know," I said, reaching out to take the bag from Nilda. "Thanks, Nilda. Thorbjorn and I are going to search for clues. Can you let the others know we'll be back by dinner?"

"Don't be late," she said, lifting an admonishing finger at me.

"We won't," I promised. Then I turned back to Thorbjorn. "I know the fire is far away. That's why I need you. Maybe it's because you're a guardian of that fire, but I get a lot of the same connected energy from you. You anchor me with our ancestors, I guess. Look, I just need you to be there while I draw. That's all."

"In that case, why should I feel slighted?" he asked. "It would be my honor to perform such a service for you."

"I've already tried drawing at the place where Freylaug was taken. I think we should walk back to where Freygunnar was last night. I'd like to try drawing there."

We walked without talking back the way I had come just minutes before. It seemed a much shorter distance than it had this morning or late the night before. The sun was now climbing towards midday, and the weather was even warmer than it had been the day before. Under different circumstances, it might've been a nice hike through the snowy woods.

But any lightness in my heart faded when the two of us reached that clearing on top of the hill again.

"It's the same as the other, isn't it?" Thorbjorn asked. "They circled around her, and she leaped up into the sky."

"I think so," I said. "But I want to see how I draw it and compare the two."

"Here," he said, taking off the cloak he wore over his wool jacket and spreading it over the snow. I sat down and slipped the strap of my art bag off of my shoulder. I took out my sketchpad and a pencil. Thorbjorn was standing directly behind me. The sun was at his back, and the shadow of him standing with feet widely planted and arms crossed fell over me and my sketchpad both.

He didn't look self-conscious at all. Like he was asked to shade someone drawing while they sat in the snow all the time.

I forced myself to focus on the task at hand. I looked up at the snowy hill, but when I started to draw, my fingers did not trace any of the forms before me. Instead, they filled an entire page with the Ur rune, then another. Only after I had filled a third page with overlapping, tumbling repetitions of that letter did I finally find myself drawing the scene.

My mind drifted free while my fingers worked their own sort of magic.

I don't know how much time passed while I drew, but when my eyes blinked back to an awareness of reality, the page spread on my lap was filled with a highly detailed drawing of what must have happened the night before.

"I'm done," I said to Thorbjorn as I put the pencil away. He sat down beside me on the cloak and looked over my shoulder at the drawing.

"There's Freygunnar," I said, not quite touching her upturned face, afraid I would blur her image. I had a feeling her mother would want to see this drawing as well.

"And the Wild Hunt with the hounds," Thorbjorn said. "What's that tree back there?" He too pointed without touching the page.

"That was where I was hiding," I said, lifting my eyes from the drawing to the world before me, then pointing out the tall, leafless tree on the far side of the hill. "I was hoping I would draw what saved me, but I don't see anything."

"Maybe if you drew just the tree?" Thorbjorn suggested. "We can walk over there so you can get closer."

"Not just yet," I said, glancing up at the sky. I sighed. "It's nearly noon already. There are so few hours of daylight this time of year."

"What is that, the face in that rock?" he asked. At first I didn't know what he was talking about, but then I realized he was still looking at the picture. I leaned in, tipping my head to one side until the contours of a rock I had drawn at the edge of the clearing became very like a craggy face.

There was a whole pile of rocks there, each with its own craggy face hiding within the thick and thin pencil lines that defined its surface.

And yet there was no such pile of rocks before us.

"I have no idea," I said. "It's not even there. What was I drawing?"

"What you were meant to," he said. "May I?" I let him take the sketchbook from me, then got to my feet to stretch my legs and warm up my body while he examined the picture.

"I know this place," he said. There was wonder in his voice.

"Do you? I don't think I do," I said.

"No, I don't think you do," he agreed. "It's... well, I was going to say it was west of here, but in these parts such things get tricky fast. And the more west you try to go, the trickier they get."

"Do you know what it means? The faces in the rocks?" I asked.

"I think they're dwarves," he said, handing me back the sketchbook.

I looked at my drawing again. "Maybe? But I've drawn dwarves before, lots of times. I've never drawn them like this. Like... wizened old carvings of stone."

"The rune you were drawing before you started," he said.

"Ur," I said, although I knew he knew the name.

"I think you drew ur-dwarves," he said. "The oldest of the dwarves. The ones who emerged in the earliest stages of the creation of the world."

"You've met them?" I asked.

"No, but I know where the entrance to their mountain lies," he said. "Or rather, where one of them is. My oldest brother Thorulv showed it to me once."

"But you didn't go inside?" I asked.

"No. They are not social creatures, the ur-dwarves. It is said that if you are not an invited guest, you will never find your way to their hall under the mountain. You will wander for the rest of your life through dark caves and cold caverns, never finding your way to the hall, never finding your way back to the surface."

"Oh," I said. "That doesn't sound good."

"Don't be silly," he said, and a sudden grin spread across his face. "You just drew the entrance to their home without ever once seeing it or even knowing it existed. What is that if not an invitation?"

"A coincidence?" I said.

"You drew their particular rune over and over again before you even started drawing," he said. "That was as good as calling out to them for someone with your power."

"But I wasn't glowing," I said. "I've contained that."

"Are you sure? Were you paying attention to that while you were in your drawing state?"

I opened my mouth to answer, but then closed it again.

"I'm not sure," I admitted.

And I couldn't tell him why that admission filled me with so much shame.

"You wanted to draw this scene to find a clue to where to go next, right?" he said. "You wanted to use your magic to find a way forward, right? So, here it is. Now, what do you want to do?"

"I guess we go find the ur-dwarves," I said, putting my sketchbook away and hoisting my bag back up onto my shoulder.

But I hoped it wouldn't be a very long walk. I was all too aware of how quickly the sun was crossing the southern sky.

CHAPTER FIFTEEN

ᚿ

WE HIKED for nearly an hour through a forest that looked just like the forest around the lodge. Then the snow cover grew sparser, and the ground rockier. The trees were further and further apart, and the hills were ever steeper.

By the end of the second hour we had left the forest behind and were navigating through a rocky landscape that was all jutting prominences thrust up from the earth like enormous, fearsome sundials.

We definitely weren't in Minnesota anymore.

The wind was stronger here and had an icy bite to it, but there was very little snow to be seen on the ground.

"Where are we?" I asked.

"We're nearly there," he said. "Beyond those rocks on the horizon there is the start of a canyon that will take us to the very foot of that mountain. But if this place has a name, I've never heard it spoken."

I looked up ahead, past the rock outcroppings he had pointed to. "That's a mountain? I thought those were dark clouds," I said. "It's so blurry." I rubbed at my eyes and looked again, but I couldn't bring it into a sharper focus.

"It looks further away than it is," he agreed. "The rules are different here."

"Which rules?" I asked.

"Distance. Time. That sort of thing," he said.

"Time? Are we in danger of being caught out here after dark?" I asked.

"No," he said, but he didn't sound as confident as I would've liked.

We reached the canyon, although at first I thought there should be another name for it. The walls of said canyon were so low I could see over them, and the little trickle of a stream that ran beside us seemed inadequate to carve out anything greater.

But as we walked, the walls grew steeper and taller. The stream and the bank of it we were following stayed the same size, but compared to the towering rock faces on either side of us, it felt smaller.

I felt smaller.

By the end of that third hour of walking, I was getting nervous. "I hope we find these ur-dwarves right away," I said. "It would be tight getting back to the lodge before sunset, even if we turned around and headed back right now."

"It will be all right," Thorbjorn assured me. "See there? That's the mouth of the cave."

At first I didn't see what he was pointing at. Then I realized the stream was coming out of the rock face in front of us, the very side of the mountain itself. I hadn't been looking up since the canyon had grown too tall to see over, but now that I did the mountain was so close it seemed to go up and up forever, never reaching a summit.

"We're not going up," Thorbjorn said, taking my hand and guiding me into the stream itself. Luckily my hunting boots were waterproof, because that water looked icy cold. We splashed our way in a zigzag through protruding rocks.

Then Thorbjorn was ducking his head, stepping inside a cave that had formed over the stream. He disappeared into the darkness.

I took a moment to summon a ball of light. I felt better holding that on the palm of my mittened hand.

I crouched down and followed Thorbjorn into the mountain.

The cave was narrow and low-ceilinged for several meters, but then to my relief it opened up into a larger cavern. I could only imagine how cramped Thorbjorn, who was easily twice my size, felt.

I added more power to the fireball on my hand, then tossed it up as high as it could go. It grew even as it left my hands, and by the time it reached the cavern ceiling it was like a small sun, lighting up everything below.

Where Thorbjorn and I stood looked like a natural cavern formed around the channel where the little stream ran.

But the far side of the cavern was all carved rock, squared off into buildings. But this wasn't like a human village. These buildings were stacked on top of each other, some tall and narrow and others long and low. Natural rock had been left in places as if a reminder, and I knew the shapes of those buildings were dictated by the nature of the stone here.

"How big is this place?" I asked. "It's like a city."

"I don't see the ends of it," Thorbjorn said. "But the stream seems to run through the center of everything, doesn't it? As long as we can see the stream, we won't get lost."

"But where are we going?" I asked.

"To find the ur-dwarves," he said with an adventurous grin. He started walking alongside the stream, through a stone gate formed out of the corners of the two nearest buildings.

"But where?" I persisted. "This city looks abandoned. Are they even here?"

"They'll find us," he said back over his shoulder.

I ran to catch up with him. It was an eerie place that swallowed up every sound we made walking through it. The squared off buildings had windows and doorways, but no shutters, doors or curtains. We could look inside any of them, but it didn't matter. They were all empty. No furniture, no sign of habitation.

The stream took a turn between toweringly high building facades to the right and an outcropping of natural rock to the left. The bank of the stream got so narrow we had to step into the water again, splashing our way around that turn.

The light from my floating fireball didn't reach around this corner.

I stopped midstream to summon another one, even as Thorbjorn kept splashing his way forward in the dark. I tossed the globe of magic light high into the air, then watched as it grew and lit up everything around us in this part of the city.

We had reached what looked like a city center. The buildings were all set far back around a large central square of smooth pavement. At the very center of the square was a fountain, the point where the waters of the stream gurgled up from some deeper well below us.

I could imagine a marketplace being set up here, or musicians and a carnival, or children playing. It was a very inviting space.

And yet it, like the rest of the city, was completely empty.

"Are we sure the ur-dwarves still exist?" I asked after once more running to catch up with Thorbjorn.

"Why wouldn't they?" he asked.

"They don't seem to," I said, raising my hands to indicate the world around us.

"But they invited you here," he said with unwavering confidence.

"Then why aren't they coming out to greet us?" I asked.

We had reached the edge of the fountain and Thorbjorn finally stopped walking. He scanned the buildings ahead of us, then turned and did the same in the other three directions.

"I can't tell which would be their main hall," he said. "Nothing looks more likely than anything else."

"And no sign of anyone," I said.

"Maybe you should call them," he said.

"You mean like yell out, 'hey, ur-dwarves?'" I asked.

"I meant like magic," he said. "You caught their attention when you were drawing. Perhaps you should try drawing again."

I looked around at the buildings clustered around us. The way they stacked on top of each other, interspersed with the native rock, so many little details to their structure and the natural stone, I just knew if I started drawing any of it, we'd be here the rest of the day.

It was just the kind of intricate detail I loved in a drawing.

"I'll try something," I said to Thorbjorn. He gave me a puzzled look when I thrust my art bag into his arms without taking anything out of it, but he asked me no questions.

I threw my shoulders back and half-closed my eyes, tuning out the world around us. Then I extended my hand out in front of me. I held it out like that for a moment, really concentrating on the power in my own fingertips. Then I drew my outstretched hand up in a straight line. I curved it down towards my left, then straightened out that curve to once more be drawing a line before the motion ended with my hand at my side.

It was like I could see what I had drawn glowing in the air before me, a dark red glow like hot embers. The Ur rune.

Then it faded, and we were still alone, and I felt more than a little silly.

"Maybe I'll try sketching, then," I said, reaching for my art bag.

But Thorbjorn hugged it tight to his chest. "Wait," he said. His eyes were staring off into the distance, and his head was tipped to one side like he was listening intently. I tried listening too, but I heard nothing.

I was about to speak to Thorbjorn again when another voice spoke just at my elbow. I jumped and nearly shrieked, but caught myself just in time.

"Welcome, volva of Villmark," said the voice.

CHAPTER SIXTEEN

ᚾ

THE DWARF'S voice was deep, old but still strong, and in no hurry to get the words out.

I turned to see a face much like I had drawn earlier, like weather-shaped stone. His hair was gray, and so were his eyes, and so was even his skin. His beard fell down past his barrel-chest and hard stomach to pool at the toes of his booted feet. His hair was sparse on top and stood out at crazy angles, as if he had just been doing experiments with static electricity before coming to speak to me.

"Hello," I said, not sure how exactly to address this man.

"We have food and drink prepared, if you will kindly follow me," he said with a little bow. He was speaking Villmarker Norse, but with an accent I had never heard before. The consonants were softer and the vowels more whispery than I was accustomed to hearing.

"Am I also invited, lord dwarf?" Thorbjorn asked.

The dwarf, who was already leading the way across the square, turned back to look at him. "You are the guardian of the volva. How can you be left behind?" Then he turned away again and resumed walking. He had a halting gait, as if his joints pained him.

Thorbjorn took my hand, and we walked together, following the dwarf across the square and then up an alley that was all one steep staircase. It took a turn but kept climbing.

The second time it turned, I looked up and saw that the top of the staircase was where the alley ended. But it wasn't a dead end, it just flowed naturally into one of the larger buildings. It certainly had the largest doorway I had seen yet, tall enough for two Thorbjorns stacked to pass through, and wide enough for him and all his brothers to go through at once, shoulder to shoulder.

Warm firelight filled that building and spilled out of that doorway, so bright I couldn't see what lay on the other side. But I could smell roasting meat and fried potatoes and beer.

The dwarf stopped at the doorway and stood to one side, bowing and sweeping his hands to tell us to go in before him. I squeezed Thorbjorn's hand even tighter as we once again stepped into a space we couldn't quite see.

At last we had found a place that was inhabited and lushly furnished at that. The light came from two fireplaces, one at each end of the room, both burning with what looked like bonfires on their hearths. The walls were hung with colorful if somewhat faded tapestries depicting elaborate stories interspersed with embroidered bits of text. Runes. I longed to get a closer look at them.

But what beckoned first was the long table that dominated the center of the room. It had space enough to sit four dozen easily, but currently held only four dwarves as old, gray and wizened as our host. They all sat together near one of the fireplaces, and the food was all set around them.

Those bowls and platters and pitchers looked puny compared to the size of the table, but more than enough for the seven of us as Thorbjorn and I sat down at two of the empty chairs, and our original host joined his fellows on the other side of the table.

"Do you know why we're here?" I asked. Thorbjorn gave me a little shake of his head, but I didn't understand what he was trying to tell me.

"Food first," one of the dwarves said. But none of them made a single move.

"This looks excellent," Thorbjorn said, standing up to pick up an immense platter of some sort of roast with a serving-fork sticking out of it. He set it beside his plate and took up a knife. He scarcely needed it; the meat fell away before the blade, slow-cooked to a butter softness. He transferred the first bits to my plate and then sliced twice as much for his own plate.

The dwarves just watched without speaking or moving.

But Thorbjorn didn't seem bothered or even remotely self-conscious. He reached for bowl after bowl of various cooked vegetables and dark rolls of bread and pickled things. He always served me first, and he didn't stop until we had a bit of everything on our plates.

I looked down at the immense amount of food before me. He had only given me the tiniest amounts of each thing, but all together it still looked like more than I could ever fit in my stomach.

But I had thought the same on many a Thanksgiving. I picked up my fork and dug in.

I was still chewing when Thorbjorn poked me with his elbow. I quickly swallowed and then smiled at our dour guests. "Excellent," I said. "Please, join us?"

"Reindeer, isn't it?" Thorbjorn said, having sampled a bit of the roast meat. "I haven't had that in ages. However did you manage to acquire it? I hope it wasn't too much trouble on our account."

"We have partners with whom we trade," one of the dwarves said. He sounded as gravely somber as ever, but something had changed in their demeanor because they each finally reached for the bowls and platters and started filling up their own plates.

I ate my pickled herring, then rested my fork-hand on the table to speak, but Thorbjorn elbowed me again and shook his head at me.

Got it. No talk at the dinner table. I turned my attention back to that overabundance of food and tried not to imagine how far the sun had traveled across the sky or dwell on how little time we had left to get back to the lodge.

Thorbjorn had seconds. First of all, I had no idea how he fit it all in, but second of all, I was anxious to get to the talking portion of the agenda. But he just winked at me and slipped a little more cucumber in cream sauce onto my plate.

Finally, the dwarves stood up and gathered up the plates and bowls, scurrying off through a doorway on the far side of the room.

Then they returned with yet more plates of sliced fruit and cheese. Thorbjorn served me first again, but at least this time when he had taken his own portion, the dwarves served themselves at once without waiting for some sign from us.

I tried a cube of white cheese, which turned out sharper than I expected but very tasty. I was still chewing it when one of the dwarves spoke.

"We are of course aware that the Wild Hunt has been haunting the forest where your people dwell," he said, as if answering some remark we had never made.

"Yes, that's true," Thorbjorn said. "Two nights in a row. Is that strange?"

"Is it?" the dwarf who had brought us up from the square asked. He sounded like a teacher leading a class discussion, waiting for us to provide the answers.

"I confess we know little of such things first hand," Thorbjorn said. "It has been more than a century since the Wild Hunt last rode through our part of the world. I'm sure that is but a moment for such as you, but for us humans it is many lifetimes."

"Indeed," the dwarf said, regarding a slice of golden pear that he was clutching in his gray fingers. He looked so much like a living statue, one crafted from flowable stone.

"It is strange," one of the other dwarves said. "Especially in the part of the world where you dwell."

"We do not know what it means," the first dwarf said, then took a bite from his pear slice. "It is outside the usual order of things."

"Outside the natural order?" I asked.

He looked at me with those stony gray eyes, and I had no clue what he was thinking. He ate another bite of pear and licked off his gray fingertips. Finally he said, "there is no such thing as outside the natural order. Everything is part of nature."

"I meant, is someone controlling it?" I asked.

All five of the dwarves gaped at me, dumbfounded.

"Ingrid," Thorbjorn said to me. "Do you know what you are saying? Remember, the Wild Hunt is a thing of Odin himself."

"I know," I said. "I just wondered. Why twice in two nights? Why two sisters?"

"It is strange," one of the dwarves said. Then they all turned their attention back to their fruit and cheese.

"But we are pleased to see a volva and a guardian working together again," the first dwarf said. "It has been many an age since we've seen such a thing. Far, far too long."

I wondered how long was too long for an ageless being who had possibly seen the creation of the world itself, but Thorbjorn spoke first. "Surely not so very long. Ingrid's grandmother had a guardian. At least, at first," he finished in almost a whisper.

"No, not the same," the dwarf said. "Not so tightly bonded as you two."

"Two sisters, you say?" another dwarf asked.

I was getting conversational whiplash with how fast these dwarves changed the subject. A weird juxtaposition with the unhurried way they got their words out.

"Yes, sisters," I said. "Does that mean anything?"

But the dwarf just shrugged.

"They cannot be freed," the first dwarf said. Somehow he made his gruff tone sound even more stern as he spoke these words.

"I know," I said. "No one returns when they're taken by the Wild Hunt. I know."

"And yet your heart is still fixed on rescuing them," he said. He was arranging dried currants on his plate as he spoke, but when he looked up, he barely glanced at me before fixing his gaze on Thorbjorn.

Thorbjorn flushed a deep shade of red.

"You intended to...?" But I broke off, not sure how to finish that question.

"I don't know what I intended," he whispered back to me. "I only meant to help you in any way that I could."

"So you were hoping *I* could rescue them?" I asked.

He said nothing and wouldn't meet my eyes, but the color in his cheeks was giving him away.

I didn't know how I felt about that. It was nice he had so much confidence in me. On the other hand, I wasn't a superhero. I was only ever going to disappoint him.

"Thorbjorn," I said.

But the first dwarf spoke over me. "We cannot help you with your task," he said.

"Oh," I said. "Well, thank you for the lovely dinner. We do appreciate your hospitality."

He made a sound like "hurm" and seemed inclined to speak no more, but the other four dwarves were all staring at him intently.

"We agreed," one of them said.

"Oh, very well," the dwarf said testily. "First, she must swear to do no foolish things. We do not share our gifts with fools."

"She swears," I said. "I mean, I swear. I know what has been lost cannot be regained. I only want to find out how this can be stopped from happening again."

"We can't help you with your task, to our sorrow," one of the other dwarves said. "We have been too long under our mountain, too little out in the world."

"But there are others who can assist you," a third dwarf said. "Others who live closer to you and your kind."

"What others?" I asked. "The women in the trees?"

"The women in the trees?" Thorbjorn repeated. I waved a hand at him, hoping he'd get the message that I would explain later.

"You have sworn," the first dwarf said.

"I have," I agreed. "I truly hope to see you all again, but the hour is late and Thorbjorn and I must leave now."

It was probably already too late, but I didn't say that out loud.

"You will find it's not so late as you fear," the dwarf said. Before I could ask what he meant by that, he reached under the table to fetch something. Then he slammed a wooden box onto the table in front of me, sending my plate of cheese rinds and fruit stems bouncing away.

"What's this?" I asked, not sure if I should touch it. But it was a gorgeous box, carved from some sort of reddish-brown wood with a knot design on the cover. It was shaped like the sort of box a necklace would come in, if a bit large for that purpose.

"The gift I mentioned," he said, sounding even grumpier than before. But the other dwarves were watching me with keen attention, like I was the birthday child about to open a mountain of presents.

I lifted the lid and saw nestled within a wand of bronze.

"Oh, lovely," I said, stroking a single fingertip down the side of the wand still in the box. It danced with light that was more than mere reflected firelight. "My grandmother has one like this."

"This one is yours and yours alone," the dwarf said. "We agreed. You needed one."

I didn't know what to say. The crafting of such an object was not a quick task. Clearly these dwarves had been aware of me longer than I had been aware of them. A lot longer.

"Thank you," I said, and realized I was blinking back tears. "I thank you."

"You'll need it," one of the other dwarves said.

There was a sadness in his voice, a sort of sadness that only a lifetime of ages could feel.

But before I could say a word about it, I blinked, and Thorbjorn and I were standing together at the far end of the canyon. The stream at our feet was dancing away from us across the wind-swept meadow off to our left, and to the right was the very edge of the forest we had emerged from what felt like hours before.

And yet the sun was barely halfway across the southern sky. Not only had no time passed while we dined with the dwarves deep under that mountain in their ghostly city, it actually seemed to have gone backwards.

"That was..." I started to say, but I had no idea how to finish that sentence.

"Yes, it was," Thorbjorn said. He was looking at the wooden box I still held in my hands.

"And yet, no clues," I sighed, tucking the box away in my bag before we started back across the meadow towards the forest.

"I wouldn't say that," he said. "Let's head back to where Freygunnar was taken. We might have some leads yet."

"I can't imagine what we missed," I said.

"We'll see," he said with a cheery vagueness. "In the meantime, what's this about women in the trees?"

CHAPTER SEVENTEEN

By mid afternoon, Thorbjorn and I were back at the hill where Freygunnar had been taken by the Wild Hunt. The marks from the horses, dogs, and weapons of the men were still visible in the snow, but the bird wing patterns were almost gone. The few that remained were mostly close to the trees, where the wind hadn't reached them nor the warmth of the sun at midday.

"Which tree?" Thorbjorn asked. We were both avoiding climbing the hill itself by mutual unspoken agreement.

"Over here," I said, leading the way just a little further south to where the lightning-blasted tree still stood. "See, there is where I was sitting when I woke up this morning."

"Where were you last night before you found yourself inside the tree?" he asked.

I looked around. I remembered shrubbery that had offered no refuge, but there was a lot of that around.

Then I saw the marks of my own boots tracing a path down the hillside to stop some meters away from the tree. "There," I said, pointing towards it.

Thorbjorn motioned for me to stay where I was as he picked out a careful path over to the spot. He crouched low, examining the snow more closely.

"Your weight was on your heels," he said, pointing to the footprints without quite touching them. "There is a bit of slippage at the toes. It's like you were pulled backwards and dragged away."

"Towards the tree," I said, following the way the motion must have gone. "But there are no marks between there and the tree."

"No," Thorbjorn agreed, straightening up. He looked up at the dead branches of the tree far overhead. "It's like you, just like Freygunnar and Freylaug were pulled up into the sky."

"I think I'd remember that," I said. "All I remember is a hand touching my shoulder. Then I was just instantly inside that tree."

Thorbjorn said nothing. He made a slow circuit around the tree, examining everything. "There's no way inside that I can see."

"Nor a way out that I could find when I was inside," I said. "I could see the sky through the top of the trunk. If you step back a bit, you can see where it was blasted. The crown of the tree is gone now, and the whole trunk is hollow."

"Interesting," Thorbjorn said. "Did you want to try drawing it again?"

"I don't know," I said, looking at the sky. "It's getting close to sunset. I want to be back to the lodge before then."

"You don't sound frightened," he said.

"Well, I am," I said.

"Not of getting taken by the Wild Hunt. You already know they weren't after you," he said.

"Not that time," I said. "But I think they would've taken me anyway if I hadn't been spirited away into the center of that tree. Something or someone saved my life. I desperately want to know who it was and why, but I want even more to be sure we're both back inside the lodge before sundown."

"To protect the others," he guessed.

"As much as we can," I said. "I certainly hope we can do better than last night."

"Agreed," he said. Then he looked up at the tree again. "I've never heard any tales of magic trees in this part of the forest. It's awfully close to the boundary to the outside world. Most nonhuman things stay well clear of that. I'm curious to know what you might draw if you tried."

"I don't think it'll be anymore than I've drawn already," I said.

"The first go around led us to the ur-dwarves. That wasn't the lead we hoped it would be, but it wasn't a waste of time either," he said, nodding towards the bag on my shoulder, where I had put the bronze wand.

"I didn't recognize what I drew until you told me what it was," I said. "Here, I want you to look at what I drew at the clearing where Freylaug was taken." I took my sketchbook out of my bag and turned to the appropriate page before handing it to him.

"I see them," he said. "You're right, they do look like they are hiding in the trees. But you sense nothing here inside this tree?"

"Nothing," I said. "By all the magic I know, as little as that is, that's just an ordinary tree."

"I think I know what these are," Thorbjorn said, looking more closely at the images I had drawn. "They have many names, but most often we call them moss-wives."

"Moss-wives," I repeated. "That's a new one for me. Do they have moss-husbands?"

"I don't know," he said, handing me back my sketchbook. I closed it, then put it back in my bag.

"Have you ever seen one?" I asked.

"No, but I know they have been seen in these woods," he said. "Or rather, in a different part of these woods, further away from the boundary I just told you about."

"They live inside the trees, or they *are* the trees?" I asked.

"Something between the two," he said. "They have a bond to their trees that's more than just a home to them, but they can move about at will."

I closed my eyes and cast out with my magical vision. I looked carefully at all the trees around the hill, then searched a ring further out, and then another ring still further out.

I opened my eyes. "I don't sense anything like that around here."

"No, I'm pretty sure that the moss-wife that saved you followed you here and used that tree because she knew you could survive inside it."

"Followed me from the lodge?" I asked.

"I don't know. But if you drew them yesterday where Freylaug was taken, which was practically outside our door, that seems likely."

"If I drew them yesterday, they must've already been aware of me then," I said.

"I think so," he said.

"But I looked at all the trees around that clearing too, and there was no sign of any magical or sentient creatures anywhere around there," I said.

"They might've been drawn nearer by the Wild Hunt," Thorbjorn said. "In the old stories, they had a tie to the Wild Hunt. Like they knew first when it was coming and would occasionally warn humans. Then again, in some tales they're the ones that scout ahead for the Wild Hunt. Perhaps they're not to be trusted."

"I don't think that's the case," I said, shaking my head with firm confidence. "One of them saved me, and all of them in that picture were saddened by Freylaug's fate. No, I think they're on our side. If asked, they might be able to help us."

"It could be they are the ones the ur-dwarves were hinting about," he said.

"Maybe," I said. "Do you have any idea where to find them?"

"I might," he said. "Like I said, I've never seen them. But there is a particular grove I sometimes pass through that feels... different."

"Magical?" I asked.

"No," he said slowly, half closing his eyes as he tried to conjure the words to describe his memory. "It feels like the trees are watching me."

"In a good way or in a bad way?" I asked.

"Neither," he said after a long moment's thought. "They're just watchful. Just making sure I move through without bothering anything."

I looked up at the sky again. The sun was no longer visible overhead; the trees were obscuring it from view. But I could infer where it was by where the light was strongest.

It was nearing the tops of the western hills, but we had some time yet. Not a lot, but some.

"Is it far?" I asked.

"No," Thorbjorn said. "It's just a little bit north of the lodge. We won't have to deviate far, and we'll be closer to the lodge there than we are here. If anything should happen."

"Then let's go," I said, hoisting my bag up higher on my shoulder. "Hopefully they will have some information they are willing to share with us. Especially if they really are tied to the Wild Hunt. They might even know a way to send it away."

"I wouldn't get my hopes up on that score," Thorbjorn said as the two of us started walking more or less due north. "I doubt if anything has that power, but if they did, surely they would've used it already."

"Maybe they don't have the power themselves, but know how it's done," I said. "Like Haraldr teaching me magic."

"Maybe," he said noncommittally.

"Or," I added, "maybe they know who's behind it all."

"Behind it all?"

"I still feel like something is luring the Wild Hunt out. Someone is picking targets, somehow getting them outside the lodge walls, and putting them into the path of the Wild Hunt," I said. "I don't know who, but I feel a hand deliberately acting behind all this."

"That's a terrible thought," he said. "The Wild Hunt is a thing of Odin. No mere mortal can control that."

"Maybe not," I conceded. I knew he knew more about these sorts of things than in all the books on Norse mythology that I had ever read. Which had been all the books I could find. Which had been a lot.

On the other hand, there was one thing I was absolutely sure I was right about. "But something is definitely going on here, and I'm going to find out what it is. We aren't going to have a third night like the last two. Not if I can help it."

"Not if I can help it either," he said.

Then we quickened our pace until we were breathing too hard to talk, while behind us, the sun sank ever lower in the sky.

CHAPTER EIGHTEEN

∏

When I was a kid, my mother and I used to go on hikes together. This was mostly through the parks near St. Paul, but sometimes we ranged further from home. Not terribly far, the farthest was probably Saint Croix Falls, just a little way up north and then over the border into Wisconsin.

My mother always knew every tree by sight, and most of the other plants too. She would show me the distinctive features on their leaves or flowers or whatever, but none of it really stuck. I usually have a vague idea of what sort of tree I'm trying to draw, but it's more "oak tree" and less "swamp white oak" or whatever.

I suppose Thorbjorn was more like my mother than he was like me, but I didn't ask. Partly because we were moving too quickly for easy conversation, but mostly because even I could tell that the forest around us had changed. The trees around us weren't the usual North Shore trees.

I didn't know what they were or where they should belong, but the forest around us even in its glittering coating of snow was darker and twistier. And the trees themselves felt older. They weren't taller, but the trunks were stouter, and their branches, even leafless as they were now, were woven together so densely that little light reached us on the forest floor.

I didn't like that last bit at all. Not that I'm afraid of the dark, but it was terribly inconvenient not to be able to see the sun when you were racing against sunset.

"There," Thorbjorn said, pointing up ahead of us. I saw nothing but more trees at first, but then I saw a patch of bare snow-covered ground that was still shining in the waning afternoon light. A break in the trees. A clearing.

The minute we reached it and stopped walking, Thorbjorn took out a kidney-shaped leather bag and opened a stopper in the top. He took a long drink, then handed it to me.

Cold water had never tasted so good.

As I took a second sip, Thorbjorn turned around in a slow circle, looking at everything around us. When he'd completed his circuit, I handed him back his water bag.

"Anything?" I asked him.

"I don't see anything," he said, his voice halfway to a whisper. "But I think something sees us."

I felt the same way, like we were being watched. But it didn't feel malevolent, not like whatever had watched me leaving the hamlet the other day. This was more curiosity, but not a childlike curiosity. More like whatever was watching us wanted to see what we would do before deciding what *it* would do.

"Hello?" I called out. There was no reply. I set my art bag down on the snow, then pulled off my hood and hat so I could see better. "I wanted to thank you for last night. Won't you come out and talk to me?"

I felt Thorbjorn's weight shift behind me as he dropped into a defensive stance. Then I saw them too: a number of squat, green figures emerging from the trees.

Not from between the trees, mind you. They were stepping out of the trunks themselves.

They all appeared to be women, mature women, but not yet crones. Their hair was a dark, pine green, their clothes a more mossy shade of green, and their skin a softer green like the first shoots of delicate herb. They stood little taller than the dwarves, but were not quite as thick-muscled and barrel-chested as they. But they were certainly sturdy enough, with rolling hips and heavy arms. They weren't young, lithe, or particularly pretty, like the Greek dryads always appeared in the illustrations in mythology books. No, their faces were all solemn and deeply lined, but they did have a noble sort of beauty to them.

They all closed in around us as a group, and I wasn't sure who I should direct my attention to. They didn't seem to have a particular leader. So I looked from one to the next as I said, "I owe you a debt. I'm sure the Wild Hunt would've taken me last night if I hadn't found refuge inside that tree. And I never could've gotten inside on my own. Thank you, all."

"It was the thing to be done," one of them said, her voice deep but still womanly.

"Do you have to do such things often?" I asked.

"We like to help when we can," another said.

"I appreciate it," I said. There was a lull while I tried to decide what to say next. They all watched me patiently with gently eager eyes but said nothing themselves. "Tell me, why do they call you moss-wives? Is it because you have no men?"

"That is not what we call ourselves," one of them said.

"That is the name the woodcutters gave to us," said another.

"Sometimes one of our number chooses to go home with a human man who passed through our grove," said a third. "Not often, not for centuries now, but sometimes."

"It was they who gave us the name moss-wives," said a fourth.

Their tone was so modulated I couldn't tell whether they found the name offensive or not. They were merely stating facts, I guessed.

They hadn't told me what they called themselves. It felt like that omission had been deliberate.

"I suppose there have never been many woodcutters here in these woods," I said. "Did you choose to come here to this world, or were you pulled along by my ancestress' magic?"

"Your predecessor Torfa did indeed have staggeringly great power," one of them said. "Some of us remember her, although we were but children at the time."

I nearly gasped aloud at that. Torfa had brought her village to the North Shore from an island off the coast of Norway nearly eleven centuries ago.

"This has always been our place, our grove," another said. "How our place moved here, we do not know. But moved we have. We no longer see our old friends from our old home. They no longer pass through our grove."

"I'm sorry about that," I said. "But what about the dwarves? They aren't so very far away. Aren't they your friends?"

"They never stroll through the woods if they can help it," one of them said, and there was a hint of laughter in her voice.

"And have no need to," another said. "They always remain in their city under the mountain. It is for others to go to them."

"Every world has a cave that leads to the city under the mountain," a third said. "It is only a matter of finding it, if one wishes to visit the dwarves. We are happy in our grove. We have no need for cities."

"It is lovely here," I said. The trees were taller just around the clearing where we stood, like the support pillars inside a cathedral where the sky itself was the beautifully decorated ceiling. And there was such a feeling of warm acceptance, although perhaps that was emanating from the women all around me. "May I ask you about the Wild Hunt?"

"We know the old stories are not true," Thorbjorn added. "We know you are not bringing it here."

"No, those stories are not true. We do not scout victims for the Hunt," one of them said.

"For the Wild Hunt to ride through the same forest twice in two nights is a very bad thing," another said.

"Unusual?" I asked.

"Very," one said.

"We have been lucky so far," another said. "None of our number has been carried away."

"Yet," a third added ominously.

"You think it will come again?" I asked.

"We fear it."

"It draws ever closer to our grove."

"We have so little defense."

"What do you mean?" I asked. "Don't your trees keep you safe? Like that tree last night kept me safe?"

"They do, but not so well as the walls of a human house. One that has been infused with slow magic over many generations. We have nothing like that. It is so long for us, the time between generations."

I had all sorts of questions about how they reproduced, and why I saw no children among them now, or even women who looked young enough to have them.

But the sun was too low in the sky for me to entertain any of them now.

"Something is calling the Wild Hunt," I said. Thorbjorn sucked in a breath but made no objection.

Which was good, because every moss-wife around us answered at once and in one voice, "yes."

"How?" he asked.

"Who?" I asked, which to me felt like the more relevant question.

But they all just shook their heads sadly.

"We wish we could help you, Ingrid Torfudottir," one of them said.

"We have watched you from afar."

"We have seen you grow stronger in your magic."

"And stronger in your control."

"But, alas, we humble moss-wives have no way to help."

"You saved me once," I reminded them.

"The Wild Hunt will not be fooled by such twice," one of them said. "It is far better for you to be inside human walls before dark."

"And the time for that grows short," another said.

"You've seen nothing at all?" I asked desperately. "No stranger wandering through these woods? No signs of magic that ought not to be here? If you've been watching me all this time, you must've seen other things as well."

"We see the sons of Valki when they patrol near our grove," one said.

"We see the one who calls himself Loke popping up all over the between lands."

"We see trolls who've wandered too far south and lost sight of their brothers."

"But we've seen no sign of the sort of things of which you speak."

"But you know someone is calling the Hunt?" I asked.

"We sense it," one of them said. "But you sense it more strongly than we."

"And you have a wand now," another said. "A fine gift to be wisely used."

"Yeah," I said, glancing down at the bag at my feet. I wasn't sure how that wand was going to be best used just yet. I had been expecting to leave it in its handsome box until I could show it to Haraldr, but now I was getting the feeling I would need to take it out much sooner.

"You must go," a few of them said together, with real urgency.

"They're right," Thorbjorn said. "We'll have to run to reach the lodge in time."

"Thank you, all," I said as I picked up my bag and slung it over my shoulder.

"We wish we could be more help to you."

"But it is we who must beg you for help."

"Please stop the Wild Hunt from riding nightly through our woods."

"I'll do the best I can," I said, even as Thorbjorn was tugging urgently on my sleeve to get me moving. "My very best. I swear."

Then we were running. I glanced over my shoulder just one time and saw that the moss-wives had gathered at the very edge of their clearing to wave their farewells. I raised my right hand over my left shoulder and tossed them a quick wave.

Then I put my head down and forced my legs to keep running.

I only hoped my very best would be enough.

CHAPTER NINETEEN

I TRIED NOT to look up as we ran. Trying to track the progress of the sun through the trees to the west was only going to make me trip over my own feet, and that would really slow us down.

Plus, it was getting cloudy, especially in the west. That, with the trees and the hills, made guessing at the time remaining until sunset more than iffy.

But by the time the lodge came into view through the trees, it was well past sunset. Cloudy or not, hills and trees or not, it was well into twilight and flirting with real, dark night.

And yet the doors were still standing open, light from the fire burning in the hall within spilling like a welcome mat over the snowy clearing.

I saw the silhouette of a woman in that doorway, as stout as a moss-wife but twice as tall. But as we burst out of the last of the trees, she disappeared within.

I was pretty sure that had been Thorbjorn's mother waiting for us. I could only imagine the worry we had given her, being out so late. But I didn't know what emotion had driven her away, what she didn't want us to see on her face when we got close enough to the light.

Was she angry? No, even in the short time I had known her, I suspect she would've lingered and given us a tongue lashing if she had been angry.

No, more likely she had felt overwhelming relief that we, or at least Thorbjorn, were safe. I further suspected she moved away so that she wouldn't display that happy emotion in front of her own still-grieving sister.

We didn't slow our run until we were safely inside those walls. It was like I could feel the change, like those walls were embracing me as they would any member of their family.

As nice as that was, it paled next to the wicked stitch I had in my side. And my normally trusty boots had rubbed the back of my heels raw. I could feel the blood making my socks sticky and knew the minute I pulled those boots off my feet would swell to double their size.

But we'd made it in time.

I stayed where I was just inside the door, hands on my knees, gasping for breath. I was dimly aware of Thorbjorn behind me, shutting the heavy doors and securing the bar across them. But my vision kept darkening in a pulse timed to my heartbeat. I hoped that would stop happening when my heart stopped hammering.

"Hungry?" Nilda asked, suddenly appearing at my side with her sister Kara standing silently beside her.

"I think right now food would just make me sick," I said between huffs of breath. "But give me a minute."

"Where did you go?" she asked.

"It's a long story," I said. "I'll tell it, but I have to get my breath back first."

"Is it safe here?" Kara asked. "Are we safe?"

"That's a definite yes," I said. I pressed the heel of my hand into the stitch in my side and managed to straighten back up and push away the hair that had plastered itself to my sweaty skin. "It is safe within these walls."

"The problem is, people keep going out of this safe space," Nilda said.

"I know," I said. Before I could say more, Thorbjorn approached the three of us.

"I'm going to speak with my brothers and my father about setting up a watch," he said to me.

"Okay," I said, lifting the strap for my art bag off my shoulder and dropping it to the floor with a thunk.

"Careful with that," he said, pointing at the bag. Or, as he and I both knew, at the wand within.

"You should sit down," Nilda said to me after Thorbjorn had left us.

"Yeah," I agreed. "I need to get these boots off."

"Then let's go over there, where no one is eating," she said, and the three of us crossed to the far side of the room where the cabinets for the bedding were. I sat down and untied my boots, but that was all I could manage before a wave of fatigue washed over me.

"Are you going to be all right?" Kara asked, frowning at me.

"I'm not used to running like that," I said. "I just need a minute."

"Here, let me," Nilda said, dropping to her knees at my feet. It took a bit of effort for her to pry off first one and then the other of my boots. The socks should've been easier, but she did it gingerly, carefully rolling them down past the bleeding backs of my heels before pulling them off.

"I'll get a tub of hot water," Kara said and headed back towards the kitchen.

"Good thing I'm not going anywhere tomorrow," I said.

"You've planned that far ahead?" Nilda asked me. "And in your plan we're not going home?"

"I hope not," I said. "I learned some things today and received a gift I hope will be of use. But let's wait for Kara to get back. I'm so tired I could sleep right now. I definitely don't want to tell this whole tale more than once."

Kara returned with a tub of hot water, but she wasn't the one carrying it. Not surprisingly, it was Thorge who set the heavy tub at my feet. But Kara had a mug of hot tea with her that she pressed into my hands as Nilda helped me lift my feet over the sides of the tub and into the water.

It was almost too hot at first, but after the first initial shock it quickly became quite nice. There was something more than water in that tub. The steam rising from it smelled minty and almost mediciny.

Then Thorbjorn and Thormund joined us with a tray laden with bowls of stew. They handed the bowls around, then spoons, and we all sat together in silence, shoveling down the stew until it was gone. I wasn't sure what sort of meat was in it, perhaps venison from the first day's hunt.

But there was also a mix of mushrooms in the sauce, which was so thick it coated the spoon if I let it linger there. Which I mostly didn't. Once I'd started eating, I realized I had been ravenous.

"You three are going to keep watches through the night?" I asked when I finally had to admit there was nothing more to be scraped up off the bottom of my bowl.

"Not just us," Thormund said. "Everyone is taking a shift."

"Is that necessary?" I asked. There were only so many hours in the night.

"No one was willing to sleep at all at first," Thorge said. "This was decided before you and Thorbjorn even got back. The only way anyone will even try to sleep is if they get a turn at the watch."

"We've divided everyone into thirds," Thormund said. "One of us on each shift, plus a third of the others will also be awake."

"Which shift am I?" I asked.

"None of them," Thorbjorn said.

"Or, I guess, all of them," Nilda said. "So far, you've always woken up just before something has happened. So there's no reason for you to sit up waiting."

"Not the first night," I said.

"You just missed her," Kara said, and Nilda nodded firmly.

"If we see anything, we'll wake you," Thorge said. "Provided you're not already awake."

"Okay," I said. But I felt guilty, like I was shirking. But, on the other hand, I was so very tired.

"We also agreed before you returned that you should do the spells here like your grandmother does at the mead hall," Kara said.

"I already did that," I said. "But honestly, this place doesn't need those sorts of spells. It has protective magic of a kind that is far stronger than anything I can do."

"You did these protective spells while everyone was out hunting?" Nilda asked. I nodded. "I think you should do them again. Now, while everyone is here and can see you doing it."

"It will help the others rest easier," Kara said.

"The others," I said, looking across the room to where Raggi and Báfurr were sipping at beer with Manni and Yngvi. "I find that kind of hard to believe, actually. They don't seem to like me, for one. I doubt they trust my outsider-tainted magic."

"What they say and what they believe down in their bones aren't necessarily the same thing," Thorge said.

"You should do it," Thorbjorn said. "Even if you're just checking the work you've already done."

"So they can see," I said glumly. But I wasn't arguing. I knew the placebo effect was a real thing.

"But also, there's the wand," Thorbjorn said.

"What's this about a wand?" Nilda asked, and Kara beside her also perked up in interest.

"You tell it," I said to Thorbjorn. I rested my head on my folded arms, not really sleeping but just sitting restfully, letting the rumble of his voice wash over me. He told the others all the events of our day, from the walk out to the clearing with the lightning-blasted tree to our final sprint back to the lodge.

"Can we see this wand?" Kara asked when at last he had finished.

I sat up and looked around for my art bag. I had a vague memory of leaving it near the front door, but it was sitting beside me now, Mjolner napping against the side of it. I carefully opened it without waking him and took out the box. I set the box on the table and the others leaned in as I lifted the lid.

The polished bronze immediately caught the orange and red light from the fire on the far side of the room. It looked like it glowed, the sort of color I could see through my eyelids if I turned my face up to the sun on a summer's day.

"Your grandmother has one of those," Nilda said. "And now you have your own."

"And a gift from the dwarves, no less," Kara said, sounding deeply impressed. "Show us what it does."

I laughed. It wasn't like this was a shiny new bow and I could string it and shoot a few arrows into a target to show it off.

But then again, I did have a spell to do, one where it was apparently important that everyone be watching.

I took my feet out of the now-tepid bath and got up from the table. Then I lifted the wand out of the box and held it aloft.

At first it felt like nothing, like I was holding a spoon or a paintbrush or any other manner of mundane thing. It's not like I was shooting sparks or making a rainbow or anything.

But then I closed my eyes and shifted my awareness until I saw the weave of magic in the walls around us. My spells from the day before and the lodge's own magic intertwined.

Everything looked just as it should.

I walked the length of the room, still holding that wand high over my head. The talk around me quieted as I passed, and I felt every pair of eyes on me as I traced the spine of the roof high above us with the tip of my wand.

It didn't feel like I did anything, perhaps because there was nothing to be done. But when I reached the doors and lowered my wand, then turned to face the others, I saw awe on every face. And respect on a few I had never expected to see respect on before.

"The walls will protect us," I announced as I slipped the bronze wand into the sleeve of my sweater. At first it was cold against my skin, but it quickly grew warmer. Like it was a part of me. "Now we have to protect ourselves. No one can go outside for any reason. But we all already knew that before. What we need to watch out for now is one of us being lured out not of our own accord."

"How will we know?" Raggi asked.

"Because they're trying to get outside," Thorbjorn said. "Any of us who does that is being lured out."

"By what?" Raggi asked.

"It doesn't matter," I said firmly. I hoped he couldn't tell that he had just spoken the question that was my biggest worry.

But there was no way to find out the answer to that question now. Not until daylight.

"First watch, gather up," Thormund said as he walked closer to the fire, clapping his hands like he was summoning a sports team to huddle up.

Nilda and Kara were already laying out my bedroll on the far side of the room.

"I'm first watch," Nilda told me, then left to join the others by the fire.

"I'm second," Kara said. "I'll be beside you while you fall asleep. Do you need anything?"

"No," I said, or tried to. The massive yawn that came out of nowhere mostly obliterated that word. "Just Mjolner."

Upon hearing his name, Mjolner got up from his resting place beside my bag and walked over to the bedroll. He waited for me to get into the covers and get comfortably situated with an excessive show of patience. Then he flopped down on the pillow behind my head, pressed his spine against the back of my neck, and promptly started purring.

Four purrs in, and I was out cold. It had been a very long day.

CHAPTER TWENTY

ᚾ

ONCE AGAIN, the middle of the night found me opening my eyes. Only this time, instead of seeing the world as anyone else saw it, I was looking at it in my meditative state. I could see the soft glow of the others sleeping around me, the brighter light from the walls themselves and the spells I had spun to reinforce them, and brightest of all Mjolner beside me on my pillow.

I could feel something approaching the lodge through the forest. Not the Wild Hunt, at least not yet. This was a solitary thing, not human, not even natural. I sensed no mind, just a mission.

I sat up and blinked to bring myself back to the real world, but nothing happened. I was still in my magical meditative state.

Although it had gotten easier to reach this place through weeks of practice, I had never accidentally found myself in it, let alone just woke up looking at the world this way. That was alarming enough, now that I was awake enough to properly think about it.

But to not be able to get out of it? I looked down and realized I hadn't even sat up. I could see my body lying behind me, looking as if it still slept, undisturbed. I looked down at my own hands and saw that I had a form, sort of. It was mostly the magical glow I was used to seeing, but now it was in the rough outline of a human shape.

And my ghostly legs were overlapping my real legs. That freaked me out, so I stood up and stepped away from my bedroll. What was going on?

That thing in the woods was getting closer. I could feel it snaking silently through the trees.

But how could everyone be sleeping around me? What had happened to the watch?

I spun around and saw everyone who had volunteered for first watch sitting together by the fire. They were dressed all the way down to their boots and each had their weapons close at hand. But every single one of them had their chins resting on their chests, lost in a deep slumber.

"Meow?" Mjolner said, and I turned back around to see him wake up and then stretch. Or stretch then wake up; it was a little unclear.

He looked up at me sleepily, and I belatedly realized that he was no longer glowing with magic. He looked just like he normally did: a black six-toed cat.

That made no sense to me. I wasn't in a different world. I was just perceiving the usual world differently.

Wasn't I?

I wished Haraldr was there. I had so many questions.

But I really wished my grandmother was there.

Mjolner was bathing his ears as if nothing particularly interesting was happening. But I could feel that thing moving over the clearing. It would be at the very door in a matter of seconds.

I spun back around but saw that the door was firmly shut, the bar in place.

But the relief that gave me was only momentary, as I sensed something moving behind me. In my magical vision world, nothing made a sound save Mjolner. But I didn't need to hear to know something was stirring. I felt it in my bones.

I turned to see Kara sitting up in the bedroll next to mine. This time I didn't let myself feel any joy that I was no longer the only one awake. I moved closer to her and saw something wrong with her magical glow.

There was another, darker light interwoven with her own glow. It was subtler, more invasive, even than my spells within the older magic of the walls.

And now she was standing up, but I knew she wasn't awake. She was moving like a zombie, slow and graceless and not at all like her usual self. She didn't stop for her boots. She just made her way across the room to the doors and the thing that was waiting outside those doors.

No, not just waiting. I had been expecting the thing to attack the doors, but that wasn't its plan at all. It was just there, waiting.

Waiting for Kara.

I floated over to Thorbjorn, but I couldn't touch him, let alone wake him. I couldn't even shout.

Then Mjolner meowed again. There was a command in that meow, and not his usual dinner-demanding tone. I floated back to the bedroll to see he was pawing at my art bag, trying to get inside.

Trying to get to the wand.

I couldn't touch the bag, but I stuck my hand through it, inside of it.

And I felt the wand. The bronze was so cold I was afraid my skin would freeze to it. But touching something real had never felt so good.

Then I blinked, and I was back in the normal world.

Standing alone inside the lodge full of sleeping people, all of them oblivious to Kara making her way towards the door.

I ran across the room and tried to tackle her, but like Freygunnar she was suddenly imbued with super strength. She tossed me back, and I slid across the wood planks of the floor. I didn't come to a stop until I collided with Thorbjorn's outstretched feet.

Not even that jostling woke him. I got back to my feet and looked towards Kara, but I had nothing more to try with her than another fruitless tackle. I needed Thorbjorn and his brothers.

I realized I still had my wand in my hand. It had snapped me out of my spell when I had touched it. On impulse, I tapped the end of it in the middle of his forehead.

He sucked in a deep, mighty breath, his blue-green eyes wide and disoriented. He blinked at me just once, then that disorientation was gone.

"Kara," I said to him, and he followed my pointing finger to see her fumbling with the bar that held the doors closed. He was on his feet in a flash, across the room in scarcely more time.

Kara tried to buck him away as she had done me. He stayed on his feet, but he was struggling to keep her hands off that bar.

He needed his brothers. They hadn't been sitting up for this watch, but I knew where to find them among the sleeping figures on the floor.

I tapped Thorge and then Thormund on the forehead and sent them to help their brother. Then I went back to the remains of the fire and made my way around the circle of the first shift watch, waking each in turn so they too could help.

Nilda was the last of the watch to wake. By the time her eyes focused on mine and she was aware of the world around us, the lodge was echoing with the angry screams of her sister trying to fight off three Thors at once. Thorbjorn stood behind her with his arms around her in a tight bearhug. He had lifted her clean off the floor, but she was kicking and shrieking like a thing possessed.

Even in her stockinged feet, her kicks against the doors were shaking them on their hinges. The bar jumped and danced, threatening to come away entirely.

Nilda ran to Thorbjorn's side and desperately tried to speak to her sister, but it was like Kara couldn't even hear her.

"Get her on the ground!" Thorge said. "If we all pile on top of her, we can keep her here until she tires herself out."

I didn't think that was likely to happen anytime soon. But then I realized that the others I had left sleeping in their bedrolls were waking up on their own.

Well, not entirely on their own. Kara's screams were ear-splitting. But not with any assistance from me.

Kara might not be tiring, but whatever was outside the doors was. It was losing its hold on the situation.

But we were running out of time. I could feel the air getting colder by the minute. I could even see frost forming on the wooden pillars, spreading out in fan-like patterns before my eyes. I had to act fast.

I lowered my wand and aimed it at the door. Raggi and Báfurr were standing there, trying to hold the bar in place. I don't know if it was the sight of my wand or just the look in my eye, but they both yelped and jumped out of the way.

I didn't think it mattered if they were there. Magic didn't work like arrows fired from a bow, after all.

Then I realized I didn't know how magic *did* work. I had my wand in position, but what was I supposed to do?

On impulse, I commanded, "be gone!" in my most impressive, magically enhanced voice.

And just like that, Kara stopped fighting.

"Open the doors!" I yelled at Raggi and Báfurr. Whatever had been outside the doors, it was retreating. I could sense it zipping away back through the trees, so fast.

"No way!" Raggi said.

I grumbled something that wasn't really articulate words, then jumped over the scrum of Thors and Kara on the floor to throw up the bar myself. I pushed both of the doors wide open.

I might've had some half-formed plan to run after the thing, never mind I was no better dressed than I had been the night before. But I didn't even put a toe past the threshold.

I looked back to see Thorbjorn still kneeling on the floor behind me. He had gotten up off his brothers and lunged to catch the back of my clothes, holding me fast.

"It's getting away!" I said desperately.

"Let it," he said. "The Wild Hunt is coming. Don't you feel it?"

I did. The cold had been the first clue, but now the wind was picking up. The first dog barked far off in the distance, and was answered by another that sounded like it was on the far side of the clearing, just out of sight amongst the trees.

"The doors!" Raggi cried. Thorbjorn pulled me back out of the doorway, and Raggi and Báfurr slammed the doors shut and dropped the bar into place.

Just in time. The doors began to shake even before they'd stepped away.

"Something was here first," I said. I hoped I didn't sound as bad-tempered as I felt, but I had just lost my best chance at catching whatever was behind all this.

"Did it summon the Hunt, like you feared?" Thorbjorn asked me as he got to his feet.

"I don't know," I admitted. "But it was definitely doing something to Kara. Luring her out. Waiting for her just outside the doors."

"What was it?" Raggi demanded.

"I don't know," I said. "I've never seen anything like it before."

He turned away from me, but not before I saw him start to roll his eyes at Báfurr.

"I know I'm new at this," I said. "I'm still figuring it all out."

"You'll get no complaints from me," Nilda said. She was sitting on the floor, her sister in her arms. There were tears in her eyes, something I had never thought to see in my lifetime. It shook me more than anything else I had seen that night.

"Nor me," Kara said, pushing back her loose hair to look up at me. "Thank you, Ingrid. I don't know what you did or how you did it, but thank you."

I didn't trust myself to speak, not pass the lump that was hard in my throat. All I could manage was a nod.

But I knew she understood. I saw it in her eyes.

CHAPTER TWENTY-ONE

NONE of us got anymore sleep that night. Not with the Wild Hunt still riding just outside our walls. The wind shrieked, the dogs howled, and the horses' hooves thundered. There were cries like from men, but only inarticulate shouts of excitement and then growing frustration.

Valki and Thormund got the fire back to roaring life. The warmth did little against that unnatural cold, but the light was much appreciated. Gunna and Jóra made large pots of strong coffee and passed mugs around.

We all huddled together, sipping that coffee, listening to the cacophony outside, and waiting for dawn.

"So what exactly happened?" Thorbjorn asked me. I was resting with my head on his shoulder, but I sat up to look at him, not sure what he meant. "You were awake before the rest of us. Tell me the whole story. What woke you?"

"Nothing, I don't think," I said. "I just was suddenly awake. Only, not really."

"I don't follow you," he said.

"Well, you know how when I meditate I can see the magic of things around me," I said.

"You said you contained your glow," he said.

"I did. This is more the opposite. I'm seeing other things. I'm not necessarily being seen."

"Were you seen last night?"

I thought about that for a moment. "No, I don't think so. I was just awake, aware of something approaching. But I don't think it was aware of me. It wasn't coming for me."

"It was coming for Kara, already?" he asked.

At the sound of her name, Kara, who was sitting across from us wide awake but with her head on her sister's shoulder, sat up straight.

"I think so," I said to both of them. "There was something wrong with the glow around Kara. Something alien was woven into it."

"Is it still there?" Kara asked.

I closed my eyes and slowed my breathing, then opened my eyes and looked at her magical glow. I searched it as thoroughly as I knew how. Finally, I blinked and was looking at the normal world again.

"No. It's gone," I said.

"You're sure?" Nilda asked.

"Yes. Very sure," I said. Nilda nodded, satisfied with my answer.

"Let me get this straight," Thorbjorn said. "You sensed something approaching, hunting for Kara, but she already had a mark. Was that mark what lured the... whatever?"

"I don't know. Maybe."

"Did Freygunnar or Freylaug have it?" Nilda asked.

"I don't know," I said, and felt my cheeks flushing. I didn't want to admit that I hadn't even looked.

"Well, you didn't see Freylaug at all, and when you followed Frey-gunnar you were pretty much running the whole time, right?" Kara said.

Now my cheeks were glowing for a different reason. It felt good to have Kara back in my corner again.

"You should check everyone now," Thorbjorn said.

"No, don't," Nilda said. She looked around, but none of the others were paying any attention to us. Still, she waved for us all to put our heads closer together before she spoke again. "Wait until tomorrow. If it's even necessary tomorrow. Check us all before we go to bed."

"She's right," Kara said before I could argue. "If anyone else was marked like I was, they'd already be trying to get outside, right?"

"I don't know. What was drawing you out wasn't the Wild Hunt. It was that other presence, the thing that retreated too fast for me to see. I wish I'd run after it," I said regretfully.

"I'm glad you didn't," Thorbjorn said. "Who knows where it was heading? And you'd have been caught by the Wild Hunt for sure. The mark might show who's inclined to sneak out in the dark of night, but there's more than one kind of obsession that can lure people out."

"Point taken," I said.

But I still wished I'd run after the thing.

"It doesn't make any sense," Nilda said. "One sister after another, but then Kara? Where's the pattern there?"

"Single women?" Thorbjorn said with a shrug.

"That accounts for half the people under this roof right now," Nilda said. "Why Kara next?"

"I'm wondering how someone put a mark of magic on me without me knowing," Kara said. "Did someone cast a spell on me from afar?"

"I don't know," I admitted.

"Because I certainly didn't encounter anyone out in the woods who could've put a spell on me," she went on. "The only people I've seen since we left home are the rest of us here."

"And before you left home?" Thorbjorn asked.

"Mostly the same people," she said. "Did I eat tainted food or something?"

"I'll figure it all out," I promised her. "Although I might have to go back home to do it."

"You're going home? Tomorrow?" Nilda asked, alarmed.

"I don't want to spend another night here if you aren't here too," Kara said.

"It's not like I'm of any use with the hunting," I said. "I could go and be back before nightfall."

"I don't want you to go," Kara insisted.

"No, I can see why you wouldn't," Raggi said suddenly. I looked up to see most of the rest of the lodge now watching us. Our voices had been rising during the course of the conversation, I realized too late.

"I'm not abandoning you all," I said.

"Like we need you around for another little show," Raggi said.

"What do you mean 'show'?" I asked.

He mimicked waving a wand around, then sneered at me. "You know what I mean."

"That wasn't a show," Kara said darkly. "Those were protective spells."

"Too little, too late, if you ask me," Báfurr said.

"No one did," Nilda grumbled.

This was getting out of hand. The constant howling outside was putting everyone on edge, but the last thing we needed was a fight amongst ourselves. "I'm still new at all this," I said. "I'm sorry for letting you all down."

"See, that implies you actually tried to do something," Raggi said. "Which I don't think you did. I think you want us all to believe you have power, but you don't, do you?"

"I don't have to prove anything to you," I said.

"No, I don't reckon it's me you're trying to impress," he said.

"Then who?" I asked.

"Doesn't matter," he shrugged. "The point is, I'm sick of being part of your little theatrical show. Go back to Villmark, or better yet, carry on to Runde and past it. Leave the rest of us in peace."

"Do you call this 'peace'?" Kara asked, waving her arms around to indicate the Wild Hunt still pounding on the walls of the lodge.

"That wouldn't be happening if she weren't here," Báfurr said.

"We don't know that," Nilda said.

"Don't we? We've been coming out here for how many years, never a sign of the Wild Hunt? Then she comes with us, and bam!" He slapped his hands together loudly, then said no more.

"You think she summoned the Wild Hunt just to pretend to fight it with magic?" Nilda asked, shaking her head. "That makes no sense. If this were all a show, wouldn't she be succeeding more?"

"Hey," I said softly. That one hurt.

"It's all part of the show," Báfurr said. "She gets rid of a few women she has no use for, just lets the Hunt take them. But not her friend. No, her friend is *special*."

I tried to argue, but all I could manage was to sputter in rage.

But Kara had no such trouble finding the words. "How dare you?" she hissed, getting to her feet and stalking over to stand over where Báfurr sat on the bench next to Raggi. She had her sword in her hand. Her arm was still at her side, but every muscle in it was tensed to move.

"Kara," I said, but she ignored me.

"How dare you imply that I was part of some ruse," she said to Báfurr. "Do you think that of me? Truly? Then you don't know me at all."

"I was just talking," Báfurr said, raising his hands in mock surrender.

"You talk too much," Kara said.

"We're all on edge here," Thorbjorn said, putting a hand on the wrist of her sword hand. She looked down as if she wasn't sure what was touching her.

"Apologize, Báfurr," Thorge said. He, too, was on his feet. He didn't have his knives in his hands, but that didn't matter. I had seen how fast he could draw and throw them. In a blink of an eye, Báfurr could have two knives buried up to their hilts in his throat.

And I could see that he knew it.

"I'm sorry," Báfurr said to Kara. He put a hand over his heart as if to indicate just how sincere he was.

"And Ingrid," Thorbjorn said.

Báfurr glanced at me. "Sorry," he said with a little nod.

Thorbjorn narrowed his eyes, but now it was my turn to calm a warrior with a soft touch.

"I accept your apology, provided you accept mine," I said. "I am honestly trying to save everyone. I know I've failed twice already, and there is nothing I can do to make amends for that now. But I swear there will not be a third failure."

Báfurr grunted noncommittally. That sound could mean anything.

"We should vote again," Raggi said to the room at large. "Whether to stay or to go."

"Better just to ask if anyone has changed their mind," Nilda said. "I haven't."

There were murmurs around the room, various people agreeing with Nilda.

Raggi threw up his hands, then slumped back on his bench, reaching for his mug of coffee.

The Wild Hunt continued to ride around the lodge. At least that meant the moss-wives were safe for this night, I thought to myself.

But this couldn't keep happening night after night. It was untenable.

"I'll figure out what's happening here," I said to Thorbjorn, Nilda and Kara. "Tomorrow, I'll devote all of my attention to it. If that means going back to Villmark, then so be it."

"But you'll be back," Kara said, as if this were already an accepted fact.

"I'll be back," I promised her. "If I have to bring Haraldr, my grandmother, or heck, even Loke with me to keep everyone here safe, I'll do it. But I'll definitely be back."

CHAPTER TWENTY-TWO

THE NOISE of the Wild Hunt left shortly before dawn, but no one felt like celebrating. We just all stayed huddled together, unspeaking, staring into space.

The fire had died back down, but the grayish light through the cracks in the shutters was brightening the room. Gunna went to the doors and lifted the bar, then swung both doors wide open.

The bird-wing patterns on the snow were fresh and as intricate as ever. Gunna looked out at them for a moment, then set the bar aside and shuffled off to the kitchen area, where her sister was already spooning porridge into bowls.

We ate without talking, then the other hunting parties headed out one by one.

"What are we starting with, then?" Thorbjorn asked me once his bowl was scraped clean.

"*You* are heading out with the others to hunt us some meat," I said. "I have some things of my own to do."

"I want to help," he insisted.

I glanced around to be sure Nilda and Kara weren't in earshot, then leaned forward to whisper, "I know you do. And I couldn't have gotten anything accomplished yesterday without you. Don't think I don't know that."

"So?" he said.

"Kara is working hard to keep her chin up. I respect her for that. But I think she's earned a day doing what she loves best. And you know that means hunting."

"It does," he allowed.

"With you," I added. He scowled at me, but I raised a hand to hold off whatever he wanted to say. "I know, and she knows, how you feel. I'm only asking for you to be there with her as a friend."

"And what are you planning to do without me there by your side?" he asked.

I looked over at my art bag, Mjolner once more sleeping while curled around it. It was clear to me he had very protective feelings about the wand stowed away within that bag.

"I have to learn how to use that wand," I said.

"What do you mean? You did great with it last night," he said.

"That was impulse. And luck," I said. "I would like to add skill to that list before I need it again. I need to get acquainted with it. And that's really something I need to do alone."

"Okay," he agreed. "Be careful."

"Of course I will," I said. I yawned, then gave myself a little shake, as if that could rouse my mind to full wakefulness. "I should get started."

"We're going north today," he said as he got to his feet. "I'm sure we'll shoot nearly more than we can haul back before we even break for lunch."

"Then I'll see you at dinnertime," I said.

I walked with the others to the edge of the clearing, hugging Nilda and Kara goodbye before heading back into the nearly empty lodge.

Gunna and Jóra were still cleaning up in the kitchen. And Freyja was trying to get a few more spoonfuls of porridge into the mouth of little Martin, who for his part was anxious to get down on the floor and play.

I crossed the room to my art bag. Mjolner was awake now, sitting patiently beside it and watching me closely with his yellow-green eyes.

"I suppose you're a part of this, aren't you?" I said to him as I opened the bag and took out the wand.

He meowed at me but didn't move. Well-trained dogs should have such an impressive sit posture.

I turned to walk back to the doors, and Mjolner got up to follow at my heels.

I paused in the doorway. I wanted to see if I could sense anything from whatever had been at the door the night before, waiting for Kara to come out. It would make sense to start inside, where I had been standing when I had dispelled it.

But while no one in the lodge was looking at me now, that could change at any moment. I didn't want to worry anybody.

And I really didn't want to work magic with people maybe looking at me.

So I went outside. Mjolner followed along as if we hadn't stopped at all. I went to the left just outside the door and turned back to face the threshold.

Of course, there was nothing to see in the normal world now. Everyone's boots as they'd headed out had churned the snow up pretty thoroughly. But I had seen the bird-wing pattern on the snow already, and it had been just like before.

I looked down at the wand shining brightly in my hand. I really wasn't sure what to do.

My grandmother had a wand of her own, but I had only seen her holding it while acting as a judge. It had been more badge of office than weapon or tool. I had never seen her use it in her own spellwork.

But with every little increment I made on my own journey of magical knowledge, I acknowledged more and more that she and I had very different ways of doing things. And the ur-dwarves had made this particular wand especially for me.

So what did that mean?

I looked down at Mjolner, who blinked back up at me. He was waiting, patiently waiting for me to figure it out.

I glared at him just a little bit. I was pretty sure he knew what I was supposed to do but was just refusing to tell me.

He winked at me.

I snorted a laugh, then turned my attention back to the wand. I started waving it around, at first just to get a feel for the weight of it in my hand, the balance of it. It was like working with some art implement on a vast canvas. I was drawing from my shoulder, using the whole range of motion my arm could manage.

I kept waving it around, my eyes half-focused as I fixed my attention instead on the sensations of the movement. But the glint of the bronze caught the light from the morning sun, like sparks of too-bright light in my vision.

But the sparks were forming a pattern before me. And not just where I was waving the wand. They were tracing out a snaky path through the air, up and down from about shoulder height to about waist height.

It started at the center of the doorway and trailed off through the woods to the north and east.

Or rather, it started in the woods and ended at the door.

"You see that, right?" I said to Mjolner, still waving my arm around.

"Meow," he said.

"This is tiring on my arm. Do you know where this trail leads?" I asked him. "Do you know where this snake thing came from?"

"Meow," he said again. And then he was gone, off like a shot over the snow, across the clearing and then through the thicket into the woods.

I decided not to put my wand away just yet and ran after him. He wasn't waiting for me, but he kept a pace that I could just keep up with. He darted through trees, over frozen ponds, and around boulders, more or less back towards Villmark.

I hoped that didn't mean he was just heading back to the markets he knew, the ones that always had fresh fish. His favorite dinner, but not one he'd had since we'd come out to the hunting lodge.

I really hoped I wasn't wasting the day chasing a cat with a craving.

But at least if we ended up in Villmark, I could implement the "come back with reinforcements" plan.

I followed him for hours. We were heading mostly in the direction of Villmark, but definitely not along the course we had taken out in the first place. Not that I'd been paying much attention to the countryside during that sleigh ride, but still. Nothing around me looked familiar.

Then Mjolner leaped up to the top of a large boulder and began washing his ears as he waited for me to catch up.

"I can't keep running like this," I told him as I leaned back against his rock and willed my heart rate to slow. "My feet are still a mess from yesterday, you know."

He gave me a sympathetic meow, then finished bathing with a snappy flick of his enormous paw. Then he turned away from me to stare off into the trees.

"What is it?" I asked, squinting to see what he was looking at. All I saw were trees, trees, and more trees.

And faintly, almost lost in the shadows under those trees, the boxy shapes of cabins.

"Is that what I think it is?" I asked him. But he just launched himself off the flat top of the rock and sprinted across the snow, far faster than I could follow. Like he was in full pursuit mode of some fleeing rodent.

Or like he was running for his life.

I spun to look behind me, but there was nothing there.

So, the former then. I jogged after him. He was quickly out of my sight, but his paw prints on the snow left a clear trail to guide me.

The vague box shapes became more definitely cabins as I drew closer. Then they were definitely cabins arranged in a circle under tall pines. There was no question where I was. This was the hamlet where the exiles from Villmark lived together.

But why was Mjolner bringing me here?

I followed his paw prints as they circled around the outside of the hamlet. Then they darted between two of the cabins, towards the center of the community.

I finally caught up with him in the center of the hamlet. He was stalking back and forth as if trying to pick up the scent again. I watched him do this for a few minutes until it became clear he wasn't going to find what he was looking for quickly or easily.

I took out my wand and unfocused my eyes as I waved it around. I could see traces of magic, but they were like random shreds of paper scattered all around me. A spell had moved through here, a powerful one, but from where and to where, I couldn't tell from what had been left behind.

I fixed my attention on the cabins themselves, looking at them carefully one by one, but nothing magical appeared to be going on behind any of those closed doors.

Meanwhile, Mjolner's pacing was getting tighter. He was moving past the same three cabins over and over. At first glance I thought all the cabins were alike, and could see nothing different about these three.

But then I realized that the one on the right was Signi's place. Her shutters had little heart shapes carved into them. I remembered that from when I had been here before.

So that meant the one in the center belonged to the man that Loke had been anxious for me to meet. What was his name? Had Loke said it? I couldn't recall.

Wait, Geiri had told me. It was Frór.

The house to the left of that, I had no idea who lived there. But Mjolner's hunting took him past it again and again.

Was the murderer I sought behind one of these three doors? Not that I suspected Signi, but she did have that mysterious houseguest. Was she watching over him because he was potentially dangerous?

That Frór man hadn't felt dangerous to me when I had met him. At least, he hadn't triggered any of my self-protecting instincts. But Geiri hadn't trusted him.

Not that I even knew if I could trust Geiri. All I knew about him was that my sketch of him had shown nothing alarming.

But who lived in that third house?

Mjolner gave a little meow, as if suddenly realizing something, and ran straight up the stairs of the middle cabin. He sat down on the porch and started scratching at the door insistently.

"What is it?" I asked him, looking around with my wand and my unfocused eyes. But I saw no more magic here than the occasional shreds that were scattered all over the hamlet.

Mjolner was still scratching, forcefully enough to rattle the door in its frame. Then he added a persistent yowling to the mix.

Which was odd. I knew for a fact he could walk through walls. He always managed it at home, whether that home was in Villmark, Runde or St. Paul.

Was this place different? Or was he just being polite?

He upped his yowling frequency, and I decided it definitely wasn't a matter of politeness.

"Mjolner, stop," I said to him. I bent to try to pick him up, but he danced out of the reach of my hands. I gave up at once and stood up to look down at him with my hands on my hips. I had to project my angriest cat-mama energy at him.

"Did you follow that spell here?" I asked. "Is this where it came from? Is the man in this house the one who's been luring women out to meet the Wild Hunt? Are you sure it's this house and not either of the others?"

Mjolner ignored me. He made a little huffing sound, then went back to scratching at the door.

"Stop that!" I said, dropping to one knee to try to grab him again.

I was still down there, completely failing to catch hold of a cat, when the door swung open. A pair of man's boots were there in the doorway, big enough and worn enough to belong to a Thor.

Then Mjolner was being lifted up into the air. Without any feline objection.

I straightened up, intending to apologize for disturbing him. It was the man called Frór, but he didn't seem to notice me there at all. His attention was all on Mjolner.

He was holding the cat gently in his arms and scratching all around his ears, just the way Mjolner liked best. He was also cooing something I didn't understand. Some of the words sounded familiar, but the accent was very different from what I was used to in Villmark. Even in a singsong, the words he spoke felt older than any I knew.

Even without his winter coat on, he was definitely a large man, tall and wide across the shoulders. The sleeves of his knit sweater strained to reach around the hard muscles of his arms. His hair was all silvery gray but still thick, and his beard was so long he wore it tucked in his belt.

He didn't exactly look like Santa Claus, but he didn't look like a killer either. I remembered what Geiri had called him. The man who could've been king. He did look like an old king, and of a hard-won kingdom at that. He had seen battles. He had probably killed scores of giants and trolls and maybe even other warriors.

But luring young women to their deaths through magic? Not this man.

And anyway, I very much doubted that Mjolner would be purring so loudly at the pets of a devious murderer. That wouldn't be like him at all. He always sensed danger, even when I didn't.

But then, why *did* Mjolner lead me here?

I realized Frór was looking at me as if waiting for me to speak. Well, I hadn't been the one rattling at his door, but I was probably still the one who should talk first.

I opened my mouth, but nothing came out.

Frór's eyes were twinkling merrily. I felt a wave of irritation at that, but that wave faded away before it quite crashed ashore.

Again, there was something so familiar about those eyes. Where had I seen them before?

"Well, come in, Ingrid Torfudottir," he said, still petting my cat as he stepped back to let me inside his cabin. "We have much to discuss, you and I."

I tried talking again, but still had no words. So I just nodded, and went inside, and shut the door behind me.

CHAPTER TWENTY-THREE

ᚾ

THE INTERIOR of his house was much like Signi's. The walls were covered in white bookshelves. They even extended for a single shelf over the doorways and windows, and the windows had two shelves below them as well.

But this place had no room for knick-knacks. And the only light which was on was a reading lamp situated to shine down on the lap of whoever was sitting in the most comfortable chair by the fire. It was a recliner, and judging by the burnt orange and brown color of the upholstery, I guessed it dated back to the 70s.

The man carried Mjolner over to that chair. He poked the fire in his fireplace back to life before settling down in the recliner. He pushed the lamp back so that its light wasn't shining directly in the cat's eyes. Then he calmly scratched all around Mjolner's ears. He wasn't looking at me, but I knew he was waiting for me to do something or say something.

But I lingered still in the doorway. I felt strange. Not like I was under a spell, more like I was looking at two overlapping realities and I wasn't sure which one was real.

I stepped further into the room, and the smell of the place washed over me. The room smelled strongly of musty paper, a scent I knew well. It was that classic used bookstore smell. There was no sign of the modern, scholarly texts that Signi had favored on her shelves. No, each of those shelves was stuffed with books on top of books, mostly old, faded paperbacks.

But there was something familiar about those books, about that smell. And it wasn't memories of shopping in used bookstores that were floating in my mind, not quite coming into focus.

No, whatever I was trying to remember wasn't so mundane as all that.

"This isn't your house," I said to the man. I was still only just inside the room, hovering with a hand on one of his over-stuffed bookcases.

"Oh, I assure you, it is mine," he said, his focus still mainly on my cat. "It's just not the house of mine that you remember. That cabin is much further north of here. I still use it sometimes, but I'm more often here."

"Mjolner led me here," I said, still confused. That strange feeling was only growing stronger. I wanted to remember what I was being reminded of, but the memories refused to surface.

"I know," he said. "Ingrid, wouldn't you like to sit down?"

"I don't know," I said. "We were following the trail of a spell. A bad spell. It should've led us back to a killer."

"I see," he said, quite neutrally. "Do you think I'm the killer you seek?"

"I don't know," I said.

"You have your wand in your hand," he said. "Touch it to your own forehead."

"Why?" I asked.

"Because it's time for you to do so," he said. "But please, sit down in this chair here with me first."

I looked down at my wand, unsure of what to do. Mjolner's loud purring was the only sound besides the crackling of the fire. If I were in danger, he would know. He would protect me. Whoever this man was, Mjolner trusted him.

So why was I so afraid?

Some of the memories rushed back into the front of the mind. My grandmother, lividly angry, but not at me. No, she has her arms around me, a very young version of me, and she's yelling at someone else. I've never seen her so angry.

Except apparently I had. This was a memory, a memory of my time before, when I had come to Villmark as a child for a single summer.

The very moment I realized that, all the memories fled to the darker corners of my mind again.

"What's happening?" I asked.

"Your mind is breaking through. But the spell has been on you for a very long time," he said, his voice kind and sympathetic. "It's far stronger than your grandmother intended when she cast it on you, but she was quite angry at the time. But please, Ingrid, sit down with me. If you use the wand to break the spell, the process will go much faster."

I looked down at my wand again, then raised it to my own forehead and gave it a little tap.

The world rushed away from me, and I was lost in my memories. I was a little girl, and I was running through the meadow at the top of the waterfall with a boy. I knew him at once by his red hair and green eyes. Thorbjorn. We were together, having adventures.

We explored every inch of Villmark that summer, just the two of us. We knew every hiding place in the village and the meadow and the woods all around. We had even been caught sneaking into the caves more than once by Thorbjorn's father, Valki.

But our best adventures hadn't been just the two of us. Our best adventures had been when Frór, the old guardian of the people of Villmark, took us out on patrol with him.

He showed us rings of standing stones, and old villages long abandoned. We had met trolls and played with troll children. We had visited dwarf cities under different mountains, if never the ur-dwarves themselves.

Then, one day, Thorbjorn and I had decided to follow Frór into the north, the one direction we were absolutely forbidden to go.

The memory of my grandmother was back again, her angry red face and stiff posture, the way she had been crackling with magic. She had been yelling at Frór, but Thorbjorn and I had been quaking in fear, uncertain what she was about to do.

The fear pushed me out of the dreamy memory place, and I opened my eyes to find myself in a heap on the floor. There was a bump forming on my temple, I guessed from where it had hit the floor.

"I did ask you to sit down first," Frór said.

"Mormor blamed you," I said, rubbing absently at that bump as I sat up.

"Yes," he agreed.

"But it wasn't your fault," I said. "Thorbjorn and I were following you after you specifically told us not to do so. It wasn't your fault."

"You assume I didn't know you two were there," he said.

"Did you?" I asked.

He picked Mjolner up from his lap and settled him against his shoulder, stroking his back in long strokes that had the cat purring in delight. "Perhaps."

I got up from the floor and unsteadily made my way over to the other chair by the fire. I looked around the room again. The books weren't the only familiar things. The bearskin rug in front of the fire was one I had seen before. The carving on the bowl full of apples resting on a table nearby was also familiar. I could even remember Frór's hands as he carved those knots into the wood.

"Do you live out here because she's still mad at you?" I asked.

He laughed. "Well, that would be reason enough, wouldn't it? But no. You're still getting memories back. It will take a few days for them all to catch up with you. But when they do, you'll recall that I've never lived in town. I'm too much of a loner for that."

"But you're here now," I pointed out.

"Indeed," he said. "It's not as overwhelming as Villmark. The people here like to keep to themselves. But perhaps I see the value of some small amount of companionship in my last days."

"Mjolner is quite fond of you," I said, nodding towards my cat, who was sleeping against the side of Frór's neck.

"Oh, yes. Well, there's a reason for that," he said sheepishly. His cheeks were even turning pink.

"What's the reason?" I asked.

"I suppose he's grateful for the last time we met," he said. He stroked Mjolner's head fondly. "I was walking a patrol far west of here when I found this little kitten with enormous paws all alone in the branches of a tree. No idea how he came to be stuck up there, him such a tiny thing. It was late spring at the time, but in the middle of a cold snap for all that. He was shaking and so thin, it near broke my heart."

"Late spring?" I asked in surprise. "Last year?"

"Just so," Frór said. "I put him inside my jacket and we walked the rest of my patrol together. I fed him bits of my food, and he stayed warm against my chest by day and close up against my neck by night. Soon he was big, although his paws were still too big for him, and strong enough to be on his own. So when my patrol ended we parted ways, I back to my cabin in the north, and he to wherever he chose to go."

"This was still in the spring?" I asked.

"Hmm. No. It was late summer when my patrol ended," he said.

Mjolner lifted his head and turned to look at me.

"I guess he came more or less straight to me, then," I said. "All the way in St. Paul. That makes no sense."

"Well, he's no ordinary cat," Frór said. He touched the collar around Mjolner's neck, admiring the hammer pendant that hung there. "You've given him a fine name."

"He gave it to himself, actually," I said. "He kept appearing in my bedroom, trying to steal that little pendant from me. Finally, I just gave it to him, the pendant and the name both."

"I can't say I'm surprised," Frór said.

I sighed. "He was supposed to be helping me follow the last traces of a spell. I thought that's where he was leading me, anyway. But now that we're here, I guess that wasn't what he was doing at all. He was just bringing me to see you."

"I've long wished to see you again, especially after I heard you were back in town. But I knew from others that your memories were still hiding from you, and so I bided my time," he said.

"I suppose he knew that," I said. "He often just seems to know things. I think he could even talk if he ever chose to do so."

"Perhaps he prefers to keep his own council," Frór said. "As happy as I am to see you, I know that you didn't intend to visit me today. Tell me about this killer."

"It's a long story," I said, and took in a deep breath to begin.

But to my surprise, Frór set Mjolner down on the floor to race off to some other part of the cabin before getting to his feet. "It's a long story, but it's also lunchtime. Two things that go together very handily. Let's go to the kitchen and once you've eaten, you can tell me everything."

"There's a good deal of urgency to the matter," I said, but the loud growl of my stomach drowned out my words.

Frór chuckled. "We'll make it a quick meal. Then, when your tale is done, we'll have full bellies to decide what to do next."

"You're going to help me?" I asked.

"Well, of course I'm going to help you," he said. "Surely you remember that much about me."

I closed my eyes and sorted through my newfound memories. I didn't remember every event that had taken place - not yet, anyway - but one feeling came through all of them loud and clear.

I trusted Frór.

As a child, I had trusted him to keep me safe, which despite how angry my grandmother had been for our last adventure, he had always done.

But more than that, even as a child I knew I could tell Frór anything, and he would hear me and take me seriously. He always treated me not exactly as an adult, but at least as someone whose thoughts and feelings were of value.

I could tell him anything, and not only would he not require proof to believe me, he would go to any length to help me solve my problems.

"Yes," I said, and smiled at him with all the warmth in my heart. "Yes, I do remember that about you."

His cheeks flushed, and I think he was actually feeling a little bit embarrassed. But all he said was, "good. Lunch, then."

And I followed him into the kitchen.

CHAPTER TWENTY-FOUR

FRÓR'S IDEA of a quick meal was more like banquet where I came from. He set a loaf of black bread on a cutting board in front of me and had me start slicing it as thin as I could. Then he took a wheel of cheese and an entire roast beef out of his refrigerator and sliced those himself. Finally he added cold sliced potatoes, fresh herbs, an urn of butter, and a variety of jams in cute little jars to the assortment of things on the table between us.

I had been to restaurants with sparser buffets.

"Beer?" he asked me as he poured a mug for himself from a barrel standing on a pedestal in the corner.

"None for me," I said.

"Tea? Or milk?" he offered.

"Tea would be lovely," I said.

He nodded and pushed a kettle over the fire in the kitchen fireplace. While we waited for that to come to a boil, we sat together at the table and began loading up the bread slices with all the various toppings.

"Oh, nearly forgot," he said, getting up again and going back to the refrigerator. He came out again with a little plate of pickled herring and set it on the floor. Mjolner gave an ecstatic meow of thanks and sat between us to eat his own special lunch.

"Now, start at the beginning," Frór told me as he spooned tea into the basket of a teapot.

And so I told him the entire story, from the moment I had left the hamlet down the path just outside his door to the moment I had appeared on his doorstep.

I told him about the feeling of being watched I had in the woods between where we were and my own little cottage, and about the Wild Hunt and the lost Freyas. I only briefly mentioned the ur-dwarves and the moss-wives, but his eyes darted over to the bronze wand I had set on the table beside my placemat when I reached that part of the story.

"And, like I said before, I thought Mjolner was going to help me find whoever cast that spell last night, but instead, he brought me here," I said, and took a big bite of my bread topped with roast beef and potato.

"Three nights in a row," Frór said, stroking his beard as he sat back in his chair. "I've never heard the like. Not in this part of the world, anyway."

"But didn't you hear it?" I asked. "I know they were riding through the woods south of here, but the galloping horses and howling dogs were so loud."

"No, I heard nothing, or I would've investigated," Frór said.

"Would you have gotten word if anyone in Villmark had noticed it?" I asked.

"Yes, definitely," he said. "No worries there. The people of Villmark are safe, save for those who are hunting with you."

I knew what I wanted to ask him next, but the thought of saying the words made my mouth suddenly dry. I took a sip of my tea, then gathered up my courage. "Do you think I'm right? That something is summoning the Wild Hunt?"

"Well, that's a tricky one," he said. "The Wild Hunt is a thing of Odin, and no mere mortal commands Odin."

"No, I don't suppose so," I said, disappointed.

"But that doesn't mean he can't be tricked," Frór went on. "Or lured somehow."

"Really?" I asked eagerly.

"It would be no simple thing," he said. "Your grandmother is the most powerful wielder of magic I've ever known, and I doubt she could do it. So that leaves us with the real conundrum. Who could do such a thing? And how are they hiding?"

"Anyone with such power could also hide it from those of lesser power, couldn't they?" I said, remembering how even I, as weak in magic as I was, already knew how to hide traces of myself from the senses of others.

"True enough," he conceded. I watched him think, sip at his beer, then think some more. I spread butter and raspberry jam on another slice of bread and ate that while I waited.

"It seems to me when you first started following Mjolner, he was doing as you thought," he said at last. "He was trying to follow the spell. But at some point he lost the trail, or he just got distracted."

"He never seemed to have lost it," I said. "It was all I could do to keep up with him until he stopped."

"Where did he stop?"

"On a rock just south of here," I said. "I could just barely see these cabins from there."

"Well, there you go," Frór said and drained the last of his beer, wiping the foam from his beard with the back of his sleeve.

"What?" I asked.

"Mjolner brought you to this hamlet," he said. "He lost the trail here, but there is nowhere else it could have gone but here. No creature lives anywhere near these parts, I promise you."

"You think one of the residents here is the one who cast the spell?" I asked.

"That seems to be the case," Frór said.

I had a sudden sinking feeling in my stomach. "Before he came to your door, Mjolner seemed to have narrowed it down to three possibilities. You, Signi, and whoever lives on the other side of you."

"Hmm. Well, I hope we can agree it's not me," he said, and I nodded. "Nor Signi. That doesn't seem remotely likely."

"No," I said. "But what about her houseguest? Have you met that man?"

"Man?" Frór said. "I suppose you might call him such. I reckon he's about your age. He's a tiny thing, looks more like boy, to be sure."

"That doesn't mean he can't be dangerous. Especially not if we're talking about magic," I said.

"No, sure enough," he said. "But I don't think so. He's very closely watched. I don't know when he'd have the opportunity. I will talk to Signi about it, surely, but I think it very unlikely."

I had another, darker thought, but I was loath to speak it.

"What is it?" he asked me.

I took a deep breath and plowed ahead. "Has Bera been here? Visiting Signi next door? You would've seen her, wouldn't you?" I waited for him to tell me I was being paranoid.

But he didn't. He just looked a little confused, like he was having a hard time placing the name. "Bera?" he said with a frown.

"Short woman, a little younger than me, mousy looking?" I said.

"I know who she is," he said. "I'm just not sure why you're asking about her. Do you think she's in danger?"

"No, I think she..." but I broke off without finishing that sentence. Because it made no sense. I knew Bera had no real magical skill. She had only ever pretended, although she had pretended so hard she had believed it herself. She couldn't have done this.

But then Frór was sure that no one he knew from Villmark could do it. Only I wasn't entirely sure that was true.

"What are you thinking?" he asked me.

"Bera spends most of her time in a cell in the caves behind the waterfall, right?" I said. "But there is another woman in those cells, one who maybe could do this. And I would totally believe she would try if she could."

"Halldis," Frór guessed, but he shook his head. "No, even she is not up to something like this."

"But, like you said, no one is," I said.

His frown deepened. "Tell me," he said.

"Halldis had an artifact, something that let her do magic far beyond her own capabilities. My grandmother took it from her, but what if she found another?"

"There is no way she could get access to anything now," Frór said. "Those cells are impenetrable. She's allowed no visitors save Signi. And she never goes out."

"Still," I said. "I worry she might be using Bera. Especially if Bera, unlike Halldis, gets to leave the cells from time to time."

"Never alone," he said, but I could see from the line down the center of his forehead that my words were worrying him.

"That just leaves whoever lives on the other side of you," I said.

"That would be Geiri," he said and pulled a face.

"He doesn't like you," I said.

Frór laughed. "Is that so?"

"That's what he said when I was here last," I said.

"Well, he's not the first. And I suppose it doesn't hurt to admit that feeling is mutual," he said.

"Why don't you like him?" I asked.

Frór shrugged. "He doesn't hide his feelings as well as he thinks he does. I don't care for people who say one thing to my face and another behind my back. I like it even less when they don't do it well."

"So he's duplicitous?" I asked. "A liar? Maybe has secrets?"

"Well, that doesn't mean I think he's a murderer," Frór said. "That's a big leap."

"No one here seems like a murderer," I said glumly.

"True enough," he said, draining the last of his beer. "And yet, someone is. And it's up to us to find them. So, what now?"

"I want to go back to that rock where Mjolner stopped," I said, getting to my feet. "I want to try looking around again from there."

"I'll go with you," he said.

Mjolner looked up from his thoroughly licked clean plate and meowed that he too was coming.

We went back outside, and I quickly realized it was much later in the afternoon than I had realized. It had been a quick lunch, but apparently a late one. How much time had passed while I was inside?

Or rather, how long had I spent sprawled out on the floor after dispelling my grandmother's memory blocking spell?

"Where to?" Frór asked.

"This way," I said, and half-jogged back the way I had come. Mjolner raced ahead and perched himself once more on the same rock.

"I guess this is it?" Frór said as Mjolner proceeded to wash the herring juice off his paws.

"Yes," I said, taking out my wand. I half-closed my eyes and then waved it around before me, the same as before. I walked all around the rock, then again in a wider circle, and then a third time in a still wider circle.

But there was nothing there. I stopped walking and put my wand away. I could feel how slumped my shoulders were, like a discouraged child. I forced myself to straighten up.

"Nothing," I said.

"It's not nothing," Frór assured me. "Look, like I said, there's nothing out here but that hamlet. And only so many cabins within it. Someone there knows something, I'm sure of it."

"So we should go door to door," I said, but I couldn't help glancing up at the sky again.

"You're worried about the time," he guessed.

"I promised to be back before sunset," I said. Then added, "But I'd like to come back with help. Haraldr, my grandmother, maybe Loke if he's around."

"Oh, that one is always around. It's just a matter of finding him," Frór said. He sounded ever so slightly annoyed, and I remembered that Loke had been very eager to be there when Frór and I met. He had missed out.

But I couldn't for the life of me guess what sort of fireworks he had been hoping for. None of my childhood memories involved him. I don't think the two of us had ever met until the day I had driven up to Runde a few months before.

"I don't know how I'm going to get to Villmark and then back to the lodge in time," I said.

"Just head back to the lodge," he told me. "I'll send your mormor after you, and Haraldr if you think you need him."

"He's been training me," I said.

Frór snorted his opinion of that, but then turned away as if he hadn't wanted me to hear that. He wiped at his face, then turned back to me. "I'll send them on first. And then I'll ask around here. As soon as I know anything, I'll be straight out to see you."

"Not after dark," I said.

But he waved off my concern. "Odin doesn't want the likes of me for his Wild Hunt, believe me."

"Why?" I asked.

"Never mind," he said. "You just get going. Tell your friends that help is on the way. We'll get to the bottom of this, don't you worry."

"Okay," I agreed. I was reluctant to go. Not because I didn't think he'd do everything he said he'd do. And not because I'd rather ask around myself, although that was part of it.

No, mostly I was just really done with running.

"Here," Frór said, and pressed something into my mittened hand. I looked down at it. It was a jagged piece of chocolate that looked like it had been snapped off a bar as thick as a gold brick. "Let it melt on your tongue. It will give you energy to keep moving."

"Thanks," I said. I put it in my mouth. It melted richly over my tongue, and my tired brain sparked back to life like he'd just given me the world's strongest espresso. Which was nothing compared to how invigorated my body was feeling. "That's more than chocolate," I said, careful not to spray any of it out of my mouth as I talked.

"Well, of course," he said.

I turned to run but then looked back. Mjolner was still there on the rock. He was no longer washing himself. Instead, he was rubbing his body against Frór's arm as he stood close beside the cat.

"You're not coming?" I said to Mjolner.

He said nothing. He just pawed at Frór's sleeve as if eager to go. Only in the other direction.

"He knows his business," Frór reminded me as he scooped up my cat. "I'll keep him safe for you."

"I know," I said. I didn't want to say out loud my real worry. But without Mjolner there, who was going to keep *me* safe?

"I'll be along behind you," Frór said, as if reading my mind. "I'll take my sleigh. I'll probably reach the lodge faster than you."

"So why don't I wait and ride with you?" I asked.

"Well, maybe not so fast as all that," he said. "Go. You need to be there before sunset. That's absolutely crucial."

"Why?" I asked. I knew the lodge was safe. The others would go inside and close the doors, and they'd be all right. Especially if Frór found who was doing this before they could do it again. But even if he didn't, I'd see that spell move past me on its way to the lodge. I was sure I could stop it. I could send it back with my wand, just as I had before.

But Frór was shaking his head gravely. "The very last thing anyone should be doing is worrying a Thor. Let alone three of them. If they come out to find you, and they will, the Wild Hunt will find them."

"Odin will take them," I guessed.

"Odin will take them," Frór agreed. "Run."

"But can't you-" I started to say, but this time he interrupted me with a roar.

"Run!"

The booming of his voice shook the trees all around us, and as I ran back the way I had come, it was with great clumps of snow raining down on me from above.

CHAPTER TWENTY-FIVE

WHEN I FIRST STARTING RUNNING AWAY FROM the hamlet, I was hyper-aware of everything I was sensing going on behind me. I didn't want to be caught off guard again if something started following me through the woods.

But once the sound of Frór's footsteps as he carried Mjolner back to the cabins faded away, I could hear nothing but my own breathing. The forest was quiet, but not unusually so.

And I felt nothing behind me, magical or otherwise. Nothing was setting off my danger sense.

But I definitely didn't have the energy for another long run. It was only a matter of minutes as what would only laughingly be called a sprint became more of a light jog. And then that jog was downgraded to a brisk walk.

Or I intended it to be brisk. But my muscles were aching, my lungs were on fire, and my feet were rubbing more and more raw with each step.

I don't know how long I was merely focused on how miserable I was. Far longer than I ought to have been. But eventually I realized that something was wrong.

I was in the right part of the forest; I hadn't gotten lost. I could see the trail of footprints in the snow I had left that morning, following Mjolner to the hamlet.

And yet, I was pretty sure the twisted pine tree I could see off to my left was too familiar. Like I had passed it more than once while enjoying my little mental pity party.

I stopped to look at it. Maybe I was just remembering it from that morning? I looked around, but the only tracks in the snow were mine following Mjolner's, and mine now going back to the lodge. If I were somehow going in circles, I saw no proof of it.

And yet, I had the nagging feeling I had seen that same tree at least three times. Maybe four.

I pressed on, paying closer attention to where I was going and ignoring all of my body's little complaints. I even tried to put on a little more speed, but that effort was short-lived. Still, I kept my head up and my senses alert and I trudged on, back towards the lodge.

I was just starting to laugh at myself for being silly - I was following my own footprints on a straight path from point A to point B, even I couldn't mess that up - when that same twisted pine rose up on my left again.

This time when I stopped, I pulled a loose strand of yarn out of the end of my scarf and tied it to one of the branches. Then I found the energy again to jog for a few minutes.

Until I reached that same pine again. There was absolutely no mistake. That was the yarn from my scarf on its branch.

And yet, the only prints in the snow were the ones from that morning and the ones I was making now.

What kind of magic was this?

I took out my wand and half-closed my eyes as I waved it around. Nothing was revealed to me, but I knew there must be some sort of spell at work.

The only other option was that I was going crazy.

I sat down on the snow, regretting that I had left my art bag back at the lodge. I had nothing to work with but the wand and the world around me.

I turned the wand around in my hand, holding it not like a magician would but like I normally held my pencil when sketching out the first lines on a drawing. I closed my eyes and settled my breathing, no easy trick after all the hard exercise.

But when I was finally in a calm, creative place, I started sketching on the snow in front of me. I didn't open my eyes to see what I was doing, I just let instinct guide my hand.

And it did. Furiously.

When at last I was done, I opened my eyes and saw an absolute jumble of lines all over the icy crust of the top layer of snow. It wasn't easy to pick out any particular shape in that abstract chaos.

I turned the wand back around in my hand and waved it between my eyes and the snow.

Now things came to life. I could see where I had drawn the lodge, up and to the left. It glowed like a bright young sun. Then I found the stick figure that was me, right at the center of the drawing. Off to the right was the hamlet. I couldn't make out the cabins, but there was a little drawing of a cat that shone even brighter than the lodge. That had to be Mjolner.

I looked up and blinked at the world around me. It still looked just like an ordinary forest. But something was leading me astray.

I touched the tip of my wand to the drawing of the lodge, then aimed the wand in the direction I was sure the lodge should be.

Suddenly something was glowing through the trees. It was bright but small, far away, with many overlapping layers of branches between me and it. But I knew it was the lodge. With this light to guide me, I wouldn't get turned around again.

I put my wand away, got to my feet, and started running yet again. The sun was behind a dense layer of clouds now, but I knew it would be sunset soon. I could make it in time, but only if I didn't get slowed down yet again.

I settled into a rhythm with the pounding of my feet and my breath. It was almost hypnotic, not a good combination with my tired body, but I kept my eyes fixed on that light and never looked away.

Not even when I started to feel that thing again, the invisible thing in the woods, slowly creeping up behind me.

When I couldn't stand it any longer, I looked away from the light from the lodge and back over my shoulder. There was nothing there. I squinted my eyes, but my magical vision wasn't seeing anything either. But I felt it. I knew something was coming up behind me.

But when I looked back towards the lodge, I realized to my horror that the light had shifted. I was running too far to the east, and somehow the point of light had moved further away from me.

I don't know how long I kept running like that, never daring to look back again or even to blink, always feeling the little tickles of being watched on the back of my neck. It seemed to go on for hours.

Worse, with my focus never moving away from that light, I wasn't sure if the rest of the forest was getting darker, or if I was just seeing it that way because the brightness of the lodge's magic was dazzling my eyes.

And I had lost all sense of where the sun was in the sky, behind those banks of dark gray clouds to the west.

But suddenly the thing behind me seemed to reach out for me. It was like I could feel tendrils of a malevolent spell brushing over my cheeks, like someone behind me with cold, cold hands about to put them over my eyes and say "guess who?"

The feeling was so revolting, and I was so beyond tired, that when my toe caught on a tree root rather than stumbling then catching myself, I went sprawling down face-first into the snow.

I tasted coppery blood in my mouth, but I didn't have time to worry about that. I pushed myself to my hands and knees, then spun around to face the world behind me. I pulled my wand from my sleeve and held it out before me.

But there was nothing there. I saw nothing and heard nothing, and that malevolent feeling was just gone.

I stayed like that for a moment, staring around and listening intently, then put my wand away and got to my feet. I brushed the snow from my leggings, but the sound of my mittens on the wool of my leggings seemed to roar loudly in my ears.

The forest around me was far too quiet. And it was dark. Even now that I was no longer staring fixedly into a bright light, it was all black and murky grays.

I was too late. I was out long past sunset, and still had so far to go.

I made a little ball of light and tried to get a better sense of where I was. I could tell I was nowhere near the lodge itself. But was I close to the grove of the moss-wives? I might get at least the protection of a tree there.

But when I looked around, I had no idea where I was. All I could tell was that the only footprints in the snow now were the ones that ended with that tree root. I had stopped following my own trail when I had fixated on the light from the lodge, and now I had lost it entirely.

I looked towards that light again, and my heart sank. Yet again, when I had stopped looking at it, it had shifted position and retreated so much further away. I had to fight the nearly overwhelming urge to sit down in the snow and just cry. So much running on top of sleepless nights was just too much for me to expect myself to master all my emotions as well.

But in the end, I won the fight against that childish impulse. There was only one thing left to do, and that was get back to running towards that light.

Frór was coming with help. Perhaps he was there already. Perhaps he had beaten me to the lodge just like he had said he would. Haraldr, mormor, Frór and Mjolner were all there now. Everyone was waiting for me.

I had to get moving.

And yet my legs were like lead. I couldn't summon the energy to move them.

Or at least that seemed true. Then the first dog howled off in the distance.

I was running for all I was worth before the second dog answered. Then I was running even harder, because that hound was right at my heels.

And there was nowhere for me to hide.

CHAPTER TWENTY-SIX

I COULD FEEL that dog's hot breath on the backs of my legs. I could feel its drool spattering against my heels. I expected with every painful breath to feel those paws land on my back and push me down into the snow.

But it didn't leap. It just kept running behind me. Pacing me. Playing with me.

I had my wand out in my hand, but I had no idea what good I could do with that. I couldn't shoot spells back over my shoulder. But if I turned to look behind me, I was lost.

I didn't want to admit to myself that I was probably lost already. There had to be some way out of this mess.

The thunder of horse hooves was all around me now. I kept my head down, looking only at the ground immediately in front of my feet. But I knew the Wild Hunt was all around me now. I could hear the men and the woman calling to each other in some strange language I didn't know. Their voices were ethereal, like they were forcing terrible sounds past frozen vocal cords.

I felt a spear bounce off my shoulder, like one of them was taunting me with a light tap.

Then those horses and the hounds as well put on a sudden burst of speed, racing past me into the forest ahead. I still didn't dare raise my head.

But I did turn and start running back the other way.

Not that it mattered. I could hear them circling around. They were turning to run me down again.

And there was still no place to hide.

But I could run no further. My legs wouldn't do it. My lungs were on fire. I threw myself down on the ground in a little hollow between two trees. The snow was deeper there, in that hollow. I had a half-formed plan that involved burrowing down under that snow.

But before I could dig into that snowbank, something caught on the back of my parka. This was no overhanging branch from a nearby tree; it lifted me up and off of my feet.

The Wild Hunt had caught up with me. They had reached out to take me.

But I still hadn't seen anything yet. I held onto that shred of hope and kept my eyes tightly shut as I pummeled whatever was behind me for all I was worth.

"Ow, Ingrid!"

And I realized it was Thorbjorn holding me up out of the snow.

"You weren't supposed to come after me!" I yelled, trying to twist around to see him. "Would you put me down?"

"Yes, if you stop hitting me," he grumbled.

"They're coming back," I said, still not willing to open up my eyes.

"I know. I have a place," he said. Then I was back on my feet, but his hand had my wrist in an iron grip as he dragged me after him. I was worn out from running, but he was still fresh, and it was a struggle to keep up with him and not face-plant into the snow and be dragged behind him.

Then he was pulling me through a thicket of branches that poked and scraped and caught at my hood and my scarf and my parka. Now I was keeping my eyes closed to avoid losing one to a sharper branch.

Then suddenly we were still. I could still hear the Wild Hunt, but the sound of the hooves was muffled.

I opened my eyes to see where we were. I couldn't see more than a glimpse. Thorbjorn had me tucked close against his side with his arms around me like a shield and my face pressed tight to his chest. But I could see we were in a sort of tent formed out of the space under the branches of a tall thicket. The branches were all covered with a thick layer of snow, so our tent was more like a soft-sided igloo.

"Thorbjorn," I started to say, but he shushed me and squeezed me tighter. I still hadn't caught my breath from the running, but I tried to quiet it as much as I could.

The Wild Hunt was galloping all around us, some riders closer and some further away, but one of the hounds was just outside of our sparse shelter. I could hear it snuffling over the snow. It bumped into the thicket and sent a shower of snowflakes down over us.

But it didn't come inside.

Finally, it gave one last discouraged wuff of breath, and then it was gone.

"They're moving on," Thorbjorn whispered, and his arms around me loosened.

"They'll be back," I said.

"We'll have to run again," he said. "But let's wait and listen. Perhaps they will ride further away, give us a better opportunity to get away. At the very least, you need a minute to recover. Here," he added, pressing something into my mittened hand.

I sat up and looked at it, but it was impossible to make out any details in the darkness of our igloo.

"It'll give you some energy. Go ahead and eat it," he said, then put something into his own mouth.

I put it on my tongue and recognized the rich flavor right away. It was exactly the same as the piece of more-than-chocolate that Frór had given me before. I held it in my mouth for as long as I could before swallowing it down.

"I've had this before," I said.

"Have you?" he asked, surprised.

"Yes. Frór gave it to me," I said. Even in the gray darkness I could see his face register delighted surprise that quickly tempered to a more cautious look.

"You met Frór? Just today?"

"Once before, actually, but not properly until today. Mjolner brought me to him," I said.

"But neither of them are with you now?" he asked.

"No, they had other things to do first. Didn't they reach the lodge at all?"

"No more than you did," he said. But he couldn't quite work up an appropriately accusatory tone. "Ingrid, when you met Frór..." But he trailed off, unable to find the words.

"I remembered everything," I said to him. "I remember all of our adventures. I remember sneaking off to follow Frór when he went to the north. I remember the fight with the trolls he had while the two of us were hiding in that little cave. And I remember my grandmother finding us there and how angry she was with Frór for putting us in danger."

"We put ourselves in danger," Thorbjorn said.

"I know," I said. "It seemed like such a good idea at the time."

I wondered how things might have been different, if we had pursued some other, safer sort of adventure that summer. Would I have been allowed to keep visiting Villmark? Would all of my summers have been spent there, having more adventures with Thorbjorn?

Could I have grown up knowing exactly who I was, and what I was called to do?

But then there was another side too. If we hadn't followed Frór into the north, if my grandmother had never wiped all of Villmark from my memory, would I have ever bothered with art at all?

No, I was sure, I would've been a completely different person.

"Ingrid, I'm so happy you finally remember everything. I wish we could reminisce for hours, but-"

"Yeah, this isn't the time," I said. "Your brothers?"

"They are also out in the forest, searching for you," he said.

"I was afraid of that. And no one came to the lodge before sundown? My grandmother, Frór, nobody?"

"Not even Loke," he said.

"Something was keeping me away from the lodge," I said. "I could see it in the distance, but I couldn't get any closer to it. Not even with magic."

"I don't like the sound of that," he said. "Especially not if the same thing succeeded in keeping your grandmother away."

"Maybe there's an upside," I said. "Maybe the Wild Hunt will get lost too."

"How is that an upside?"

"If anyone back at the lodge had gone outside, I'm sure they would've zeroed in on them. If they are wandering still, no one has gone out."

"Maybe," he said. "But it's not very late yet. When the others went outside, it was more than an hour later than it is now."

"If this lost-in-the-forest spell holds, they'll never get close enough to the lodge for that to matter," I said.

"Do you think there's yet another person of incredible magical power casting this new spell?" he asked. "Because if it's the same person who's been luring people out of the lodge and locking the doors behind them, I don't see them also keeping the Wild Hunt running in circles."

"No, you're right," I agreed. "Maybe this has been happening every night. The Wild Hunt circles around without finding anything until the person coming out of the lodge draws them that way like a beacon."

"But what can we do?" Thorbjorn asked. "You said you couldn't get to the lodge before, even with magic. Is that still true?"

"I'm afraid so," I said, wrapping my arms around my legs and resting my head on my knees. I wanted nothing more than to curl up under the thicket and sleep until dawn. Or, better yet, noon.

But then a thought struck me, and I looked up to grin at Thorbjorn. "It doesn't matter. We don't have to get to the lodge to keep everyone there safe."

"What do you mean?" he asked.

"It's what you said, the people who go outside lure the Wild Hunt to them like a beacon," I said.

"You want to lure them yourself?" he asked. "But they didn't take you just now."

"No, but that's because I was trying to hide from them. I wasn't looking at them," I said.

"I am not letting you go out there and challenge the Wild Hunt face to face," he said.

"No, I don't need to see them," I said, although a part of my heart longed to do just that. I had drawn them well enough from the memory the places they had been retained of them, but imagine what I could do after I'd seen them with my own eyes? Had soaked up every detail I could discern by moonlight?

I was just picturing the final drawing, trying to imagine just what those details would be. I wanted a better look at their faces, just to start.

But Thorbjorn interrupted my thought processes. "What's your plan?" he demanded.

"Simple," I said. "I'll be the brighter beacon. I'll make sure they follow me."

"You want to lure them away from the lodge?" he asked, intrigued.

"Not just away from the lodge," I said. "Towards that hamlet hidden in the forest."

"What hamlet?" he asked.

"The one where Frór lives," I said. "And also where our murderer is hiding, somewhere."

"You can do that?" he asked.

"I'm sure I can," I said.

"How?"

"Everything I'm doing to contain my magical glow from the awareness of others? I'm going to stop doing that. More, I'm going to reverse the process. I'm sure I can do it. Then I'll glow like nothing they've ever seen."

Thorbjorn didn't look like he liked my idea much. But he didn't object. "Do you want to wait for them to get closer?" he asked.

"No, better now," I said. "I want them far from the lodge before the usual hour."

"Then let's go," he said.

We crawled out from under the thicket. The snow all around us had been churned up by horses' hooves and the paw prints of large dogs, but there was no sign of the bird-wing markings. At least, not yet.

Then I dropped all my mental shields. I could see myself glowing, even brighter than the beacon I had created to lead me to the lodge. I was confident I could be seen through the trees for miles by those with the eyes to see magic.

Then we started running. I led the way back towards the hamlet. I couldn't see my own trail through the snow since the Wild Hunt had obliterated all signs of any passage but their own. But I knew we were headed the right way.

Whatever spell had had me running in circles only prevented me from getting to the lodge. The way to the hamlet was unimpeded.

Which was good, since we'd only been running for a minute or two before we could hear the sounds of the Wild Hunt drawing nearer behind us.

I looked over at Thorbjorn and we shared a crazy grin at the success of our plan, but neither of us had enough air to speak on top of the running.

The way back was much shorter than I remembered, or I had never made it even as close to the lodge as I thought I had. Whichever was the case, I realized we were nearly to the rock where Mjolner and I had said farewell.

But the Wild Hunt was all but on top of us. I could feel the hot breath of that hound close behind me and didn't even dare look over at Thorbjorn beside me, lest I accidentally see something close on his heels as well.

Then the thing I had been fearing most happened. The breath of that hound stopped puffing against my heels, but only because it was pulling its weight back to leap.

Its mighty paws landed on the backs of my shoulders, and I was going down. My body hit the snow hard enough to knock the wind out of me.

The hound backed away, surely trained to do so. It's not for the hounds to make the kill, after all. That's for the hunters.

I tried to get up, but I had nothing left in me. I couldn't even draw in a proper breath.

"Ingrid," Thorbjorn said. I realized he too had been knocked to the ground. He sounded as weary and sore as I felt, but the hand that closed over mine was strong.

We would have to get up and keep running. I could hear the hooves pounding all around us. There was a huntsman towering over us, but I didn't dare look up.

Then the sky was filled with blinding light, far brighter than my own most powerful fireball spell. The horse screamed, then bolted away.

And my grandmother was saying, "are you two going to get up or are you planning on lying there all night?"

CHAPTER TWENTY-SEVEN

ᚾ

EVEN THOUGH I knew my grandmother was there and I knew she had driven the Wild Hunt away, I couldn't bring myself to open my eyes.

I didn't let go of Thorbjorn's hand either.

"Bring them inside," I heard Frór saying. Hands lifted me to my feet, but Thorbjorn tucked me close to his side protectively. I kept my eyes closed and let him guide me until we were safely indoors.

"I should have been told far, far sooner," my grandmother was grousing from somewhere behind me.

"I told you the minute I knew myself," Frór told her.

"Not the very minute," she snapped back.

"Please, no fighting amongst ourselves," I said, still with my eyes closed.

The two of them fell quiet. Thorbjorn guided me up a short flight of stairs and then through a doorway. Only when I heard that door close behind us did I dare to open my eyes.

I looked up at Thorbjorn. His eyes were tightly closed, but as if he felt me gazing up at him he blinked them open then looked me over as if checking me for injuries.

Past him, I saw my grandmother and Frór also in the entryway with us, shaking snow from their clothes and deliberately not looking at each other.

There was a step up from where we were standing to the hall that ran between the living room and the kitchen. Haraldr and Loke were both standing there, watching us. Haraldr's face was lit up with relief at the sight of us. He had one hand clutching at the front of his sweater as if his heart had ached, waiting for us all to return.

But Loke, as usual, was just grinning at me. Then I realized I was still pressed up against Thorbjorn's side. That was the source of his amusement. But for the life of me, I couldn't make myself to step away from Thorbjorn. I needed the support.

"I missed the meeting," he said with an exaggerated pout.

"Don't take this the wrong way, but I'm glad you weren't there," I said. "It was a private thing."

"What are we talking about?" Thorbjorn asked. But before I could answer, my grandmother seized my arm in an iron grip and dragged my attention to herself.

"You look terrible," she said with a frown, but then she pulled me into a tight hug. Frór and Thorbjorn behind me both cleared their throats uncomfortably, then brushed past us to get to the hall. I suspected Haraldr and Loke had already fled.

Did they think we were about to explode with sentimental emotions or something?

Well, I was sniffling back some tears, but it had been a very exhausting day. Or rather, a chain of exhausting days.

For her part, my grandmother was hugging me so tight it was nearly impossible to breathe.

"I should've told you sooner what was going on," I said, my voice muffled against her shoulder. "Don't blame Frór."

"Don't blame Frór?" she repeated and pushed me back at arm's length to look into my eyes. "So you remember."

"Finally," I said. "I have loads to say to you about that, but this isn't the time."

"No," she agreed. "Come. Let's join the others in the kitchen."

It was a true sign of how dire things were that everyone was tromping through Frór's house with their boots on. As much as we'd all stamped the snow off our feet at the door, there were still grimy puddles of melting snow all over his floorboards.

My grandmother all but pushed me down into one of the chairs at the table, and Frór set a steaming mug of tea in front of me. Loke was buttering slices of black bread and setting them one by one on a plate in front of me. The tea was too hot to dare a sip from yet, but I greedily lunged for that bread.

"How long will your spell last?" I asked my grandmother.

"Without my concentration, it's gone already. But we're quite safe here," she told me.

"I'm worried about the others back at the lodge," I said. "Why didn't you go there like you were supposed to?"

"We tried," Frór said. "None of my forest craft or your mormor's magic was enough to overcome whatever enchantment is at work in those woods. We kept finding ourselves back in Villmark, over and over again."

"Not even I could get there," Loke said, handing me another slice of buttered bread.

"You never got near the lodge?" I asked.

"Nowhere near it," my grandmother said, settling herself into the chair next to me. She looked nearly as worn out as I felt. She must have been pushing herself very hard. "Do you know how close you got?"

"I did a spell to guide me there. I could see it in the distance, but the minute I lost eye contact with it, it would suddenly get so much further away," I said.

"Then you got closer than we did," Frór said.

"You have a new wand?" my grandmother asked.

"Yes," I said, taking it out and setting on the table. She looked at it without touching it.

"Lovely workmanship," she said. "I can feel the power coming out of it already. And you've only had it a day?"

"I guess," I said, the hours running together in my mind. "But I've been using it a lot since I got it."

"Yes, I can see that," she said. Haraldr moved to stand over her shoulder and lean in to look at it himself.

"Very fine," he said with a nod. "Very fine indeed."

"It's not been helpful yet in finding who's behind all this," I said with a sigh. "Just that it's coming from this hamlet. I'm guessing you didn't find anything when you went door to door?" I asked Frór.

He shook his head. "No one was acting suspiciously, and I saw nothing that would indicate anyone had access to magic."

"Signi's house guest?" I asked.

"That's a long story," Frór said with a sigh. "It's too long to go into, but trust me, that boy is not our problem."

"I found him in the woods a few days ago," my grandmother said after giving Frór a hard look. Like asking anyone to trust him was a huge deal. "He's been missing from Villmark for eleven years, more than half of his young life. He seems to have been moving between our world and the larger one around us, I think at random. It's been very traumatic, which is why Signi is keeping him apart from other people. But Frór is right, that boy is not the cause of this problem."

"Are you sure?" I asked. "I feel like whatever is doing this is very powerful magic, nothing like anything I've seen in Villmark. If he's been wandering deeper into the other worlds from here, who knows what he found?"

"*I* know," my grandmother assured me, squeezing my hand.

"All right. But we still have to do something," I said. "Everyone back at the lodge is in real danger. It might be happening even now." I looked around the kitchen until I found Thorbjorn standing in the shadows on the far side of the fire.

"It's about that time," he said. "And as fast as that Wild Hunt can move, they could easily be there by now."

"Your brothers," I said, remembering that they too had gone outside to look for me.

"They'll be fine," he assured me.

"But Frór said-" I started to say.

"Oh, you listen to him too much," my grandmother said testily.

"They will be targets," Frór said firmly. "But they have been taught by the best. They will be on their guard."

"They'll be fine," Thorbjorn said again. But I wasn't sure he was as confident as he was trying to sound. In fact, I had the impression that, not being able to go out and help them, he was trying to convince himself that they didn't need him.

"Let me think," my grandmother said, pressing a hand over her eyes. "If the spells are coming from here, there must be a way to detect them."

"You didn't manage it before," Frór said. "It certainly looked like you tried everything."

"I'm far from having tried everything," she snapped, still sounding irritated. Frór just really rubbed her the wrong way, I guessed.

But his warm voice was kind despite her tone. "Nora, I can see you've depleted yourself. You may have things left to try, but you don't have the energy to fuel them. And I won't watch you burn yourself out."

"I'm fine," she said firmly, but the hand over her eyes was trembling.

"Mormor," I said. "Did you try just getting to the lodge, or have you searched for magic here in the hamlet?"

"Both," she said, lowering her hand to look at me. "The spell to drive off the Wild Hunt is what did me in. I'm not so frail as some may think."

"I would never use the word 'frail' to describe you," Frór said.

"No, but I know what words you would use," my grandmother shot back.

"This isn't helping," Haraldr said to both of them.

"Come on," Loke whispered close to my ear and tugged at my sleeve.

The others didn't notice us slipping away. Thorbjorn had disappeared further into the shadows beyond the fireplace, either still brooding about his brothers or else engrossed in the argument between my grandmother and Frór that was just getting heated up.

Haraldr was between those two trying to moderate their discussion, but I could see that he was doomed to fail.

But I didn't listen to whatever the argument was about. I just followed Loke into the quiet of the living room.

"You knew about all this," I said to him as we settled into the chairs by the fire.

"You mean how those two are always instantly at each other's throats? Yes," he said.

"Did you know seeing him would trigger my memories?" I asked.

"No. Honestly, I always expected that Thorbjorn would be the one that would set that off. Color me surprised," he said with a shrug.

"You honestly tried to get to the lodge? You're sure you can't?" I asked.

"Yes and yes," he said. "But I don't think you need to worry too much about that. Whatever is happening, it's happening here, in this hamlet. This is the best place for us to be."

"It would be if we were actually *doing* anything," I said glumly. We lapsed into silence for a minute, but then I asked, "Have you met the boy next door?"

"He's nearly our age, so I'm not sure those of us who aren't older than time would want to call him a boy," Loke said. "But no. Not yet. Signi is very protective of him."

We were quiet again for another length of time, and I realized that I was in the process of falling asleep there in that chair. But maybe a little nap would be just what I needed?

I let myself drift, but instantly my not-quite-sleeping mind conjured up an image of that horse and rider that had been standing over me before my grandmother's spell had driven them away. I could see the wildness in the horse's red eyes, the hair of its face covered in ice from its own freezing breath. The man leaning down from the saddle had splotchy black skin, layer after layer of frostbite having necrotized his flesh.

I jerked awake, my heart still pounding. I had never seen them. My eyes had been closed the whole time. And yet, I knew that vision was real.

"Are you okay?" Loke asked me.

"Geiri, next door," I said. "Do you know him?"

"I was with Frór when he called on him," Loke said. "He's not fond of Frór and made no attempt to hide his contempt. But he seemed awfully milk toast to me. You think he's the guy?"

"I want to talk to him," I said, but my eyes were drifting closed again.

"Listen, they've stopped arguing in the other room," he said. "I'm going to see what they've decided. Why don't you just rest here for a minute, and I'll tell the others we have to talk to Geiri again. I really don't think he's capable of summoning the Wild Hunt to do his murderous bidding, but if there's nothing better to do, we should start with him. In the meantime, get at least a cat nap, will you?"

"No," I said. But I waved him towards the kitchen. "Go, do what you said. I'm just going to meditate a bit. I'm not going to sleep. Because when I do, I don't intend to wake for days and days."

"A proper Odin sleep," Loke said. "Another tea while I'm in there?"

"Sure," I said. I wasn't sure I even wanted it, but it seemed the fastest way to get Loke out of the room.

The minute he was back in the kitchen, I sat down on the rug before the fire. I closed my eyes and quieted my breathing and slowed my heartbeat.

Then I felt a warm glow all over the front of me. But it wasn't from the fire. No fire could warm my very soul the way this glow was doing.

I opened my eyes and saw Mjolner sitting pertly in front of me, tail wrapped around his paws, just waiting for me to notice him.

The moment I did, he winked at me. Then he got up and went out through the entryway.

Without another thought, I followed.

CHAPTER TWENTY-EIGHT

MJOLNER MUST HAVE DONE his walking through walls trick to get outside. I had to take the more conventional route, quietly opening and closing the door behind me. Then I stayed there on the porch for a moment, looking around for signs of trouble.

My grandmother's spell had indeed disappeared, and the center of the hamlet was still and dark. With so many trees close around the cluster of cabins, the moon was creating more shadows than light.

But even in the darkness I could see that Mjolner was hunting again, his tail snaking back and forth as he stalked with his face low to the ground. I watched as he made a large circuit of the center of the hamlet, but when he started zeroing in his attention on a smaller area, it was the same three cabins as before.

One was Frór's, and I already knew he was not our killer.

The other was Signi's, with her mysterious, never seen house guest.

And the last was Geiri's. Geiri, who had seemed benign when I had drawn him and who Loke didn't consider a threat.

But he was the only suspect left. I couldn't just cross him off my list without being very, very sure.

I took out my wand and waved it around while I unfocused my

eyes. The fragments of the snaky spell were still lying all around like mystical confetti, the same as before.

But this time I walked outside the circle of cabins. Waving my wand around in front of me, I walked a slow circuit around the outside of the hamlet.

I sensed Mjolner stalking along at my side, but I didn't look down at him. I was afraid I'd miss something if I glanced away, even for a second.

And I nearly did anyway. Not only was it subtle, it was far over my head.

But as I stood under one of the tall trees, there was no mistaking the twists of magic that were caught in its branches. It looked like a long strip of something, maybe magical cloth.

Or a strip of snake skin.

"I'm not imagining this, am I?" I asked Mjolner as I stood at the bottom of the tree and squinted up towards the sky.

Mjolner meowed in a way I was pretty sure meant no. He saw it too.

"It went up," I said, looking off to my left, through the trees, to the rock where Mjolner had lost the trail before. "The snake spell thing. It ran along the ground from the lodge to that rock, and then it was up in the air. And somehow got disrupted over the hamlet, leaving all those fragments all over the place. Deliberate, I suppose, so we couldn't follow the trail. But that's not a confetti fragment up there. That's a real piece of that snake thing. Isn't it?"

Mjolner meowed noncommittally.

I looked around and found the cabin with all the lit-up windows: Frór's place.

We were behind the cabin next to it.

"Geiri's house," I said. Mjolner made a low yowling warning sound. "No, I'm not going in alone. I'll get the others and we can knock on his door."

Mjolner gave a curt meow of agreement, then yowled his objection again as I tucked my wand away and reached for the lowest branches of that tree.

"I'm not going in alone, I said! I'll get the others, I just want to check out what's up there first. Maybe I can see something more from up there. I don't need help climbing a tree," I told him.

I pulled my way up the tree, branch after branch. It was a deciduous tree; I wasn't sure of what kind, but the branches were thick and could unquestionably hold my weight. They were also plentiful; it was an easy climb. After the day I had had, anything easy was something I was grateful for.

But Mjolner still didn't like it. He didn't climb up after me. He just sat on the snow at the bottom of the tree and chewed me out worse than my grandmother ever could.

At last I reached the level of that twisting bit of magic. I didn't try to grab it. Instead, I pulled myself up to sit on a nearby branch with the trunk at my back and my feet dangling. I held tightly to another branch and leaned over to catch on to the end of the glowing thing with my wand.

It snagged on the wand easily, as if I were picking up iron shavings with a strong magnet. Then I held it before my half-closed eyes.

I didn't really know what I was looking at. On the one hand, it looked like snake skin, the scales shining like polished bits of jade. It was beautiful, and it glowed so brightly I knew it was a finely crafted spell. Only my grandmother's mead hall with its layers and layers of spells had a brighter light to it when I looked for magic.

But it was inert. It wasn't attached to anything and couldn't do anything. I let it go, and it drifted away as if on a breeze that I couldn't feel.

Then I looked down. I was intending to see if the confetti formed any sort of pattern, but there was something much more obvious going on below me.

Another snake was moving around the trunk of my tree, not at ground level but not so high as I was either. It was just curling around it, like the tree was an obstacle it had to slither past. It went past Mjolner's rock before plunging to the ground, then shooting much faster through the woods beyond.

Towards the lodge. I knew that for a fact because my beacon still shone on the horizon. Even after everything that had happened, my spell was still working.

I spun back the other way to see where the snake spell was coming from. There was no mistaking it. It was Geiri's house.

Only so far as I could see, it was appearing out of the walls of the cabin itself, on the second floor.

I blinked and looked with my normal eyes. It was hard to pick out details in the moonlight, but I was sure I could see the outlines of a bedroom. Not through a window, but through the wall itself. I could no longer see the snake, but I could see where it moved through the wall. It wasn't an insubstantial thing passing through a solid mass. No, it was making that solid mass insubstantial to let it through.

Or, I realized with a shiver, to let something inside out. Or someone. They could just step through a solid wall, or a barred and locked door.

I thought I saw someone standing in that bedroom, but I couldn't be sure. Perhaps I was looking at a coat rack or something. If it was a person, they were certainly standing unnaturally still.

I waved my wand in front of my unfocused eyes and looked at the snake spell again. I tucked my wand away so I could use both my hands to support myself so I could lean in to look more closely. The spell was so intense, it couldn't just be coming out of nowhere. And yet from everything I could see, that was what was happening.

The figure below, if it truly was a person, wasn't casting a spell. They had no glow of magic to them. And I saw no glowing artifacts anywhere in that cabin.

What was going on?

Suddenly I heard a loud crack. It took me a long, stupid eternity to work out that this sound came from the branch beneath me.

Only then, as if I were some cartoon character who could hover until they realized they were standing on nothing, I started to fall.

I reached out, trying to catch the branches around me. I failed to break my fall, but I banged up every one of my arms and legs on the way down. I managed to catch on one of the last branches, not for long enough to stop my descent, but just enough to redirect my body towards the thickest patch of snow below me.

Then I met the ground with an audible slam.

I lay still for a moment as the snow I had sent flying up into the air drifted back down all around me. I twitched my fingers and toes, then my hands and feet, and finally my arms and legs. My body hurt all over, and I was sure I was going to be stiff all over by morning, but nothing was broken.

Not even my wand. I could feel the length of it pressed against my arm under my sleeve.

But half of my vision was obscured. The fall had shoved my hat down over my eyes. I raised a shaky arm to push it back, but froze with my hand still on the fold of wool over my eyes.

That sinister feeling was back. But it wasn't watching me from afar this time. It was standing right over me.

"Geiri?" I said, trying to sound lightly conversational. As if we'd just happened upon each other in the middle of the night in his backyard.

I still held out hope that my initial sketched impression of him hadn't been wrong. That he was really an okay guy. The spell was coming out of the second floor of his house, sure, but if it were him doing it, how had he gotten outside so quickly?

But my hopes were quickly dashed when he said, "Geiri? Not anymore."

Which really weren't comforting words.

I pushed myself up onto my elbows, then shoved my hat back out of my eyes. "Sorry for wrecking your tree," I said, still hoping to pass myself off as not a threat. He was standing over me, just as I had sensed, but he wasn't looking at me. It was hard to tell since he was just a black silhouette against the midnight sky, but I decided he was looking towards the lodge.

"Not my tree," he said shortly, then raised a hand. Despite myself, I flinched, but his attention was still off on the far side of the forest. He made a movement with his hand like he was adjusting something, like a dial on a control panel only he could see.

"What are you doing?" I asked him.

"Making them pay," he said. "Making them all pay."

"Making who pay?" I asked. It took a supreme effort, but I managed to sit up, then get my feet under me in a low squat. He still didn't seem to be looking my way, but I kept my motions slow so he wouldn't get distracted by movement in the corner of his eye.

"All those women," he said with a sneer. "All those women who never had a minute for me when I lived here and certainly don't have a minute for me now."

"I see," I said. I tried to get to my feet, but my legs just wouldn't do it. I rested a hand against the tree for support.

And noticed for the first time that Mjolner was gone. Had he fled when I fell, or sooner? I couldn't remember at what point I had stopped hearing his nagging meows as I climbed. Where had he gone?

"If you hate the women of Villmark so much, why did you come back here?" I asked, still looking around for any sign of my cat.

"You think this is just about the women of Villmark?" he demanded.

"All women, then?" I asked conversationally.

"You know nothing," he said, then turned away from me as if dismissing me from his mind.

Finally, I got to my feet and moved back into his field of view. "What do you have there, Geiri?" I asked him. I knew he had something in his hand, not the hand that was from time to time making more little adjustments, but the other one. But it was too dark to see with my normal eyes, and maddeningly, I saw nothing magical going on with my other vision, nothing save the snaky spell which was now far off to the south. I could just see the tail end of it slipping through the trees.

"Nothing that needs concern you," he said.

"Geiri, I'm the volva. This absolutely concerns me," I said.

"Stop saying my name, *volva*," he said with real bitterness.

"All right," I agreed. "But my point still stands. I don't know how you're doing this magic, or why I can't see it happening even now, but it has to stop."

"You can't stop me," he said dismissively.

"Maybe not," I conceded as I fumbled for my wand.

"But I can," I heard Thorbjorn say. I looked up just in time to see him swing a punch at the side of Geiri's head. Geiri collapsed like a puppet whose strings had just been cut.

And then Mjolner, who had been perched on Thorbjorn's shoulder the entire time, gave a triumphant meow.

"He had something in his hand," I said, trying to scrabble over the snow towards Geiri's inert body.

"This?" Thorbjorn asked. He bent over the body and picked something up.

It was like a thousand voices suddenly shrieking at once, all inside my head. I curled into a ball, wrapping my arms over my head for all the good that could do.

I think Thorbjorn called out my name. I know he took a step closer to me, because those voices in torment grew louder.

"Put it back!" I shrieked at him.

I felt him hesitate. I rolled to sit up on my knees and lowered my arms to look up at him. I could see something in his hand glinting in the moonlight, some sort of arm ring fashioned from metal.

It hurt to look at it, like those voices were somehow now screaming inside my eyeballs.

"Give it to me!" my grandmother shouted, her magically amplified voice carrying even over the cacophony in my skull.

Then everything suddenly fell silent. I could hear the snow shifting around me in the slightest of breezes, a slivery whisper of sound.

"What was that?" I asked, my voice hoarse. I suspected I had joined in the screaming at some point.

"Something he absolutely shouldn't have had," my grandmother said. Then she knelt by Geiri's side. First she touched the side of his neck to make sure he was still alive. Then she took something from his hand.

I sat up and scooted closer to see what she had. She turned and showed it to me.

It looked like a pouch made of black velvet, something jewelry might come in, or that someone might keep gaming dice in.

"Do you see the enchantments worked into the fabric?" she asked me.

I nodded. The traces were faint, but definitely there. Magic of some sort. But I didn't know what they meant. "Why did he have that?" I asked.

"To hide what he was doing from the two of us," my grandmother said. "Come, let's get back inside. There's been enough excitement for the night. It's time for you to go to bed."

"But the Wild Hunt?" Thorbjorn said as he helped me to my feet.

"That was the thing," I told him. "What he was holding. That was what was summoning them."

"Are you sure?" he asked me.

"You didn't hear it?" I asked.

"No, he wouldn't," my grandmother said. But I could tell from the tightness of her face that she had.

"What was it?" he asked.

"The voices of those who have been taken from the Wild Hunt," she said grimly. "How such a thing can even be done, I shiver to think. But this is very old magic. These souls are lost to life and afterlife both. They long not to be alone, dangerously so. And the Hunt wants them back very badly. I'll have to figure out a way to free them from this accursed object. But in the meantime, I promise you, this is over. We can rest now."

If I got back into Frór's house and up to his spare bedroom under my own power, I don't remember it. For all I knew, I just curled up there in the snow and finally fell into that Odin sleep I had been promising myself.

And, thankfully, it was a dreamless sleep.

CHAPTER TWENTY-NINE

I WOKE to the familiar experience of being half off my own pillow, displaced by the cat sleeping against the back of my neck. I sat up and looked around. At first it was disorienting. Nothing around me was familiar.

Then memories started coming back. I was in the spare bedroom of Frór's cabin. I wasn't entirely sure how I had gotten up there. I was even less sure how long I had been sleeping. It looked like morning outside the small window beside the bed, but it felt like I'd just slept for days.

I got up, careful not to wake Mjolner, and found my clothes on a chair. They weren't the clothes I had been wearing before. Someone, probably my grandmother, had fetched me fresh things from my house in Villmark. I got dressed and took a brush to my matted hair, then headed downstairs, hoping to find someone awake or at least a cup of coffee.

I found both the minute I set foot inside the kitchen. But it wasn't Frór waiting for me there, already pouring me a cup of coffee after hearing me come down the stairs. It was Loke.

"Good morning," he said, handing me the cup.

"Which morning?" I asked, soaking in the smell of roasted beans before taking my first sip.

"You missed a day, but only because your grandmother did a little..." he finished his sentence with a vague wiggling motion of his fingers.

"She used magic to keep me asleep?" I asked. I wasn't sure I liked the sound of that.

"She'll say it was because you needed the rest," Loke said.

"But you think it's because?" I prompted.

He shrugged. "Probably that."

"Loke," I said warningly.

"I'm not making trouble," he said, holding up his hands as if in surrender. "I'm just saying, she had a lot of decisions to make."

"And she wanted to make them without me?" I asked. "No, that doesn't sound like her at all."

"If you say so," Loke said.

"Where is she now?" I asked.

"At the trial," he said.

"Geiri's trial? Already?" I asked.

"Like I said, it's been a day," Loke said. "A momentous day. And you slept through it."

I rubbed at my face, then drank more of Frór's strong coffee. "So he's guilty then? He was the one doing the spell?"

"There were three spells," he said with a grin. "But he was only doing two of them."

"He had a cursed arm ring that had the power to summon the Wild Hunt," I said.

"And a bag to keep it in," he agreed. "That bag cloaked the ring's magic. That's why you and I and your grandmother couldn't see it, even when it was right there. Not until Thorbjorn took it out of that bag. And how horrid was that?"

"I don't remember you even being there," I said with a frown.

"I was in the house. That screaming was loud," he said.

"Why didn't the arm ring bring the Wild Hunt straight to it?" I asked.

"The bag again," Loke said. "Geiri was just using the arm ring to summon the Wild Hunt to this general area."

"So how was he getting the women outside?" I asked.

"He had marked them beforehand," Loke said. "At the bakery. He had some sort of magical ointment that soaks into the skin and stays in the bloodstream for days. He marked all three of the youngest sisters, the unmarried ones. Nilda and Kara were at the shop at the same time, and he touched them too. He was targeting single women, and he knew who was going to be outside of Villmark on that hunting trip. Just a little touch of his thumb on their bare skin when shaking hands or just brushing past them in passing. They never knew, apparently. They'd all forgotten a hooded stranger lurking around the bakery, touching them all on the hand. Although they did remember it happening after your grandmother asked them about it."

"They're here?" I asked. "They're safe?"

"They've been sworn to secrecy regarding this little hamlet, but they're all outside at the trial," he said. "No one else was taken."

"So after my grandmother took that arm ring from Geiri, she could get to the lodge?"

"That's the funny part, actually," he said. "They all just showed up back in Villmark yesterday afternoon. They gave up on hunting when you and Thorbjorn disappeared. Good thing too; no one else was ever going to reach that lodge. It's not possible. Only blood members of the family can find it."

"Part of the protective magic," I guessed.

"Exactly. Gunna and Jóra never told anyone, but they did make sure that the hunting parties always had a family member in them. Otherwise, if you walk more than a mile or two away from the lodge, you'll never find it again. Although apparently *you* got very close."

"It didn't seem close at the time," I said. Then a sudden thought had me laughing out loud. At Loke's puzzled look, I said, "I was just laughing at the irony. If Thorbjorn and I had decided to try for the lodge rather than running back to the hamlet, we would've made it. I guess he didn't know."

"No, he didn't know," Loke said. But there was no laughter in his own voice.

"What is it?" I asked.

"No," he said, shaking his head firmly. "He's going to have to talk to you about that."

"About what?" I asked, but he just shook his head again. "Well, where is he now? Wait, let me guess. At the trial."

"It's just outside the front door," he said with a tip of his head in that general direction. "But I'm not going that way. Eat a couple of those hard-boiled eggs before you go. You need the protein."

"Are you my honorary grandmother now?" I asked him, but took one of the eggs and rapped it on the table before setting to work peeling it.

He ignored my quip, draining the last of his coffee and setting the mug in the sink. "I have to go, but I'll see you as soon as I can."

"When's that?" I asked, my eyes still on my egg.

"Oh, whoever knows?" he said. He sounded tired and frustrated, and I glanced up at him. But he was already disappearing out the back door.

I blinked hard as the door clicked shut behind him. For a second there, I thought I had seen another, more modern kitchen through that doorway. But that made no sense. I took a bite of the egg, then crossed the room to open that door.

I was looking out over an expanse of snow and snow-covered trees, just as I should be. Clearly, I needed more coffee.

It was a little remarkable that I saw no sign of Loke walking away, but if he had gone around to the other end of the hamlet, there'd be no sign of him from where I was standing.

Then I looked down. There wasn't a single footprint in the snow.

That was a mystery for another day. I put another egg in my pocket, then headed to the entryway where my boots and parka were waiting.

As promised, the minute I stepped outside the door, I was on the fringes of the trial already in progress. A small dais had been set up on the northern end of the village circle, and my grandmother in her volva regalia sat on her three-legged stool upon that dais.

Geiri was in chains at her feet. Thorge and Thormund were standing in front of the dais, close enough to grab him if he moved. But I doubted he would. Those chains looked incredibly heavy, and his entire posture was slumped and despondent.

My grandmother looked over at me, the briefest of glances, before returning her attention to Geiri. But others had noticed that glance, and faces in the crowd turned my way. Nilda and Kara gave me little nods, which I returned. Raggi and Báfurr scowled at me; no surprise there.

But Thorbjorn, who had already been standing at the very edge of the crowd, walked over to me, his pace so swift he was all but running.

My stomach knotted. Every face in the crowd gathered before my grandmother was grave, but his was particularly so.

Just what had Loke refused to tell me before about Thorbjorn? Was I about to find out?

"Ingrid," he said in a whisper when he reached the bottom of the steps. "Walk with me?"

I nodded and came down to him. Then we walked together between Signi's cabin and Frór's, heading out into the forest.

"Shouldn't we be back there?" I asked as soon as we were far enough away where not whispering felt appropriate.

"Not really," he said with a sigh. "That's all just for show. He has nothing more to tell us. He'll go into a holding cell in the caves, and that will be the last anyone in Villmark will ever have to see of him."

"Nothing more to tell us?" I asked, suddenly very irritated. I stopped walking and turned to face him directly. "Did he say every-thing yesterday while I was still sleeping?"

"Ingrid," he said, and I realized my tone was far harsher than I had intended it.

Or was it? I was pretty mad. "Why did you let her do it?"

"Let her do what? Leave you to finally get some sleep?" he asked.

"Is that what she did?" I asked.

"You know it is," he said. "That wand of yours is a powerful object, and you were using it a lot. Without training. Haraldr and Nora were both concerned. We all agreed to let you recover. *I* agreed to let you rest and recover. Are you angry with me?"

"No," I said, but too quickly. "It just feels like I was being kept out of things."

"No one intended that," he said.

"All right," I said, and turned to start walking again. He quickly fell into step beside me. "What did Geiri say, then? From what little he told me, I guess this was some sort of misogyny thing."

"For his part, yes," Thorbjorn said. "He left Villmark years ago because, he says, all the women rejected him. He thought he had found his one true love and had followed her all the way to Minneapolis. But then that relationship didn't work out either, so he just drifted back here."

"Loke told me about the ointment he used to mark the Freyas and Kara," I said. "But they're all so young. Surely they weren't the ones who had rejected him before?"

"No, they weren't. He wanted to punish all of Villmark by removing all the single women one by one, starting with those on the hunting trip. I gather he wasn't sure how all this magic was going to go, so he wanted to start with an isolated group and then work up to all of Villmark."

"So where did he learn magic?" I asked.

"That's just it. He knows nothing," Thorbjorn said. "The ointment was something Halldis used to make. He still had a vial from his younger days when she sold it to him as some sort of love spell. Just touch the woman you long for, and in the dark of night you can lure her out to you."

"And she sold this?" I asked.

"Not out in the open," he said. "But your grandmother has gone through everything we found in her cottage after she was arrested, and there were other vials there. She says in normal circumstances the victim would indeed slip outside without her family knowing, but the minute she was disturbed in any way, she would snap out of it."

"Well, they didn't," I said.

"No, he did something to it to increase the potency," he said.

"Without knowing any magic," I said skeptically.

"Someone probably told him what to do," he said.

"Who?" I asked.

"That's just the thing," he said, and now it was his turn to stop walking and face me directly. "He can't tell us."

"What do you mean 'can't'?" I asked.

"Just that. Someone or something of great power told him how to concentrate that ointment. And it gave him that cursed arm ring as well as the bag to hide it. And it told him exactly what to do. He thought he was getting his revenge, but he was really working in the service of something else."

"But what is this something else?" I pressed.

He closed his eyes, tipping his head back as if to feel the warmth of the sun. But the sky was overcast.

"Thorbjorn," I said. "What's going on?"

"All of Villmark is in danger," he said. "And that means I have to go."

CHAPTER THIRTY

"WHAT DO YOU MEAN 'GO'?" I asked.

"Let's walk back," he said, not answering my question.

"Thorbjorn," I said warningly.

"We should walk back," he insisted. "I'll just have time enough to tell you before I have to go."

"Go *where?*"

"On patrol," he said. But I could tell that, as familiar as those words were coming from him, this time he meant something very different.

"Why are you saying that like you're never coming back?" I asked.

"This arm ring your grandmother took from Geiri, it's the second thing of ancient power to show up in Villmark in a matter of months," he said.

"Since I got here, you mean," I said.

He gave me a wounded look. "I didn't say that. None of this is because of you."

"Maybe not," I said. But it didn't feel that way. Still, I pushed my feelings aside to focus on what I knew. "Roarr found the talisman he had because Halldis told him where to go."

"Right, but who told Halldis?" Thorbjorn asked.

"We could try asking her," I said.

"We have," he said. "I don't think the same thing is going on with her as with Geiri. It's more like she just doesn't want to say."

"What do you mean? What's going on with Geiri?"

"Didn't I tell you?" he asked. I shook my head. "That's why there's no point in watching the trial. He is incapable of saying anything about the arm ring or where he got it or who gave it to him or anything."

"A spell?" I guessed.

"A very powerful spell, one your grandmother cannot break," he said. He gave me another nervous glance. "I've never seen her so frightened."

"Does he remember, or can he just not say?" I asked.

"It seems like the latter, but who knows?" Thorbjorn said. "Frór has already gone out to hunt for whatever is causing all this. He left yesterday when it became clear that Geiri was going to tell us nothing. Now my brothers and I are all heading out as well, if not so far into the deeper places as Frór."

"You were just waiting for this trial to end?" I guessed.

"No, Ingrid," he said. "I was waiting for you to wake up. I couldn't leave without seeing you one last time."

I closed my eyes. "Would you stop saying it like that?" I asked. "Like we're never going to see each other again?"

He grabbed both my arms until I opened my eyes and looked at him again. "I *know* we'll see each other again. I just don't know when. That's the uncertainty that is eating at me."

"You've been on long patrols before," I said.

"Not like this," he said. "All five of us are going out at once. My father and Nilda and Kara are going to be guarding the caves and tending the ancestral fire. Everything is changing."

"Is that so strange?" I asked. "Someone else did it before you and your brothers were old enough, right?"

"For a long time, Frór was Villmark's only guardian," he said. "Don't you remember?"

"Yes," I said. "Sorry, I'm not used to remembering, if that makes any sense. The memories are there when I search for them, though.

When I came here as a kid, your father tended the fire and Frór patrolled."

"But do you remember what we promised each other?" he asked, his fingers on my arms gripping almost painfully tight.

"That I would grow up to be volva, like my grandmother. And you wanted to be the guardian, like Frór. Mission accomplished. Good job, us. Not that we knew what we were signing ourselves up for," I said with a nervous laugh.

"We promised more than that," he said, his tone still earnest.

"I know," I said softly, my own laughter gone. "We promised to do it better. We promised to be a better team. To support each other more."

"There are things you don't know yet," Thorbjorn said. "Things about your grandmother and Frór. Things I learned after you left and never came back."

"Hey, I came back," I said.

"You know what I mean," he said. "You weren't really back until just a few days ago, and we haven't had time to have a proper talk since."

"And what's this?" I asked.

"A very rushed conversation," he said, as if it pained him.

"Frór left at once, mostly to get away from my grandmother, didn't he?" I guessed.

"He needed to go," he insisted. "But yes, to outside eyes, it always looks like they're trying to stay far away from each other."

"That isn't going to be us," I promised him. "That will never be us. Look, I didn't even remember what we said to each other until a few days ago, but we've already been working as an unstoppable team. Nothing is going to change that."

"I want to believe that with all my heart," he said.

"Well, I already do," I said.

"The crowd is dispersing," he said, looking towards the hamlet. "Your grandmother will want to speak with you. Haraldr too, I think."

"They can wait," I said.

"But I cannot," he said. "Thorge is already heading this way with my pack. The two of us are going into the mountains in the north to find any sign of whatever it is that plots against us." Then he looked at me with real regret in his eyes. "This isn't how I wanted to part from you."

"It's *not* forever," I said. "I'll be thinking of you every minute. Every magical protection I can extend to you from such a distance, you know you'll have it."

"I know," he said. He planted a lingering kiss on my forehead, then turned to take his pack from his brother.

I watched them go, only slowly realizing that Kara stood by my side, doing the same. Our hands found each other, and we squeezed them tight in silent support.

"They'll be back," my grandmother said as she walked towards us. She was leaning very heavily on her walking stick, something I had never seen her do before.

"Mormor?" I asked, but she quickly waved my concern away.

"Just need a little Odin sleep of my own. Which I'll get, now that this matter is dealt with," she said.

I felt ashamed then for how angry I had been with her before. Why had I thought she was putting me out of the way like an unwanted competitor? Why hadn't I believed she just wanted me to rest?

Was I that susceptible to Loke's muck-stirring?

"I didn't get to say goodbye to Frór," I said after too long of an awkward silence between us.

"Well, he'll be back too," she said, albeit a bit more grumpily than before.

"Nilda and I have to get back to Villmark. We have watch duty tonight," Kara said to us.

"Yes, I've heard," I said.

"It's a heavy responsibility," my grandmother said, "but one I expect you and your sister will lift easily. And Ingrid and I shall always be there if you need us."

Kara just nodded, then ran to catch up with her sister already on her way back into town.

"I'm heading back down to Runde myself," my grandmother said.

Now that it was just the two of us, she stopped making even the small pretense she had been attempting before to not look as tired as she felt.

"Someone must have a sleigh," I said, looking around. But everyone around us was walking themselves.

"I'll be fine," she said. "But you have work to do here before you can come home."

"Here?" I asked, looking at the cabins around us.

"Signi has books for you," she said, pointing towards the cabin with the little hearts just visible on the shutters. "And Haraldr is there with her, waiting to speak with you."

"Oh," I said. Now I was the one feeling epically tired despite my daylong nap. On the one hand, I was about to get weighed down by a mountain of books on abnormal psychology.

And on the other hand, there was that rune I had never quite gotten around to practicing.

But after hugging my grandmother goodbye, I headed up Signi's steps and knocked on her door.

Haraldr himself opened the door.

"Signi's not here," he told me as he let me in. "She and her house guest made themselves scarce before half of Villmark came down into this hamlet. How this will stay secret now, I have no idea. That was your grandmother's decision, even though the council didn't like it. But that boy isn't ready for all of Villmark. Not yet, anyway."

"I'm sorry I got so little rune work done," I said. "But I was busy. I mean, you know I was busy, right?"

"Nonsense," he said, that one word exploding out of him. I couldn't help but flinching. At first I thought he was denying that I had been busy. But then he said, "the ur-dwarves and the moss wives both sought you out? I'd say that's a sure sign you've got a handle on the power of this particular rune."

"So I'm here to get the next assignment already?" I asked. I didn't do a very good job of hiding how stressed out that thought made me.

But he just laughed. "No, not quite," he said. "A little more medita-tion on this one wouldn't kill you. Tomorrow morning is soon enough to start with the next one. No, you're here for quite another reason entirely."

"What's that?" I asked apprehensively.

He smiled at me. "I've convinced the council that you have earned yourself a bit of a reward. A night, just one night, back among your friends down in Runde. Your grandmother has sworn to be your chaperone, not that you'll need one."

"I can see my friends?" I asked, all but blinking back tears.

"From sunset tomorrow until sunrise the next day," he said. "I'll even let you catch a little nap in the morning. We can push our meeting that day back to lunchtime. What do you think?"

"I think... thank you!" I said, throwing my arms around him. I wanted to squeeze him tight, but his bones felt too fragile for that.

"You've earned it," he said. "It's not every volva who can take on the Wild Hunt and live to tell the tale." Then his face took on a mock stern expression. "Not that you will tell such tales. Not to outsiders."

"Of course not," I said, even though I knew that I would. How could I not? They were my friends.

"Until morning, then. Enjoy your night," he said.

"I will," I promised.

But as I walked back towards Villmark, Mjolner appearing out of nowhere to walk beside me like a loyal guard dog, I couldn't get that last look in Haraldr's eyes out of my mind.

I couldn't help but feeling that he wasn't giving me this night with my old friends as a reward. Maybe that was a part of it, but it wasn't the main reason.

No, I was pretty sure Haraldr knew that with Thorbjorn gone for who knows how long, and with Nilda and Kara now taking over so many of his duties, I was going to need the support of my other friends.

And not just emotional support either. Something was coming for Villmark. There could be nothing more pressing on the minds of the council than that. And at least one of their number was willing to entertain the notion that the help of outsiders might play a part in the days to come.

But for now, it was enough just to know I'd be seeing them again.

"Sunset to sunrise. That's not much time," I said to Mjolner as we walked. "But probably enough to squeeze in a dinner of fish and chips. How does that sound?"

Mjolner made a happy sound, and the top of his tail twitched from side to side contentedly.

If I had a tail, I would've been doing the same.

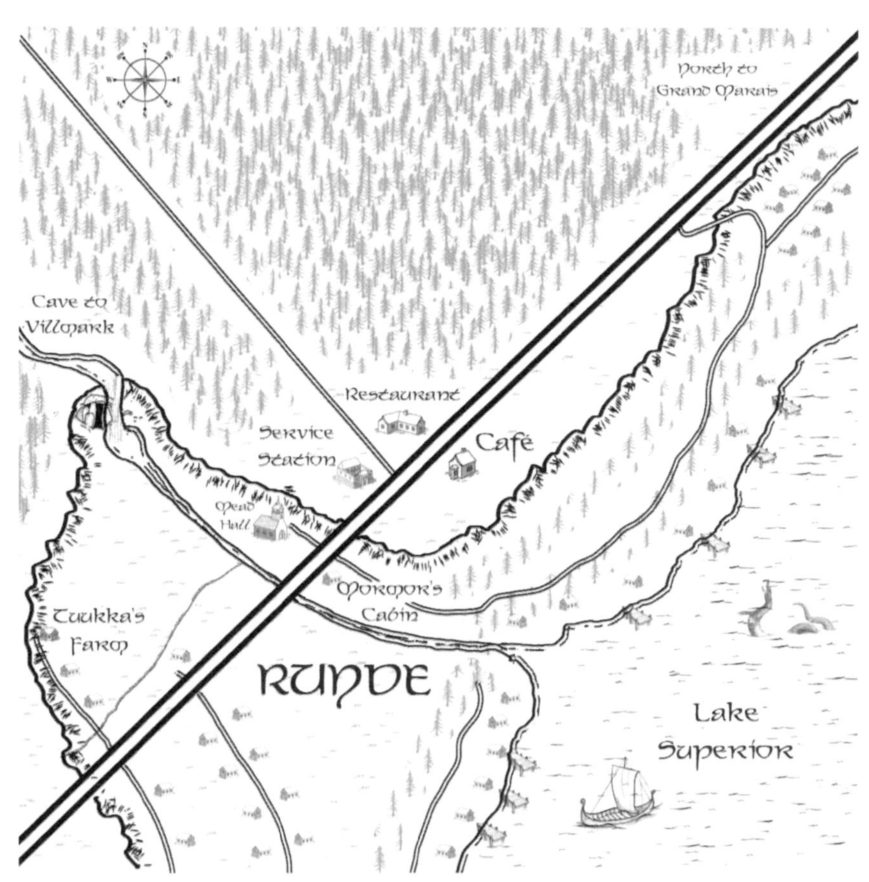

North to
Grand Marais
Cave to
Villmark
Restaurant
Service
Station
Café
Mead
Hall
Mormor's
Cabin
Tuukka's
Farm
RUNDE
Lake
Superior

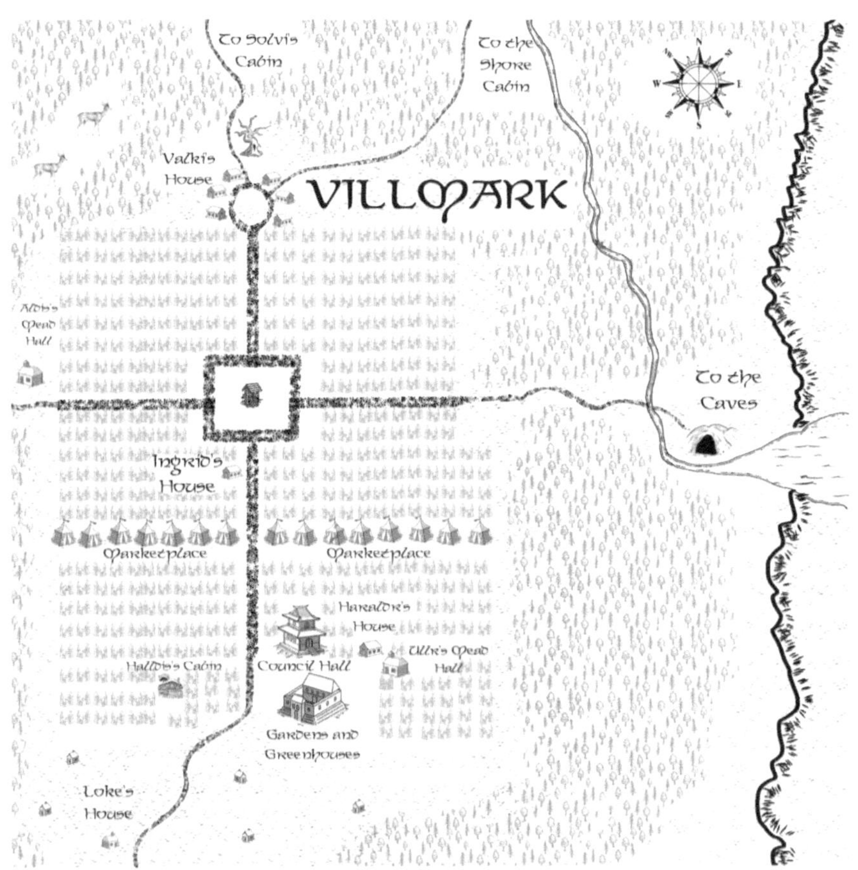

To Solvi's Cabin
To the Shore Cabin
N
W E
S
VILLMARK
Valki's House
Aldi's Mead Hall
To the Caves
Ingrid's House
Marketplace
Marketplace
Haraldr's House
Halldis's Cabin
Council Hall
Ulfr's Mead Hall
Gardens and Greenhouses
Loke's House

CHECK OUT BOOK SIX!

The Viking Witch will return in **Corpse in the Mead Hall**, available now!

By day, a drab pole barn used as general store, post office and meeting place all-in-one by the people of Runde, Minnesota, a fishing village on the North Shore of Lake Superior.

By night, a Viking-style long house filled with tales and singing, roasting meat and flowing beer, and of course mead.

Ingrid Torfa can imagine no better place for a much-needed night of R&R.

The mead hall run by her grandmother lies where modern small town life brushes up against the old world lifestyle of the people of Villmark, proud descendants of a lost tribe of Northmen. All of her friends mingle there from the server who works in the restaurant on the side of the highway to the guardians charged with protecting the sacred flame of their ancestors.

The spells that her grandmother casts over her mead hall nightly keep everyone within safe and harmonious.

Or so everyone always believed. But when a murder interrupts

CHECK OUT BOOK SIX!

Ingrid's night off, she finds herself questioning everything. Because her chief suspect is her own grandmother.

Corpse in the Mead Hall, Book 6 in **The Viking Witch Mystery Series**!

THE WITCHES THREE
COZY MYSTERIES

In case you missed it, check out **Charm School**, the first book in the complete **Witches Three Cozy Mystery Series**!

Amanda Clarke thinks of herself as perfectly ordinary in every way. Just a small-town girl who serves breakfast all day in a little diner nestled next to the highway, nothing but dairy farms for miles around. She fits in there.

But then an old woman she never met dies, and Amanda was named in her will. Now Amanda packs a bag and heads to the big city, to Miss Zenobia Weekes' Charm School for Exceptional Young Ladies. And it's not in just any neighborhood. No, she finds herself on Summit Avenue in St. Paul, a street lined with gorgeous old houses, the former homes of lumber barons, railroad millionaires, even the writer F. Scott Fitzgerald. Why, Amanda can practically hear the jazz music still playing across the decades.

Scratch that. The music really, literally, still plays in the backyard of the charm school. Because the house stretches across time itself. Without a witch to protect this tear in the fabric of the world, anything can spill over. Like music.

Or like murder.

Charm School, the first book in the complete **Witches Three Cozy Mystery Series**!

THE WEAL & WOE BOOKSHOP
WITCH MYSTERIES

In case you missed it, check out **The Teashop Terror**, the first book in the complete **Weal & Woe Bookshop Witch Mystery Series**!

No one knows more about every branch of magic than Tabitha Greene. She devoted years to studying the most esoteric texts, hunting down the most obscure source materials, and deciphering the most cryptic ancient scrolls. But her career in academia hits a dead end when no wizard will take her on as an apprentice.

Just because, despite being descended from two long and prestigious lines of witches, her attempts to actually perform any magic always fail. Often spectacularly.

But no more college means no more dorm life. And no magical skills means no real job skills, at least, not in the witchy world. And a life spent moving from school to school every few months was a life without real friendships. She finds herself alone with nowhere to go.

Then an uncle she barely remembers offers her a summer job, running his bookstore over the summer. The Weal and Woe Bookstore, located in a magical pocket world within a block of buildings just north of the old Mill District of Minneapolis, Minnesota.

Not exactly the pinnacle of all her hopes and dreams. But it's just for one summer, right?

Or so Tabitha tells herself. But unbeknownst to her, the Weal and Woe Bookstore is about to change her life.

The Teashop Terror, the first book in the complete **Weal & Woe Bookshop Witch Mystery Series**!

ALSO FROM RATATOSKR PRESS

The Ritchie and Fitz Sci-Fi Murder Mysteries starts with **Murder on the Intergalactic Railway**.

For Murdina Ritchie, acceptance at the Oymyakon Foreign Service Academy means one last chance at her dream of becoming a diplomat for the Union of Free Worlds. For Shackleton Fitz IV, it represents his last chance not to fail out of military service entirely.

Strange that fate should throw them together now, among the last group of students admitted after the start of the semester. They had once shared the strongest of friendships. But that all ended a long time ago.

But when an insufferable but politically important woman turns up murdered, the two agree to put their differences aside and work together to solve the case.

Because the murderer might strike again. But more importantly, solving a murder would just have to impress the dour colonel who clearly thinks neither of them belong at his academy.

Murder on the Intergalactic Railway, the first book in **The Ritchie**

and Fitz Sci-Fi Murder Mysteries, available everywhere books are sold.

FREE EBOOK!

Like exclusive, free content?

If you'd like to receive "A Collection of Witchy Prequels", a free collection of short story prequels to the Witches Three Cozy Mystery and Viking Witch Mystery series, as well as other free stories throughout the year, go to my website CateMartin.com to subscribe to my newsletter! This eBook is exclusively for newsletter subscribers and will never be sold in stores. Check it out!

ABOUT THE AUTHOR

Cate Martin has written stories which have appeared in **Mystery, Crime and Mayhem** quarterly magazine as well as in the annual **Holiday Spectacular** Advent calendar of Christmas stories. She is also the author of three witch mystery series: **The Witches Three Cozy Mysteries**, and **The Viking Witch Mysteries** and **The Weal and Woe Bookshop Witch Mysteries**. She currently lives in Minneapolis, Minnesota. You can learn more about her work at CateMartin.com.

ALSO BY CATE MARTIN

The Witches Three Cozy Mystery Series

Charm School

Work Like a Charm

Third Time is a Charm

Old World Charm

Charm his Pants Off

Charm Offensive

The Witches Three Cozy Mysteries Books 1-3

The Witches Three Cozy Mysteries Books 4-6

The Viking Witch Mystery Series

Body at the Crossroads

Death Under the Bridge

Murder on the Lake

Killing in the Village Commons

Bloodshed in the Forest

Corpse in the Mead Hall

Slaying on the Lake Shore

Bones by the Forest Road

Sacrifice Behind the Falls

Body Under the Café

Assassination in the Glade

Bewitchment After the Storm

Predator in the Lanes

Threat From the North

Snare in the Blind Alley

Ashes Beneath the Tree (available July 14, 2026 direct from me or August 11, 2026 in stores everywhere)

The Viking Witch Mysteries Books 1-3

The Viking Witch Mysteries Books 4-6

The Viking Witch Mysteries Books 7-9

The Weal & Woe Bookshop Witch Mystery Series

The Teashop Terror

The Salon & Spa Scandal

The Bookseller Blunder

The Entrepreneur Enigma

The Novelty Shop Nightmare

The Courtyard Conundrum

Short Story Collections

Bubbly, Bicycles and Brides

The Dorothy Lundegaard Mysteries

Fruitcake, Festivities and Firelight